CLAIMING HIS DESERT PRINCESS

Marguerite Kaye

MILLS
BOON®

First published in Great Britain 2017
By Mills & Boon, an imprint of HarperCollins*Publishers*
1 London Bridge Street, London, SE1 9GF

Large Print edition 2017

© 2017 Marguerite Kaye

ISBN: 978-0-263-06778-1

Printed and bound in Great Britain
by CPI Antony Rowe, Chippenham, Wiltshire

Marguerite Kaye writes hot historical romances from her home in cold and usually rainy Scotland, featuring Regency rakes, Highlanders and sheikhs. She has published almost thirty books and novellas. When she's not writing she enjoys walking, cycling (but only on the level), gardening (but only what she can eat) and cooking. She also likes to knit and occasionally drink martinis (though not at the same time). Find out more on her website: margueritekaye.com.

Books by Marguerite Kaye

Mills & Boon Historical Romance and Mills & Boon Historical *Undone!* eBook

Hot Arabian Nights

The Widow and the Sheikh
Sheikh's Mail-Order Bride
The Harlot and the Sheikh
Claiming His Desert Princess

Comrades in Arms

The Soldier's Dark Secret
The Soldier's Rebel Lover

The Armstrong Sisters

Innocent in the Sheikh's Harem
The Governess and the Sheikh
The Sheikh's Impetuous Love-Slave (Undone!)
The Beauty Within
Rumours that Ruined a Lady
Unwed and Unrepentant

Stand-Alone Novels

Never Forget Me
Strangers at the Altar
Scandal at the Midsummer Ball
'The Officer's Temptation'

Visit the Author Profile page at millsandboon.co.uk for more titles.

Author Note

First of all thank you to Tahira, whom I met at a Mills & Boon 'New Voices' workshop. I thought she had a fabulous name—fit for a desert princess. She very kindly permitted me to use it. I hope she likes her namesake and thinks I've done her justice.

More thanks for a name suggestion are due—this time to Mairibeth MacMillan, writer, friend and coffee mate, who named Tahira's sand cat Sayeed (Hunter). Sayeed owes his slightly vicious predilections to two of my previous pet cats, both of whom were feral by nature, and loved by me and no one else!

My final thanks go to a fictional character, Lord Henry Armstrong—is it permissible to thank your own creation? He made his first appearance in *Innocent in the Sheikh's Harem*, as a conniving and ruthless diplomat with a bevy of daughters he was determined to marry off. That book spawned the Armstrong Sisters series, and at the conclusion of the last story, *Unwed and Unrepentant*, I thought I was done with him and he with me. But, like the proverbial bad penny, he just kept turning up unexpectedly. Thank you, Henry, I've loved delving into your secret and dark past in this book, you cad, you!

This book rounds off the Hot Arabian Nights quartet. I hope that it finishes the series on a high, and that you enjoy reading it as much as I enjoyed writing it.

Chapter One

Kingdom of Nessarah, Arabia—July 1815

The moon was little more than a scimitar-shaped crescent in the night sky as Christopher moved stealthily towards the summit of the rocky outcrop which would provide him with the perfect vantage point. The heavens were strewn with hazy stars tonight, a scattering of dusty diamonds rather than the usual pincushion of bright-silver discs. Though he was pretty certain that the site he had come to reconnoitre was deserted, he had taken the precaution of leaving his hobbled camel at the nearest well, located over a mile away. The soft sand had given way to gravelly rubble underfoot. Patches of sparse scrub had forced their way through the hard-packed mud. Dusty and bereft of any greenery, their thick thorns snatched at his cloak as he crept forward, his soft-soled boots making no sound.

The rock formation which was the focus of his interest rose out of the gentle swell of the ground like the battlements of an ancient keep. In this light it looked russet red in colour, the vertical striations glittering. A clearly identifiable track had been hacked through the scrub leading towards a cleft in the rock. Stooping to examine the ground, Christopher could make out the indentations created by heavy cart wheels rumbling across the terrain. He was definitely in the right place.

His heart began to race with anticipation, but he mustn't get ahead of himself. The whispered conversations he had overheard, the careful questioning of local contacts, his own research, might yet prove unfounded. The familiar tightening in his gut, the flicker of excitement which always accompanied such discoveries, was on this occasion leavened with a healthy dose of desperation. Never in his entire career had so much been riding on a mineral find.

A single black cloud traversed the moon, casting a shadow over the rugged desert landscape laid out before him. For six months he had been scouring southern Arabia in search of the perfect confluence of natural resources without once finding this, the most elusive of them all. He had now exhausted his list of potential locations. Nessarah was pretty much his last throw of the dice.

'But this time, I know I'm in the right place,' Christopher muttered resolutely to himself. The answer had to be here. He had grown weary of this self-imposed quest, longing for it to be over. He could not contemplate failure.

'And so I must succeed.' His hand felt automatically for the pouch containing the amulet. He did not need to remove it to trace the shape cast from beaten gold, the smooth enamel interior, the setting of each individual precious stone, and the oddly-shaped gap which might hold the key to the origin of the piece. He carried it with him everywhere, a tangible reminder of all he had lost, not least his own identity.

His entire life had been shown to be a sham built on false foundations on that fateful day shortly after the funeral when he had discovered the relic, along with the document which explained its presence. He had barely been able to comprehend the contents at the time. Even now, six long months into his search, nine months after that life-changing meeting which had taken place in London, he felt sick to the pit of his stomach when contemplating the ramifications.

And so he did not allow himself to think of them. His fingers tightened around the amulet, a priceless, ancient artefact, a potent symbol of the lie he had unwittingly been living, the bribe which had been paid to ensure the hateful, sordid truth of his past remained buried. He wished he had never discovered it, but having done so, he could do nothing until he had rid himself of it, returning it to its historical home. Only then could he put an end to this shattering chapter in his life, wipe the slate of his own history clean, make a fresh start and new man of himself.

But he was not there yet. First he had to prove that this new mine could provide him with the vital connection which had so far eluded him. Force of habit made him check that the pouch containing the amulet was securely fastened, that his belt was also securely buckled, that the scimitar and the slim dagger which hung from it could be easily drawn, and that the smaller dagger was still strapped to his leg. A man never knew when drastic action might be required. A final scan of the area with his spyglass assuring him that he was quite alone, Christopher got to his feet and went in search of the mine entrance.

An hour later, Tahira tethered her camel to a gnarled acacia tree. The moon was faint, hardly ideal for exploring the site, but that did not matter greatly. This was her first visit, a reconnoitre to familiarise herself with the terrain, to have a cursory look for the tell-tale signs of ancient occupation—or the lack of it. She pulled off her headdress and cloak, folding them neatly under the acacia. Her tunic and trousers were tobacco-brown, the same colour as her riding boots, designed to allow her to easily blend into the shadows, though such caution would not be necessary tonight, for the excavations had only just begun, too early as yet to merit the posting of a guard.

She had never before explored the site of a working mine, considering the risk of discovery too great, but she had never before needed to distract herself from such a dire situation at home. Her brother was determined to force her into obeying his will. She could not resist thumbing her nose at him by exploring this, his latest pet project, even though he would never know.

Excitement made her heart flutter. There was

nothing quite like it, being out here all alone in the desert. Nothing compared to that tingling sense of anticipation, wondering what hidden treasures she might uncover. She had always possessed a strong, vital sense of connection with the past that she never could explain to her sisters. They simply couldn't understand the affinity, the way her blood stirred when she held an ancient artefact, or stood on a spot where her antecedents once stood. Not that she would dream of admitting to such first-hand experience. Her sisters would be horrified if they ever found out about her night-time escapades, terrified by the consequences were she to be caught. She would not risk compromising them by sharing such information, preferring to keep her secret firmly to herself, and in doing so, keeping the three people she loved most in the world safe.

The three people in the world who, if her brother had his way, she would soon be forced to abandon. With the pressure on her to comply increasing daily, she was determined to make the most of her fleeting moments of freedom, storing up these precious nights as ballast against the future that others were determined to force upon her. A future she neither wanted nor had any say in. Here, under cover of darkness, released from the gilded cage she inhabited, she could cast off the burden of her birthright, forget the fate she was trying so assiduously to avoid, and inhabit another world, where no one but herself could dictate her actions.

Doing so was not without considerable risk, but as her sense of impending doom increased, so too did her determination to reward herself with these stolen hours. She would not think about the consequences of discovery. She refused to believe she would be caught. Besides, she reasoned, her activities were so improbable, it was highly unlikely that anyone would imagine her capable of them. There were advantages, after all, to being a mere female. Her brother and her father would not believe such defiance possible even if they gave it a second's thought—which they would not. How satisfying it would be to confound them, to see the incredulity on their faces. Or it would be, if by doing so she would not immediately guarantee at the very least an abrupt cessation of her nocturnal activities.

A soft breeze whispered through the scrub, ruffling her tunic, tugging at the scarf which tied her hair back from her face. A gentle reminder that she had work to do. Shouldering the leather bag which contained her notebook and tools, Tahira began to explore the site.

She had completed a full circuit of the circumference of the rock formation, and had just clambered up to examine the entrance to the mine when the flicker of light from a lantern coming from inside the tunnel made her freeze in horror. There was a guard on duty after all. Heart bumping, mouth dry, Tahira turned away, bracing herself to flee down the steep incline towards her camel. He must have moved with the litheness and lightning speed of a sand cat, for she had taken no more than two steps when one very strong arm encircled her waist, lifting her clean off her feet.

'How dare you! Release me at once.'

She could not decipher the guard's response, for it was uttered in a foreign tongue, but he set her down immediately before turning her around to face him. 'A woman! What in the name of the stars are you doing here?'

He spoke in Arabic now, though his accent was odd. Tahira blinked up at him in astonishment. 'You are not a guard. What are you doing here, creeping about like a thief in the middle of the night?'

He laughed brazenly, holding the lantern higher. 'I might reasonably ask you the same question.'

He was tall, dressed in dusty, everyday garb, a drab brown tunic and trousers rather like her own, a cloak that might have been white at some point in the distant past, and brown-leather riding boots, but there was nothing at all everyday about the man himself. In fact, Tahira's first thought was that here was a man one would never forget meeting. Her second was that he was not only memorable, but at a visceral level extremely attractive. His tousled hair gleamed gold in the lantern light. His skin was deeply tanned, he had a strong nose and a sensual mouth, but it was his eyes which drew her attention, for they were the most extraordinary piercing blue rimmed with grey and, even more than the vicious scimitar which hung from his belt, proclaimed him dangerous.

She shivered as a mixture of fear and excitement coursed through her. 'You realise that you are trespassing? This mine is the rightful property of King Haydar.'

'As are all the mines in the kingdom of Nessarah, I believe, but it appears I am not the only trespasser.' He adjusted the lantern so it illuminated her face. 'I would hazard a guess that you are not a miner, though if you are, you are the most extraordinarily attractive one I have had the good fortune to meet. And believe me, I have encountered my fair share of miners.'

His supreme self-assurance in the face of what he must realise was a perilous situation was astonishing. And intoxicating. If he showed no fear, why should she? He made no attempt to prevent her leaving. Tahira knew she ought to do just that, but now she was sure she had not been recognised, she didn't want to leave. She had no reason at all to trust this man, yet her instincts told her he meant her no harm. Besides, she was very curious. And, yes, very attracted too. His smile made her catch her breath. It made her wonder, shockingly, what it would be like to feel his lips on hers—she, who had never in all her twenty-four years been kissed even once.

'Your deductive powers are to be admired,' Tahira said, unable to resist returning that smile. 'You are quite correct, I am not a miner.'

The stranger exhaled sharply. 'But you *are* a beauty. What are you doing out here alone in the desert at night?'

'I am quite accustomed to being alone in the

desert at night, and until now, have been adept at protecting my solitude.'

His teeth flashed white as he grinned. 'Then we are kindred spirits, Madam…?'

She hesitated, but it was highly unlikely he would make anything of her first name. 'Given the informal nature of our introduction, I think you may call me Tahira.'

His eyebrows quirked. 'A woman of discretion. It is a pleasure to make your acquaintance, Tahira. Permit me to introduce myself in a similarly informal manner. My name is Christopher,' he said, making a flourishing bow. 'At your service.'

'Christopher,' she repeated slowly. 'An English name?' she hazarded, and when he nodded, added, 'You are very far from home.'

'I have no home.' His expression clouded momentarily, but then he shrugged. 'And you, Tahira, are you far from home?'

Now it was her turn to shrug. 'Not so very far.'

'You are mysterious as well as discreet.'

She laughed. 'Significantly less mysterious than you, a stranger to these lands.'

'I beg to differ,' the Englishman said with another of his devastating smiles. 'Your presence here raises a multitude of questions. What is a beautiful woman dressed in male garb doing examining the workings of a mine, quite alone and in the middle of the night? How did she get here? Where did she come from? Why the disguise? You cannot, surely, expect anyone to be fooled into thinking you a man?'

Though his tone was teasing still, she had the distinct impression that his questions had a point to them. It was natural enough for him to be curious, she supposed, given her unorthodox appearance, but she could not risk him becoming too curious. 'My clothes are merely practical, like yours,' Tahira said.

She had underestimated him. 'Made from considerably more expensive material than mine, and considerably less worn too. Proof, if proof were needed, that you are not a miner,' he said. 'And yet you knew of the existence of this mine. It has only just been opened up, excavation is in its infancy. How came you by your information?'

Tahira's stomach knotted. She shrugged in what she hoped was a careless manner. 'I could ask you the same question.'

'You could,' the Englishman responded, 'but I asked it of you first.'

There was no change in his tone, which remained pleasant enough, no change either in his expression, yet she knew beyond a shadow of a doubt that he meant to get an answer. What could he possibly suspect? Instinctively she knew he would see through any lie, but the truth—no, that was impossible. The safest thing would be to leave without comment, but she found she didn't want to play safe.

'I have no interest in the mine itself,' Tahira said, opting for a partial version of the truth. 'I am interested only in the possibility that the seam may have been excavated in ancient times, and that the miners left evidence of their settlement here.'

She did not expect her answer to have such a startling effect on the Englishman, nor had she truly believed it would distract him from his original question, but it did. His fair brows shot up, all traces of a smile fading. 'And have you found any such evidence?' he demanded. 'Do you have any idea how old such a settlement might be.'

'This is my first visit to this site, but a number of our—of Nessarah's reserves of minerals and ores have been mined to some degree since ancient times,' Tahira replied, struggling to understand the change in him. 'Goodness, is it possible—are you yourself interested in such sites?'

Her incredulity made him smile again. 'I am more than interested. In fact, I'm a passionate antiquarian.'

Now it was her turn to stare in astonishment. 'Are you teasing me?'

'No, I assure you. For some years now, I have been involved in a number of archaeological digs. Some in Britain, but the majority in Egypt. I have to say, though, that in all my travels I have not encountered a female antiquarian. Are you working alone?'

'I am not working as such. It is an interest with me, that is all.'

'An interest you choose to pursue in the hours of darkness?'

That look again, it was silly to imagine he could read her thoughts, but it was how she felt. Tahira crossed her arms, meeting his bright blue eyes square on. 'As you do?'

'As you have already deduced, I don't have permission from the King to be here, any more than you. I wonder, what is it that drew you here, to this particular mine on this particular night?'

She couldn't understand the edge to his voice.

What on earth did he suspect her of? 'You cannot possibly be imagining that my presence has anything to do with yours?'

She had spoken flippantly, yet she had, astoundingly, hit the mark. 'It is rather a coincidence, you'll admit,' Christopher said.

'A coincidence and nothing more,' Tahira countered, quite nonplussed. 'Who are you, to imagine I would go to such extreme measures to make your acquaintance?'

He had the grace to look sheepish. 'Forgive me. I am simply suspicious by nature. And also innately curious. If this encounter of ours is mere coincidence, then it is a most delightful one. Do you happen to know what it is they expect to find here?'

He had turned his attentions to extinguishing the lantern, but she was not fooled. 'Do you?'

She did not expect him to answer, but after a brief hesitation he did. 'Turquoise.'

'That is supposed to be a very closely guarded secret.'

Too late, she understood the speculative look, realised that she had walked straight into his trap as his eyes lit up. 'So it's true!'

'Are you a speculator?'

He grasped her arm. 'Is it true? How do you know for certain? If this is indeed a turquoise mine it would signal the end of a very long journey for me.'

There was a fervent light in his eyes, a rapt expression on his face. Bitterly disappointed, she pulled her arm free. 'So you *are* a speculator after all, in search of riches.'

But Christopher shook his head vehemently. 'If I was, don't you think I'd be more interested in locating a new diamond or gold mine? Nessarah is well endowed with both, and not all of it has been worked yet, by any manner of means.'

'How on earth do you know that?'

'It is of no import. What's vital is confirming beyond doubt that this is indeed a turquoise mine.'

'It isn't any sort of mine as yet,' Tahira exclaimed, becoming quite frustrated. 'If you're truly an antiquarian as you claim, why are you more interested in the mineral being mined than the possibility that it was mined in ancient times?'

'The truth is that both are crucial to the successful conclusion of my quest.'

'Quest? You make it sound like some noble undertaking.'

'There is nothing noble about it, quite the opposite, but it is an undertaking and a solemn one at that.' The Englishman pursed his lips, frowning deeply. 'I have no idea who you are, why you're here alone, or how you have come by your information, but if you possess knowledge of Nessarah's ancient mining history, you could be a precious find worth a great deal more than diamonds to me.'

Which admission could not but capture her interest, though she tried not to let it show. 'I would not claim to be an expert, but the study of Nessarah's history is a passion of mine,' Tahira said cautiously. '*I* did not lie about my reason for being here.'

'I promise you, I didn't lie either. I too came here in search of an ancient settlement, because it would bring me one step closer to solving an ancient mystery.'

'By the stars, what mystery?' she asked, abandoning any attempt to disguise her interest.

But Christopher, having come tantalisingly close to confiding in her, now seemed to be having second thoughts. 'How do I know I can trust you? How do I know that you won't head back to wherever it is you came from and tell your husband, who will report me to the authorities?'

'Firstly, because I have no husband. Secondly, and more importantly, the very last thing I would do is inform anyone of our encounter. As you must already have surmised, I'm not supposed to be here. And if it were discovered that I was, and not where I should be—' Tahira broke off, suppressing a shudder. 'Be assured, I would not be so foolish as to betray you, when to do so would be to betray myself.'

'Do you mean that you have run away?'

'Escaped, in a manner of speaking, but only temporarily.'

'Escaped from what?'

'My life. My home,' she amended, not wishing to sound over-dramatic, even if it was the truth.

Christopher's brows rose. 'So you're supposed to be tucked up in bed safe and sound, but you've escaped into the night in order to pursue your interest in Nessarah's ancient heritage?'

'Is that so hard to believe?'

'Tahira.' Christopher touched her arm lightly. 'I'm not mocking you. I'm simply—I'm impressed. To take such a risk shows a true love of the past which certainly equals if not exceeds mine.'

'Oh.' She was absurdly pleased by the compliment. 'I am only—it is something I do only for myself. No one else—well, they can't know. Do you understand now why I would not betray you?'

'You assume that I am not going to betray you either.'

She had done exactly that. Was she being utterly naïve? 'Why would you, when you have just described me, in rather melodramatic terms, as a precious find? Unless of course that was a crude attempt at flattery. More tellingly, your presence here in the dead of night proves that, for whatever reason, you have no more desire to be discovered than I.'

'You are, of course, quite correct,' Christopher said, visibly relaxing. 'But I was not flattering you. Your knowledge of Nessarah's history could well prove to be of great assistance to me. If you are not in a hurry to melt back into the night, perhaps I can explain why I am here?'

This man was a foreigner as well as a complete stranger. She really ought to get on her camel and head home. But she knew she would regret it. An ancient mystery. A quest which was solemn but not noble. She had to know more. Besides, she had never before felt so drawn to a man. Hardly surprising, since her circumstances meant she met very few, but this man was different. He shared her fascination for the past. And, yes, he was handsome too, but it was his eyes which set him apart. And that smile, which seemed to connect directly with her insides, making her certain, despite her utter lack of experience, that the attraction was mutual.

'I am in no great rush,' Tahira said. 'I do not promise that I can help you, but I would very much like to hear more.'

The masculine clothes this exotic female wore made Christopher acutely aware of the very feminine and extremely voluptuous body beneath. Following Tahira down the steep slope of the rock formation to where he could now see she had left her camel, he couldn't drag his eyes away from the sensuous sway of her hips, the long, glossy sheath of hair that rippled down her back, the scarf which tied it fluttering like a pennant, urging him to follow. She moved with the careless grace of a dancer. That first glimpse of her perfect countenance had been like a punch in the stomach. No, he amended wryly, it was not his stomach which had reacted to those big almond-shaped eyes and that cherry-red mouth, and that heart-shaped face, and the sweet curves of the body beneath. He had never in his life met a woman so lovely and so innocently alluring. Who the devil was she? His curiosity was aroused, but what mattered even more was whether or not she could help him.

As they reached the softer sand, Tahira sat down gracefully and Christopher joined her, sitting cross-legged. 'So tell me,' he said, 'do you think this is likely to prove an ancient site?'

She raised a delicately arched brow. 'Is this a test of my expertise, before you confide in me?' When he did not deny it, she gave a charming little shrug. 'Understandable enough. I told you that I am by no means an expert. I am fortunate enough to have access to some manuscripts, histories, maps of Nessarah. Over the years, I have made a study of my kingdom's ancient history and traced a number of the older mines—the diamonds and gold which we are famous for, but also some emerald, silver, of course, and semi-precious stones. My practical experience, however, is severely limited.'

'Due to the fact that you have to confine any excavation to the hours of darkness, I presume?'

'Yes. I know it sounds unlikely...'

'Tahira, it's so unlikely that I believe you. You would not make up such a preposterous lie.'

'That is very true. In fact, it's so preposterous that it is one of the reasons I think it unlikely my occasional absences will be discovered. Though of late...' She sighed, averting her gaze momentarily, before giving herself a little shake. 'There is no real method to my work. My process is not scientific, my notes and drawings rudimentary, as would be obvious to an experienced archaeologist like you.'

So he was not to ask what had been happening 'of late'. Christopher accepted this grudgingly. Fascinating as she was, at this point in time, her knowledge mattered a great deal more to him than her circumstances. 'I am actually a surveyor to trade, but my heart belongs to the ancient world.'

Which remark earned him a delightful smile. 'It is so wonderful,' Tahira said, 'to meet someone who understands the thrill of standing in the remains of dwellings built thousands of years ago, of holding pots used for cooking, plates that food was eaten from, cups that wine was drunk from—it is the most thrilling—there is nothing quite like it, is there?'

Her eyes sparkled. Her lips were curved into a

soft smile that made his groin tighten. 'No,' Christopher said, 'there really is nothing like it.'

'My sisters tease me when I say that I sense a—a connection of some sort with our ancestors. When I stand amid the ruins of an ancient mining village here in Arabia, one that existed deep in the mists of time, I feel the ghosts, the spirits of the people who lived there.'

'How many sisters do you have?'

'Three, all younger than I, and their only interest in ancient mines is the jewellery made from the precious stones unearthed there. Ish—my next sister says that our ancestors are unlikely to have been miners and she is probably right, but—oh, I don't know. I like to think that there is something, some inherited fragment of memory, which connects me to the few settlements I have uncovered, the artefacts I have found there.' Tahira looked away, embarrassed. 'You probably think that's fanciful.'

'As a matter of fact,' Christopher confessed, 'I understand perfectly. I too, occasionally, feel a similar connection. A memory—though it can't possibly be a memory. Or a ghost—though I'm not sure I believe in those either. But I do know what you mean.'

'Really? I don't know anyone else who thinks as I do.'

Her shy smile was dazzling. Dear heavens, but she had no business to be looking at him like that. Christopher tore his gaze away, focusing on the rocky outcrop over her shoulder. 'I take it your sisters aid and abet you in your nocturnal excursions?'

'Oh, goodness, no. They would be horrified if they ever found out, and frightened for me too. The stories I tell them—they think my only sources are books. I dare not show them any of my finds. Not that they would be interested, since none of them are valuable.'

'So you keep all your work hidden away?'

'It is not so very difficult, since my work is not so very extensive. One day perhaps hundreds of years from now, someone might find my little collection of papers and artefacts, and wonder how it came to exist. I would like to think of it as my own contribution to Nessarah's history, but I doubt very much it's of any real worth save to me.' Tahira gave a bitter little laugh. 'My life's work. There is not much to show for it.'

'As yet, perhaps. You are very young, you have many years of exploration ahead of you.'

She had a habit of turning her head to one side, of lowering her lids to mask her eyes and her emotions. 'I'm twenty-four. My father and brother think that I am already past my prime. If they have their way, which they will imminently, I have very little time left in which to indulge my passion.'

'What do you mean?'

But Tahira shook her head, forcing a smile. 'I intend to make the most of what little time and freedom I have, that is all. Tell me, what is it that you survey?'

It was an obvious change of subject, but he followed her lead, for she was clearly upset and just as evidently determined not to be. 'I specialise in the discovery of minerals and ores,' Christopher said, 'and by doing so, I fund my archaeological research.'

'Including your trip to Arabia?'

'It is not business that brings me to Arabia.'

'No, indeed, you are here on a quest to solve an ancient mystery which I may be able to help you with.'

'Precisely. I propose, if you are amenable, that we work together, pool our resources. Time is of the essence here. It's likely that the evidence we're looking for will be destroyed once mining gets underway.'

'That is very true and also rather flattering,' Tahira said, giving him a straight look, 'but you still haven't told me why you wish to explore the site in the first place?'

A simple question, and one he must answer if he was to enlist this fascinating woman's help. Yet Christopher hesitated. Could he trust her? Clearly she had not been sent to spy on him, as he had somewhat ridiculously assumed. In the course of the last six months here in Arabia, the agents he had been so reluctantly given access to had been a diverse and frequently dubious group, but none had been a woman. Might she be a speculator? Equally ridiculous, surely. No, he was pretty certain that her claim to be an antiquarian was true. Whatever else she was…

Was not relevant, he decided. 'It is the turquoise which matters,' Christopher said. 'I need to prove that it was mined here about fifteen hundred years ago, and I need somehow to obtain a sample of the mineral.' Feeling slightly sick, he reached for the leather pouch, took out the amulet and handed it to Tahira. 'In order to match it with this.'

Chapter Two

Tahira gazed at the artefact in astonishment, turning it over and over in her hands. The gold links of the chain were the intensely deep-yellow colour which indicated purity. The amulet itself was round, the rim studded with alternating diamonds and turquoise. An intricate design composed of narrow bands of vivid blue enamel on gold had been overlaid on to the main pendant, forming petal-like segments, into which were set much larger diamonds surrounded by more turquoise. But the centre of the amulet was empty.

'There is something missing here,' she said, tracing the oddly-shaped inset with her finger. 'Another stone?'

'Possibly. That is something I'd very much like to find out, though I doubt I ever will,' Christopher replied. 'What do you make of it?'

'I think it is the most beautiful piece of jewellery I have ever seen.' Tahira scrutinised the amulet more closely. 'The design is very distinctive, and typical of this region. I have seen pictures of similar examples in ancient manuscripts. It almost certainly originates from southern Arabia and is clearly very old and very valuable. The light is too poor for me to make a proper examination, but the clarity of these diamonds looks to be peerless. And the turquoise—again, I cannot be certain, but I don't think I've ever seen stones of this particular hue.'

'They are indeed very rare. I have not found a single match anywhere. Yet.'

'Oh!' Realisation finally dawned on her. 'Do you think that this mine…?'

'I very much hope so.'

'Mined on this very spot, fifteen hundred years ago,' Tahira said dreamily, running her fingers over the turquoise. The amulet was warm in her hand. Her fingers traced the design compulsively. 'How absolutely wonderful if you could prove that to be the case. I have never felt so drawn to anything as this. How on earth did you come by it?'

Christopher's smile became rigid. 'It came to

me through my mother. Though not directly. I never knew her. She died giving birth to me.'

'Oh, Christopher.' Tears sprang to Tahira's eyes. Even now, after all this time, her own loss could catch her unawares. 'My mother too died in childbirth, but at least I had ten precious years with her. I am so very sorry.'

'One cannot miss what one never knew, nor mourn what one never had.'

He spoke curtly, as if he would not have cared to know the woman who gave birth to him, but that could not be. He was a man, that was all, and as such did not care to show his pain. 'Then this amulet must mean a great deal to you,' Tahira said. 'A very precious connection to your past.' She reached inside the neckline of her tunic, pulling free her gold chain. 'My mother gave me this. It is a Bedouin star. The traveller's star. I wear it always. My most precious connection to my past. I would never wish to be parted from it.'

'Be that as it may, I am determined to sever mine.'

Tahira's jaw dropped. 'Sever?' she repeated, thinking she had misheard him, or that he had translated the word wrongly.

'Sever,' Christopher repeated. 'By returning this object to its true owner.'

'But surely you are its true owner?' she said, utterly bewildered and a little intimidated by the turn in his mood.

Sensing her confusion, Christopher made an obvious effort to lighten his tone. 'I'm sorry, I should not have spoken so vehemently. I have been six months in Arabia, attempting to match the stones set in the amulet, and am grown weary of the task.'

'But why attempt such a task in the first place? I don't understand, do you believe the amulet to be stolen?'

He laughed shortly. 'Almost certainly, by tomb-robbers, centuries ago. But as to its recent provenance...' His lip curled. 'I have it on unimpeachable authority that I am the legal owner.'

'Yet you wish to give it away? It must be very valuable. Why not sell it, if it pains you to own it?'

He shuddered. 'To profit from such a thing—no, unthinkable. I could not square that with my conscience.'

Tahira furrowed her brow. 'Because it is a sacred object? I can understand that, but why then don't you put it on display in a museum?'

Another curled lip was his reply to what Tahira thought a perfectly reasonable suggestion. 'A solution suggested to me by another. You cannot understand, though he most certainly should have, why that too is impossible. The amulet belongs here in Arabia, and nowhere else.'

'Your sentiments do you great credit,' Tahira said, which was true, though her instincts told her those sentiments were very far from the whole truth. 'But to come all the way to Arabia on a—a quest, as you call it, which you may not be able to complete seems—honestly, quite an extraordinary thing to do. What if your quest proves futile?'

'It cannot prove futile. Until I rid myself of this thing, I can't—' Christopher broke off, screwing his eyes tight shut, clearly struggling for control. 'I must return it,' he said with a finality that made it clear that the subject was closed, 'there is nothing else to be done.'

Why? she longed to ask. Why do you gaze at this beautiful object as if you loathe it? Why must you *rid yourself* of an heirloom, a bequest from the mother you never knew? Why is it so important to you that you have spent six months of your life on a near impossible task? But he would answer none of those questions, that much was very clear. 'How will you confirm the origin of the piece?' Tahira queried instead. 'And to whom will you return it?'

'The stones hold the key,' Christopher replied, his deep frown lightening at the change of subject. 'The combination of this particular shade of turquoise and the clarity of these diamonds, along with the purity of gold, is unique. If I can locate the sources, link them closely geographically, prove that all were being mined at about the time this amulet was made, then I will know I am in the right place.'

'How many wrong places have you visited?'

He shrugged, but she was pleased to see the faintest trace of a smile. 'I have confined my wanderings to the southern region, concentrating on the kingdoms where I already knew diamonds and gold had been mined.'

'How did you come by such information?'

'Well, you said yourself that the amulet is distinctly southern Arabian in style, and I'm a surveyor to trade, as I told you. Ores and minerals are my business, and I have a—a talent for it. It was fairly straightforward once I'd narrowed down the general location.'

Proof—not that she needed it—of just how

much this quest of his meant to Christopher. 'You must have traversed any number of kingdoms,' Tahira said, awed. 'To travel so widely, you must have gone to a great deal of trouble. Papers, permissions...'

'Oh, I can produce papers if I'm required to,' he replied, waving his hand dismissively, 'but I prefer to avoid getting entangled in red tape. Officials trying to be helpful can sometimes be— well, over-inquisitive. And over-suspicious at times too—let's face it, you were suspicious of me yourself.'

Was he teasing her? No, that light in his eyes, it was more of a challenge. He could play by the rules, but he preferred not to. She didn't know whether to be impressed or appalled. 'But—but now I understand why you are here, and I am not an official, Christopher. If you were caught snooping about at this mine, you would be in serious trouble.'

'Hence my decision to come here in the middle of the night. I have no time to jump through official hoops, Tahira. I must find a way to lay my hands on a piece of ore from this mine as soon as possible. While the turquoise on the amulet is the least valuable component, its rarity is the key

to its provenance. And so, like you, I've no intentions either of curtailing my activities or of being
caught in the act. We'll make a good team, don't
you think?'

She thought she must be a little mad to be agree-
ing to this. She thought his recklessness must have
infected her. There was no getting away from the
fact that the more often she escaped, the more
chance there was of her being discovered, but time
was no more on her side than on Christopher's.
This man, this stranger who attracted and intimidated her by turn, wanted her help with his most
improbable, most intriguing quest. She would
never get such an opportunity again. There was
no possibility of her refusing.

'I think we will make an excellent team.' Smiling, Tahira turned her attention back to the amulet, examining the stones in question more closely.
'The turquoise is undoubtedly very distinctive, but
it's likely to be a few weeks before any samples
are unearthed.'

'How do you know that?'

She could have kicked herself. 'An educated
guess, nothing more,' she said lightly.

Christopher looked sceptical, but he chose not

to press her. 'Then I have a few weeks' grace in which to match the gold and diamonds.'

'Ah, now I finally understand how I can be of assistance. And I'm pleased to say that I think I can, if what you want is confirmation that diamonds and gold were mined in Nessarah fifteen hundred years ago.'

'That's exactly what I need,' he responded warmly. 'It would save me a great deal of time and legwork. In return I can help you to explore this site, and by doing so, I very much hope, obtain the final proof I need. A mutually beneficial arrangement, I think you'll agree?'

She would agree to almost anything when he looked at her like that, his smile teasing and wicked and reckless. 'I do,' Tahira said, handing him the amulet back and trying to prevent her own smile from betraying her pleasure. 'That would be wonderful. Even more so if I can help you prove that this came originally from Nessarah. Though if you do mean to restore it to its owner, and if it is indeed fifteen hundred years old, then presumably you hope to track down a descendant?'

'You've said yourself that it's extremely valuable, which means it was almost certainly created for a member of the ruling family. In Nessarah's case, that would be King Haydar.'

'By the stars!'

'It seems the obvious conclusion to reach,' Christopher said. 'I don't know why you're so surprised.'

'I suppose so,' Tahira said, trying desperately to contain her astonishment. 'I am simply—it is all so strange, isn't it? I came here tonight hoping to find a few shards of pottery or a crude flint. Instead I found you, a man who shares my passion for the past, seeking to resolve the provenance of a beautiful artefact which may have been fashioned right here, in the kingdom I call home. To think that I may even be able to play a part in proving this, that is the stuff of my dreams, Christopher. This encounter—surely it has been arranged by the fates?'

'I would not go so far as to call it destiny, but I would agree it is serendipitous.'

His smile made her lose her train of thought. Her breathing quickened. He leaned towards her, and as if they were connected by some invisible force, she leaned towards him. He pushed a tendril of her hair back from her forehead, his fingers trailing down her cheek. 'You smell delightful. What scent is it?'

Her heart was pounding. 'Jasmine.' Her voice had faded to a whisper.

'I have the absurd conviction that your kisses would taste of peaches.' His mouth hovered mere inches from hers. 'It is absurd, isn't it?'

Her mouth went dry. 'I don't know. I've never been kissed.'

Christopher groaned. 'The ultimate temptation and the ultimate deterrent. Do you have any idea how utterly delectable you are?' He shook his head, sitting back. 'No, of course you don't, and I should not have said so.'

'Because you don't mean it?'

He laughed. 'I never pay empty compliments. Utterly delectable does not do you justice. I have never met a woman like you.'

'Now that is a compliment I can very easily return, for I have never met a man like you—though no doubt you will have deduced I have met very few men, and may think it's not that high a compliment. But I have a feeling it would make no difference if I had.'

'Tahira, you should not say such things, and you ought not to look at a man with those big eyes when you do, and smile that way, and—you can have no idea of the effect you have when you smile at me like that.'

She felt as if her veins were full of sherbet. She was sparkling, alight. And she felt quite wicked. 'When I first saw you tonight, I thought to myself, there is a man one would never forget. A dangerous man. With a very dangerous smile.'

'When I first saw you tonight, and you smiled at me...' Shaking his head, Christopher looked up at the stars and frowned. 'Speaking of danger, delightful as your company is, I don't want you to risk returning in the daylight to wherever it is you've sprung from.'

Reluctantly, Tahira too looked up at the sky, and gave a startled exclamation. 'I had no idea it was so late—or rather, early. I will do everything in my power to help you, but I must go now. Will we meet again here, tomorrow night?'

Christopher jumped up, helping her to her feet. 'Is it safe for you to do so?'

She rarely risked two night-time excursions in a row, but time was of the essence in so many ways. 'I'll be here,' Tahira said emphatically.

'Then so too will I.' He watched her as she pulled on her cloak and headdress, securing her leather satchel to the camel's saddle. A click of the tongue, and the beast was on its knees waiting for her to mount. Christopher took her hand, pressing it lightly before she clambered into the saddle. 'Until tomorrow.'

A quick wave, and she headed off, urging the languid beast into a trot. She didn't look back, but she sensed him watching her fading into the desert landscape.

Later, as she lay exhausted on her divan, she wondered if he had been a mirage, a figment of her imagination conjured up by the desert sands, a beguiling vision who would melt away in the harsh light of day, never to return. Burying her head under the pillow to block out the light filtering through the high oriel window, Tahira smiled to herself. She would have her answer soon enough.

The next evening, Christopher closed his notebook, placing it first in a waxed cover before concealing it behind a loose stone in the wall of the abandoned house which had been his temporary home for the last few weeks. It was highly unlikely that anyone would happen across it and if they did, impossible to imagine that they could break his ingenious code, but its very existence, the fact that his work *was* encoded, would give rise to suspicion, even without the incriminating sketches and maps.

The contents of his notebook went well beyond the remit of the dossier he had offered to compile for Lord Henry Armstrong, payment for the official strings the diplomat had pulled to expedite Christopher's journey, and the local contacts he had provided. Thankfully, their bargain could be concluded without another face-to-face meeting. Christopher was determined never to set eyes on that loathsome countenance again. When he was done here, the shameful personal tie which neither of them welcomed, the existence of which Christopher had been oblivious almost his whole life, would be severed for ever. That dark past would be obliterated, the slate wiped clean. He would be master of his own destiny, free to embrace the future on his own terms.

A very lucrative future it could be too, if he chose to remain here in Arabia. Ironically, during the last six months, while seeking the owner of the amulet and collating the contents of Lord Armstrong's dossier, Christopher had also discovered a plethora of hitherto untapped natural resources. The so-called Midas Touch which made him highly sought after as a surveyor was proving every bit as effective here in the Arabian landscape as it had proved in Britain and in Egypt. There was a wealth of ores and minerals just waiting to be exploited. He could easily make his fortune, or facilitate the making of others' fortunes, if he were so inclined.

He was most emphatically not so inclined, though his meticulous habits dictated that he record every potential location, regardless. In the wrong hands, his very comprehensive findings could prove to be politically explosive.

Reminded of the hands his dossier was due to be delivered into—white, long-fingered, aristocratic, atavistic hands that he never wished to lay eyes on again—he shuddered with revulsion. He would make damned sure he provided only what he had agreed and no more. Bad enough that his lordship would benefit even to the degree Christopher had promised. It would be some consolation to deprive that peer of untold and as yet undiscovered riches. He could think of no man less deserving than that particular man, who had stolen his family, laid waste to his history. A man who placed his ruthless ambition before all else, who cared naught when others bore the consequences of his vile actions, and who bought silence with blood money. Recalling their one and only meeting, Christopher's hand curled into a tight, painful fist, his mouth set into a vicious snarl. The day he rid himself of the connection could not come a moment too soon.

And it would come. For the first time since he set out on this long journey, he believed the end might be in sight. Unfurling his fist, firmly confining Lord Armstrong to the dark recesses of his mind, Christopher rolled his shoulders, stiff from hours hunched over his makeshift desk. Heading for the outbuilding containing the well, he hauled up a fresh supply of water, stripped himself of his dusty tunic, and made his *toilette*. The underground spring which fed the well was deep, the water icy as he doused himself with it, stinging his freshly shaved chin. His spare tunic was almost as threadbare as the one he had taken off, but at least it was clean.

Pulling his boots back on, he sat down at the entrance of his temporary dwelling, staring up at the sky as it segued from pale blue to indigo. It was going to be a clear night. A propitious beginning to their exploration of the mine's environs? Finally, after all this time, he must surely be on the right track. Closing his eyes, he could almost see his future, wavering like a mirage on the edge of his mind, so tantalisingly close.

Perhaps even closer than he imagined, with Tahira's assistance. Christopher smiled slowly to himself. He was looking forward to seeing her again. Draping his cloak around him, and fastening the *igal* which held his headdress in place, he closed the door of his makeshift abode and went out to saddle his camel. Who would have thought that a chance meeting would bring about this collision of two people from such impossibly different worlds? He could not have dreamt of encountering a more beautiful, intriguing, exotic companion. That she not only shared his love of the past, but would, with luck, help him close the door on his own shameful history—fate, she had called it, and he had disagreed. But perhaps he had been wrong to do so. It might be that, every now and then, the stars did indeed align.

The third and innermost courtyard of the Royal Palace of Nessarah was a vast enclosed space, surrounded on all sides by a colonnade of twenty-two marble columns, the walls of which were set with huge mirrors interspersed with elaborate plaster-work covered in gold leaf, the pattern repeated on the ceiling. Divans covered in crimson velvet, tas-selled with gold, lined the colonnade at regular in-tervals, the overall impression being one of lush, shaded opulence. In contrast, the central square of the courtyard was flooded with light.

The high domed ceiling was painted in ultrama-rine and studded with gold stars. The lower walls were covered in blue and white tiles, the higher ones painted a soft dove-grey, and the arched win-dows, deliberately set far too high for anyone to peer either in or out, allowed light to dapple the rich silk carpets and terracotta floor tiles. The inner courtyard was, like every other room in the harem complex, beautiful, luxurious, and utterly closed off to the outside world. Or so King Haydar and his only son, Prince Ghutrif, believed. Tahira, the eldest of the royal princesses, knew better.

The crystal chandelier which hung from the central point of the dome held exactly one-hundred-and-twenty-two candles. Tahira knew this for certain, for she had counted them nu-merous times in an attempt to pass the hours until darkness fell, forcing herself to lie still on the divan, refusing to consult her little jewelled timepiece yet again. She could feel it ticking now where it nestled, concealed beneath her clothing, marking out the hours, minutes, seconds, until she was once more free.

Out of the corner of her eye, she saw her brother's wife, Juwan, enter the courtyard from the door which led to the Crown Princess's official quarters. Heavy with her second child, which she determinedly proclaimed to all would this time prove to be a prized son, Juwan scanned the room, a frown drawing her finely arched brows together, which cleared as her gaze alighted on her prey.

Quickly closing her eyes, Tahira feigned sleep, but as Juwan sank on to the divan beside her with small sigh, she accepted the inevitable and sat up.

'Juwan, you look fatigued, don't you think you should rest, given your condition? It would be better if I left you in peace to do so.' She stood, arranging a number of silk and velvet cushions invitingly, but although her sister-in-law lowered herself slowly down, rubbing the small of her back, she shook her head when Tahira made to leave.

'No, stay with me a while. I wish to have a little talk with you.'

Tahira's heart sank, for since the official visit from Murimon's Chief Adviser two weeks ago which put an abrupt end to her betrothal, she had endured several such little talks or, more accurately, lectures. Juwan had made it clear—as if Tahira could possibly be in any doubt—that she was very deeply in disgrace. Resigning herself to the inevitable, from force of habit keeping her expression carefully neutral, Tahira pulled a large cushion to face the divan and sank down on to it, crossing her legs.

'Only a few more weeks now, until your baby arrives. You must grow weary of waiting,' she said brightly, in an attempt to divert her sister-in-law on to her favourite subject.

Juwan folded her hands over her mountainous stomach. 'When the time is right, my fine son will grace us with his presence. It is his father who is impatient. Your brother is naturally anxious,' she added hastily, lest her words be construed as any form or criticism, 'to finally welcome his long-awaited heir. A man needs a son. I pray I do not let my husband down again.'

Ghutrif had demonstrated little interest in his daughter. Little wonder that Juwan refused to countenance the possibility of a second female child. Though every fibre of her being rebelled, Tahira could not dispute the facts. Here in the royal palace, patriarchal rule had always been both culturally entrenched and rigorously enforced, regardless of the slowly changing outside world. Here in the Nessarah harem, the female of the species was defined by her ability to produce more males to continue the line, or alternatively to enrich the kingdom by means of advantageous marriage contracts.

'As you know,' Juwan said, returning to the subject of her visit, 'this most unfortunate second broken betrothal of yours has upset your brother and father a great deal.'

'My first betrothed died unexpectedly. That was far more unfortunate for him than me, wouldn't you say?'

'Indeed it was. And only a matter of weeks before the marriage, in a most tragic and untimely accident.'

Tahira bit her tongue. Of course she would never have wished Prince Butrus dead, but she could not lie to herself. The tragic news had also come as a huge relief.

'Clearly no blame can be laid at your door for that first instance,' Juwan reluctantly conceded, 'but now it has happened again, and involving the very same royal family. It does not reflect well on you.'

'I was not the one who tore up the marriage contract,' Tahira retorted indignantly. 'And Prince Kadar, I understand, compensated our family far more generously than is customary in such circumstances.'

Juwan pursed her lips. 'You see, this is another example of the many character traits which cause my husband great concern. Dowries, compensation, these are not matters we women should be discussing. No matter how much recompense your family may have received, the stain of shame clings to you, yet your behaviour in no way reflects this.'

'What do you expect me to do, hide in a corner crying, or simply keep my head permanently bowed and my mouth permanently closed?'

'That would certainly be a good start,' Juwan replied tartly. 'You set a very poor example to your sisters, continuing as if nothing has happened.'

'Because as far as I'm concerned nothing did happen!' Tahira exclaimed, her temper rising. 'The one and only time I met Prince Kadar of Murimon, we were heavily chaperoned, and all communication was carried out on my behalf by my brother. I did nothing and I said nothing. The outcome is not my fault.'

'You forget,' Juwan said, 'that I was one of the chaperons present to protect your honour. Though your father and my husband may have been oblivious, you overlook the fact that I too have been raised in the confines of the harem, and I too understand the unspoken language, the nuances of the body women such as we have learned to perfect. You made your indifference to the prince very clear without recourse to words.'

There was no point in denying the truth of this. Tahira had from the first fought both betrothals as furiously as was possible against the implacable wall of her brother's determination to marry her off, to absolutely no effect. The fates had twice intervened in her favour, but she doubted they would do so again.

It was time to deploy a risky strategy. 'If there is such a very large stain of shame attached to me, perhaps we should accept that I am simply not marriageable,' Tahira said. 'Very soon now, you will have your hands full taking care of your new son as well as your daughter. You will not wish to be distracted by having to look after the welfare of my younger sisters too. Let me be their official chaperon. Let me take the burden of that responsibility from you. I would be content with that role and would carry it out dutifully.'

'So now, finally, you allow your true colours to show,' Juwan said disdainfully. 'Ghutrif and I are of one mind, Tahira. Your one and only duty, the purpose for which you have been bred, is to enhance the power and wealth of Nessarah through marriage. As the wife of the Crown Prince, it is *my* duty to ensure that your sisters are taken care of and married appropriately when the time comes, not yours.'

'Juwan, I promised my mother...'

'Tahira, that is another lesson which you have signally failed to learn. Your allegiance is not to a woman fourteen years dead, but to your brother, and to myself as his consort. Our wish is to have you married as soon as possible, sparing us all the pain of your most childish behaviour in defying us. Ghutrif will have his way. The easiest thing for yourself and the sisters you claim to love is to accept the inevitable with good grace.'

'I do not *claim* to love my sisters. I love them with all my heart. Ever since our mama died...'

'Spare me.' Juwan made no attempt to hide her

animosity. 'You think yourself a surrogate mother to those three, but you are serving them very ill. It is not only my husband who believes you are an unhealthy influence. I see it for myself, the effect you have on them—but Tahira says, but Tahira doesn't think—so many times every single day I hear those words. I am the wife of the Crown Prince, this is my harem, those girls have a duty to obey me without question.'

'I don't teach them disobedience, but I will not deny that I do encourage them to question what does not seem right or fair. My mother raised me to—'

'Your mother is long dead,' Juwan spat. 'Your mother, who put her daughters before her only son, who failed to give Ghutrif his rightful place as the King in waiting. Your mother is no shining example to follow.'

Tahira struggled, but no amount of deep breaths and clenched fists could hold back the tears which gathered on her lashes. It was far too late now for her to rein her emotions in. 'Ghutrif was always jealous, especially of me. You must not believe the stories he tells, for you must know how he slants things, colours things...'

'How dare you criticise my husband!' Juwan

heaved herself to her feet. 'Ghutrif is right. The sooner you are gone from here, the better. We cannot risk those other three following your bad example. It is time they learned that it is in everyone's interests, not least their own, to let you go. Time they learned how selfish they have been. Alimah and Durrah in particular are forever begging me to ask my husband not to make another match for you.'

'They are young. Do not judge them too harshly. Ishraq is more reconciled to her fate.'

'Perhaps, but where you lead they will all follow eventually, even Ishraq. Do you really want them to reject the excellent marriages your brother will make for them? Do you wish to deprive them of the joy of children of their own?'

'No, of course I do not! Quite the opposite, in fact. I'm offering to give up any prospect of marriage in order to better prepare them for theirs.'

'Have you asked them if that's what they want, for their dearest sister to sacrifice so much for them?'

'It's no great sacrifice from my perspective.'

Juwan shook her head, smiling in that condescending way that made Tahira wish to knock her turban off. 'You have been a mother to those three for many years, but they no longer require a mother. Ishraq is almost twenty years old, more than ready for marriage. You are spoiling her chances and, fiercely loyal as she is, you may believe me when I tell you that she is becoming frustrated with your intransigence. She wants to establish her own harem, to raise her own family. As for Alimah and Durrah, they may be young yet, but in three or four years' time they too will wish to fly this nest. It is the natural order of things. Only you are behaving unnaturally. Fortunately, though you may not believe it, my husband and I know what is best for you. The Murimon alliance would have been an excellent one, but that ship has sailed,' Juwan said brusquely. 'What matters now is to find you a replacement husband as a matter of urgency. You are twenty-four years old, a full three years older than I, but not yet past marrying age. The match being arranged for you will not be so prestigious, but you had better make sure you accept it with alacrity.'

Panic made Tahira forget herself. She clutched at Juwan's sleeve. 'Has my brother—or goodness, don't tell me that my father…?'

Juwan carefully removed her fingers. 'As you know perfectly well, our beloved King Haydar is far too frail to take an active role in any matters of state, and entrusts my dear husband to act on his behalf. Ghutrif is expending a great deal of energy in order to secure a suitable husband for you and is making excellent progress. I hope you will be suitably grateful. This harem has become a place of turmoil when it should be an oasis of calm while I await the birth of my son. If you cannot act out of a sense of duty towards me or my husband, demonstrate your avowed love for your sisters by embracing the next offer made for your hand.' Juwan glanced up at the row of high arched windows. 'It grows dark, long past time for me to retire. I bid you goodnight.'

Tahira watched her sister-in-law sway across the courtyard like a dhow in full sail before making swiftly for her own quarters, her thoughts already turning to the night ahead. She would have to be extremely careful. The merest hint of her sense of excited anticipation might arouse suspicion. Her sister-in-law saw a great deal more than she let on. They all did, here in the stifling atmosphere of the official harem, and no doubt it was the same over the wall, in the unofficial harem inhabited by her brother's concubines. There was little else to do save to observe and to gossip, for those who had not the key to freedom.

But Tahira did. Her heart jumped. Butterflies fluttered in her tummy. Juwan's *little talk* had left her feeling both furious and defiant. She did not want to accept the stark truth which had been laid out before her. She did not want to think of the fate which imminently awaited her, or the pain of separation it implied. She did not want to admit that there was any truth in anything Juwan said. All she wanted was to escape. The sensible thing would be to keep her head down, play the supplicant, act the penitent. But that was for tomorrow. Tonight, Christopher was awaiting her.

Christopher. The perfect antidote to her unpalatable reality. A man with no surname and precious little background. A man of mystery with a mystery of his own to resolve. He had most certainly not told her the full story behind that priceless amulet, a fifteen-hundred-year-old relic that might even prove to be part of her very own heritage. How she had managed to contain her astonishment when she realised it might actually have been passed down through the generations of her own family was anyone's guess. One of her own ancestors might actually have worn it. When she touched it, she had sensed the connection, she was certain of it. Just thinking about it gave her goose bumps. It was not just serendipity. The fates had placed her there at the mine last night, they meant her to help Christopher solve the mystery of the amulet. She, who knew better than anyone in the whole of Nessarah the history of the kingdom's mines. She, who might even be a direct descendant of the person for whom the amulet was fashioned. No wonder it seemed to speak to her heart. She laughed at herself for being so fanciful, but she believed it to be true all the same.

Christopher, however, felt no such attachment to the amulet. Her smile faded as she recalled his expression when he looked at it. Not a precious link to a distant past, but an unwelcome link to his own history that he wanted to sever. How quickly his mood had swung last night. He had looked at the beautiful piece of jewellery with such loathing. That devil-may-care façade she found so attractive hid a much darker, more tortured soul. Christopher was not a man she would care to cross.

But he was definitely a man she wanted to know better. Tahira wrapped her arms around herself.

A man who saw *her*, a woman without a royal title or impeccable blue-blooded lineage, but like him, without a name and with precious little background. Christopher had made it very clear he liked what he saw. That a man so vital, so wildly attractive could be attracted to her—she couldn't quite believe it. Last night, she had rather desperately wanted him to kiss her. The ultimate temptation and the ultimate deterrent, he had called her innocence. Was it wrong of her to wish that innocence away?

Yes, Tahira acknowledged with a wicked smile, very wrong but very appealing. Not that she would ever dare surrender what amounted to her most marketable asset, but there was no harm in travelling a very little way down the sinful path, when no one would ever know, was there? If one thing had become clear from her discussion with Juwan, it was that the days of her current life were severely numbered.

Talking of time! Tahira checked her watch, and gave a gasp of surprise. It was later than she realised. More than time for her to assume the garb of her alter ego and escape from the harem under cover of darkness, to keep her assignation with the mysterious and brooding foreigner. After all, it would be foolish not to take maximum advantage of what little time, and personal freedom, she had left.

Chapter Three

'Do you think the early indications are encouraging?'

Christopher dropped down on to the sand beside Tahira. They were sitting at the base of the rocky outcrop, on the opposite side from the mine entrance. 'It is too soon to make any judgement as yet, we have only examined a small section of the site so far.'

'I understand that. It is only that I so desperately want this to be the turquoise mine you have been searching for.'

'No one could wish that more than I.' They had not uncovered a shred of evidence of mining activity in ancient times in the course of the night. Could his instincts be wrong? Christopher wondered. No, he would not contemplate that possibility. Instead, he contemplated the woman seated opposite him. While they worked together, her knowledge and enthusiasm had made it easy to become absorbed in seeking evidence of the past, but now, seated within inches of her graceful, sensuous body, her glossy fall of hair, he was once again acutely aware of her allure.

'It is a beautiful night,' Tahira said, looking wistfully up at the sky. 'How I would love to sleep under the stars. To wake in the cool, fresh dawn, to see the desert come alive at the beginning of a new day, to have nothing around me save the sky and the sand.'

'What's stopping you?' he asked, distracted by the image of her newly woken, rumpled from sleep.

'I cannot risk returning in daylight,' she answered, and he castigated himself for his thoughtless question, when he saw her sad little smile. 'Though to be honest,' she added, 'if I were caught, I can't see how the punishment could be any worse than the fate they have already planned for me.'

'Fate? What fate? What do you mean, punishment? Tahira, do they suspect—?'

'Nothing,' she interrupted hastily. 'I only meant…' She looked away, shielding her eyes with her lids, and gave a heartfelt sigh. 'My brother's wife had one of her little talks with me earlier. They have become a tediously regular thing, and she put me quite out of temper for her words were obviously his, but he does not deign to speak to me himself. I have always known that my freedom would come to an end eventually, now I know it will be sooner, rather than later. This could well be my last opportunity to explore our ancient heritage. I hope for my sake as well as yours that it proves fruitful.'

Her smile was forced, her voice forlorn. Christopher covered her hand with both of his. 'Why so? If no one knows that you escape...'

'I cannot escape marriage, and that is my fate. One I have been raised to, after all, and so one I should be able to accept with good grace.'

He should not have been surprised. What was more surprising was that such a beautiful woman was not already married. Christopher dropped her hand. 'You are betrothed?'

Tahira shook her head. 'I was. Have been. Twice. And both times, it has come to nothing.' Another sigh, and a little shrug. 'What I deem to be two fortunate escapes, my sister-in-law tells me have placed a shameful stain upon my character. A stain so obvious that I am surprised you have not commented on it.'

'Good Lord,' Christopher exclaimed, resorting to English. His travels had taught him to be wary of criticising the customs of the many kingdoms he had traversed, but his own recently discovered history meant this was one thing guaranteed to make him reach instinctively for his scimitar. He did so now. 'Are they forcing you to marry against your will?'

'No!' She covered the hand resting on his sword hilt with her own. 'No, it is not like that.'

'You do not have to do as they bid you, Tahira.'

She sighed, shaking her head. 'If I do not do as they wish, it is not only I who would suffer the consequences, but my sisters. The reason my sister-in-law's little chat has put me so out of sorts is that I can't dispute the facts, much as I'd like to. It is my duty to marry, my brother's duty to provide me with a suitable husband.'

'Your brother! I thought you said your father was still alive.'

'He is, but he is very frail. It is my brother who reigns, in all but name.'

'Holds the reins, you mean?'

'Oh! Yes, that's what I meant, of course.'

The situation could not but revolt him, could not but remind him of another young woman destined to play the dynastic pawn, powerless to resist the will of her family, no matter what her own wishes might have been. Had she lived, would she have braced herself, as Tahira was doing, to bend her will to theirs? Or would she have resisted, and by doing so reshaped both their lives?

He would never know, and it was pointless speculating, Christopher told himself sternly. Thirty years ago, it was ancient history now. He should be wary of making comparisons, wary of allowing his judgement to be clouded by doing so. 'Your brother,' he said gruffly, 'he will surely take your wishes into account? If you did not like the man…'

'My brother would probably mark that a point in his favour,' Tahira interjected bitterly.

'You can't mean that!'

'Do you have any brothers, Christopher?'

I have five daughters, sir. That hated voice. 'No,' he said, 'no brothers.'

'You are fortunate. My brother is two years younger than me, but he has always demanded deference from everyone, and when he does not receive it, he is adept at finding ways to punish any miscreants. When I was little, it took the form of childish vindictiveness. Spoiling my games with my sisters, breaking our playthings, pinching, kicking, biting. It is no wonder that my sisters and I despise him. But now that he is in charge of our household, he can happily play the despot, pay us back for all those years when we would not love him, or pay homage to him.'

'You exaggerate, surely? A grown man would not act so pettily.'

'My brother's actions are—they cannot be questioned,' Tahira said, her lip curling. 'Now he has decided that I am a bad influence on my sisters, he is determined to separate us.' She blinked furiously. 'That is why I find it so hard to reconcile myself to doing my duty. I have another duty, to the dead. I promised Mama, you see, that I would look after my sisters.'

'You clearly love them very much.'

'Yes.' She clasped her arms tightly around herself. 'More than anything. When Mama died, I was ten years old, four years older than my next sister. I have kept my promise to look after them all these years. The youngest two don't know another mother.' She bit her lip, clearly making a huge effort not to cry. 'When my brother finds a husband for me I will be forced to break my promise and leave them. My sister-in-law said only tonight that I am making everyone unhappy, that I am being selfish, spoiling my next sister's chances. She says that they no longer need me. I know she wants nothing more than to have me gone, but I can't help wondering if some of what she says might be true.'

A single tear ran down her cheek. She brushed it hastily away, and his hand too, when he reached instinctively to comfort her. 'No, don't say you feel sorry for me. In my heart I have always known this day would come, but I simply hoped—however, I can no longer hope. You see now why it means so much to me, to explore this site, to help you with your quest?'

What could he say? Certainly not what was on his mind, which was to suggest that she told her brother to go and drown himself in an oasis. So he clutched weakly at a straw. 'Your brother has not yet found another suitable candidate for your hand?'

'Not yet, but he is actively seeking one.' Tahira had control of herself now. She unfolded her arms, pushing her long plait of hair back over her shoulder. 'My sister-in-law was right about one thing.

I have been making everyone's lives miserable, myself included, but most especially my sisters. I had not quite appreciated—but now I do. I must resign myself to my fate and try to reconcile them to my leaving.'

Christopher clutched at another straw. 'It won't be for ever,' he said. 'I'm presuming your husband will be a local Nessarah man. You will be allowed to visit your sisters regularly, I'm sure.'

She flinched, opened her mouth to speak, then closed it again. Gazing down at her hands once more, her brows drew together in a frown. What was she thinking? The frown cleared. When she looked up, her smile was forced. Whatever it was, she wasn't going to share it with him. 'There,' Tahira said, 'now you know my all-too-common fate, let us talk no more of it. You are fortunate, being free to go wherever you choose, whenever you choose. Unlike me, you are in charge of your own destiny.'

'Not yet, but I will be.' It was no good, he couldn't let it go, no matter how much she wanted him to. 'Your situation, however, is intolerable.'

'No. In many ways I am very fortunate. There are many women who would give a great deal to be in my shoes. I should remember that.'

'But…'

'I must accept the inevitable because there is nothing I can do to change it. I am trying very hard to do so, Christopher, please don't make it even harder for me.'

He swore under his breath. 'I'm sorry. We are from very different worlds, but it seems there are some things—I was informed recently that I was fortunate to be born a man. Though it goes against the grain with me to accept any words spoken by that particular man, it seems he was in this instance right. Is there truly nothing you can do?'

'Only what I have already decided, which is to make the most of my time, helping you here. Unless you can spirit me away on a flying carpet, of course.'

This time, he accepted her change of subject. Further discussion was futile. 'I'll check if there is a magic carpet stall at the bazaar,' Christopher replied. 'Where would you like to fly to if there is?'

Relieved, Tahira smiled. 'Somewhere far away from here. Somewhere which doesn't exist, or a place that is hidden by the mists of time, visible only to me. A ruined city, or even better, my own little oasis, a place where I can pitch a tent and keep goats and grow fruit.'

Christopher laughed. 'You wish for the life of a peasant. Why not wish for a sumptuous palace, a posse of servants to gratify your every whim?'

'The very last thing I'd want,' Tahira replied with an inward shudder. He did not understand. How could he, when he had no idea of her true station? Was it wrong of her to keep him in the dark? But if she told him, it would change everything. She would no longer be simply herself. He would look at her and see all the trappings she left behind at the palace—if he looked at her at all, for wasn't it more likely that he would put an immediate end to their time together? And rightly so, for if they were discovered together, everyone would assume the worst, and even though his nationality might earn him some protection, at the very least he would be thrown into prison.

It *was* wrong of her. While Christopher could admire the courage of an ordinary female for escaping her home, pursuing her dreams, rebelling against the fate her family planned for her, he would be shocked that a princess of royal blood could behave so indecorously. Her breeding, her position, would form an impenetrable wall between them.

Yet the chances of them being caught together were so very slim. And even if they were discovered, she had never been seen in public without her cloak and veil. No one would recognise her. No, it was too unlikely to worry about. If she were to be caught at all, it would be entering or leaving the palace, and since that had not happened yet, despite a few close shaves—she was worrying over nothing.

Besides, she desperately wanted to help Christopher to solve the mystery of the amulet. She wanted time to prove that the ancients had mined turquoise here. The conclusion of his quest would bring their time together to a natural end soon enough. Surely it wasn't too much to expect, to make the most of however many days or weeks it turned out to be? Too much to expect, yes, but surely not too much to ask. She needed to store up memories to sustain her for the rest of her life.

A quirked eyebrow told Tahira that she'd been silent for too long. 'I was dreaming of my life as a goatherd.'

'You don't mean it, do you? That's what you'd have, if you could have any wish?'

'No, I am not so silly as to think I could really survive in such a way.'

'What would you wish for then?'

'Right now? Oh, silly things. I'd like to take a swim in an oasis. Race a horse across the desert. Climb to the top of a huge sand dune and slide down it. Awake in the desert dawn. But I've already mentioned that one.'

'But these are things anyone could do.'

'I can't,' Tahira said simply. 'I am not free to spend the night in the desert. Even if I could find an oasis big enough to swim in, I would not dare do so for fear of drowning alone. I have no horse, and as for the dune—I can imagine the feeling, but the practicalities elude me—how does one slide down sand? You see, they are modest dreams, but no more achievable for me than flying on a magic carpet.'

'And that is it, the sum total of your desires?'

She recalled her earlier thoughts. Dare she? He was so close, she could feel the heat from his body. He smelled of warm skin, lemon soap, something else distinctively masculine. Her heart was pounding. What if he refused? But if she did not ask…

'I wish that you would kiss me, Christopher.'

He inhaled sharply. 'Tahira…'

'That was unfair of me. Ignore me.'

'Tahira, you are impossible to ignore.' He slid his arm around her waist, pulling her to him. 'Your wish is my command.'

He kissed her. He could not resist kissing her. She did not taste of ripe peaches. She tasted of spices and of heat, exotic and sultry, exactly as she looked, and she set him on fire. Christopher struggled to keep the kiss gentle, struggled not to crush her delectable body to him. He flattened his palm over the sweep of her spine, the swathe of her hair silky against his calloused skin.

She sighed, the sweetest sound, and nestled closer to him. She was all sensuous curves, scented with jasmine. He licked his way along her bottom lip, then kissed her again as her mouth opened in response. Her fingers curled into his hair. Her breasts brushed against his chest. She angled her mouth, and she kissed him back, and he felt his groin tighten, felt the blood rush, and Tahira let out that soft sigh again, an invitation to pleasure he could not refuse. He kissed her again, his mouth shaping hers, but only for moments before she responded and he pulled her tight against him into a kiss he could easily have drowned in.

Which realisation made him tear himself away. She stared at him wide-eyed, lips parted in an innocently seductive smile that made him want to pull her back into his arms again for more. 'Tahira...'

She shook her head vehemently. 'I beg you do not apologise. I wanted you to do that.'

'The desire,' Christopher replied with a short laugh, 'was entirely mutual.'

'Really? Though that was my first kiss, I could tell it was not yours.'

Her words were an apt reminder—not that he needed one. 'Which is precisely why I should not have kissed you.' He could do nothing about his tainted heritage, but he had no intentions of allowing history to repeat itself. *He* was no seducer, nor ever would be! 'Your innocence is entirely safe with me, I promise you. To take such a liberty, I of all people—' He broke off, shaking his head to dispel the memory her words had unwittingly stirred.

'But you did not. My instincts told me last night that you are an honourable man.'

'It is not simply a matter of honour, Tahira.'

'It was just a kiss,' she said, clearly perplexed by his vehemence. 'I don't understand why—oh!'

She covered her mouth, looking horrified. 'Do you mean that you have taken such a liberty in the past?'

'No! Absolutely not. I do not refer to myself.'

'Then who…?'

'It doesn't matter. You are right. It was just a kiss.'

Just a kiss. He took her hand. Her fingers were long and slim, her nails patterned with henna. His bloodline did not define him. He was nothing like that man, nor ever would be. 'Just a kiss,' he repeated, 'but a very delightful one.'

She was blushing charmingly. 'Do you mean that? You forget, I have no experience and am therefore in no position to judge.'

'I don't forget, Tahira.' He cupped her chin in the palm of his hand. 'Your innocence is something I would never forget, never take advantage of, I swear.'

'If I was betrothed, you would not have kissed me, would you?'

'Of course not.'

'So I may assume you are also free?'

'I am neither betrothed nor indeed married, if that is what you are asking. In fact, I doubt the woman exists, who would tolerate my investing every penny I earn in excavating holes in the ground. Nor would any, I am certain, endure the travails of traipsing around Egypt, living in caves and tents while I spend most of my waking hours digging up bones.'

'It sounds to me like paradise,' Tahira said whimsically. 'I wish I could live such a life.'

'Be careful what you wish for. The reality is hot, exhausting, uncomfortable, often tedious, extremely hard work for little reward.'

'What you mean is that I'm completely unfit for such a life.' Her smile wobbled. 'I do understand the difference between dreams and reality, Christopher. And my reality—at least I can be reasonably sure that I'm fit for purpose as a wife. It's what I was raised to be, after all.'

'I'm sorry, I didn't mean to patronise you.' Or hurt her, which he clearly had.

But Tahira shrugged. 'You spoke the truth. We are, as you have pointed out, from very different worlds.'

'Yet here we are, together.'

She smiled at that. 'A hiatus from reality.'

'Sadly,' Christopher said, looking up at the sky, 'one which must draw to a close for tonight. Isn't it high time you left, if you are to be back before dawn?'

'Yes.'

Turning away, Tahira stumbled. As he caught her, peering down at the sand to see what had tripped her up, Christopher saw not a rock, not the gnarled root of a shrub, but something gleaming dully. Pulling it free from the sand and dried mud which encased it, he stared at the object in astonishment. 'It's a pot.'

His heart began to pound as he rubbed the surface clean. 'A silver vessel,' he said, turning it over in his hands to examine the patina and shape. 'Very old.'

He could see his excitement reflected in her face. 'I've never seen anything—never found anything—Christopher, what do you think it means?'

He shook his head, though he couldn't suppress his own smile. 'This is not the kind of item a lowly miner would own.' His laughter echoed into the desert night. 'It means we most definitely have more work to do here.'

Christopher had visited many souks and market places throughout Arabia, but the bazaar in the centre of Nessarah's main city, which he decided to visit the next morning, not to buy a flying carpet but for a far more serious purpose, took his breath away. The building itself was unremarkable, white painted with narrow slits for windows which were cut seemingly at random into the fortress-like walls. The geometric octagonal shape of the structure was the only clue that what was contained behind the massive wooden doors which stood open wide to the early morning sunshine was the antithesis of plain.

The entrance led through a narrow passage to a huge central atrium which soared the full height of the building. Light poured down from the apex of the vaulted ceiling, a dome which had been sliced open to the sky. The dome itself was moulded in an elaborate pattern to give the impression of overlapping tiles in gold and turquoise, while the supporting pillars and columns were also brightly patterned in vivid colours of emerald, mustard yellow, cobalt and white. Terracotta tiles paved the ground, a fountain populated by a shoal of tiny fish stood under the open dome, and low divans were scattered invitingly for weary shoppers to rest their feet and pass the time of day.

The bazaar was bustling with women gossip-

ing, men haggling, children playing. Inured to
the curiosity his shock of blonde hair and distinctive blue eyes aroused, Christopher made no
attempt to disguise his foreignness and instead adopted the air of bland indifference which, while it
did nothing to suppress the stares and whispered
asides, at least discouraged the curious from approaching him directly.

The arcade of shops ran around the outer walls
on two levels, the arched entranceways to each
decorated in highly individual styles, the startling
variety of goods on sale evidence of Nessarah's
wealth. This kingdom was reputedly the richest
in the whole of southern Arabia. It appeared that
claim might be justified. Wandering past a spice-
seller, Christopher was struck as he always was,
not just by the heady aroma, but by the myriad
colours, the care the owner had taken with the dis-
plays of produce, stringing up dried chillies like
jewellery, moulding powdered spices into pyra-
mid shapes ranged in an order that segued from
the warm gold of turmeric to the deep, dark red of
paprika and the burnt ochre of sumac. The confec-
tionery stall next door housed sweetmeats stacked
into complex towers, and next door again, nuts,
pulses and grains were laid out in boxes and sacks

with a pleasing symmetry. Beaten copper in every form was the province of the next shop in the arcade. Polished platters in every size, precarious stacks of cooking pots, ewers and bowls, trays and moulds, plain and decorated, the choice was infinite. Next door, a glittering display of decorative silver dishes, pierced and chased, urns and vases, mirrors, jewellery boxes and bonbon dishes.

He wandered on, intent on finding the section of the market which had brought him here, yet careful to let none see that he had a purpose other than aimless browsing. Silver gave way to gold. Decorative items gave way to jewellery. Finally, he found it, tucked away, behind a closed screen, the entrance to the area of the bazaar given over to the trade in precious stones. But what to do? A huge mountain of a man dressed in the royal livery of crimson and white stood guard. A massive paw placed on his chest forbade Christopher from proceeding any further. 'By invitation of Prince Ghutrif only.'

Christopher bowed and backed away, his suspicions confirmed. The diamond trade in Nessarah was indeed tightly controlled by the royal family. It was frustrating, but after all, no less than he had expected. He would simply have to formulate a strategy, for he must match the stones of his amulet against those being mined here. He smiled to himself. As a last resort, he would find a way to confront the man who controlled the trade, Prince Ghutrif himself, though he wasn't absolutely sure that a previously successful tactic of deliberately getting himself arrested was such a good idea. It had worked well enough in Qaryma, but Prince Azhar was a well-travelled man of the world. The little he had heard of Prince Ghutrif led him to think that that he was unlikely to be received with civility, let alone hospitality.

He would think of something. There was certainly no need to show his hand just yet. With a polite nod of farewell to the watchful guard, Christopher retreated. The tinkling of a fountain drew him to a small courtyard, where mint tea was being served. A pleasant place to gather his thoughts, and to listen to the gossip. One never knew what nugget of valuable information one might overhear, but he had taken only one sip from his glass, when a squad of guardsmen entered. They wore the royal colours. He braced himself for arrest. Despite his low profile, his presence in Nessarah had clearly been detected, and was being investigated. After visiting so

many kingdoms in the past six months, he supposed it was inevitable that word had got out. He
set down his glass, careful to keep his expression
one of mild enquiry.

'Greetings, Stranger.'

Christopher made a formal bow.

The palace guard in Nessarah were considerably
more polite than some others he had encountered.
'With regret, we must ask you to leave the bazaar
with immediate effect.'

Extremely polite!

'The bazaar is temporarily closed to the public in order to allow a royal shopping trip to take
place. You may return in two hours.'

'I would have thought King Haydar would have
any number of people to do his shopping for him,'
Christopher exclaimed in surprise.

The man cast a glance over his shoulder. 'It is
the royal princesses who are gracing the bazaar
with their presence. Please,' he added hastily as
another of the coterie approached him, 'you must
go now, quickly.'

He did as he was bid, following the crowds of
people making for the central atrium. There were
small posses of royal guards everywhere, some
standing sentry, others sweeping through the war-

ren of shops and stores, still others issuing urgent instructions to anxious-looking storekeepers. He left the rapidly emptying central atrium and stepped out into the blazing mid-morning sunshine, where most of the people stood, clearly eager for a glimpse of the royal cortège. Fascinated, Christopher stood too, finding a position on the far edge of the crowd.

The royal entourage arrived in a magnificent caravan of camels, flanked by two sentry lines of heavily armed guards on foot. Ten women, female attendants or ladies in waiting, in two rows of five were cloaked and veiled in finest silk. Their camels were also elaborately dressed, with colourful tasselled saddle bags, silver bells tinkling from the reins, braided necklaces and chest bands adorning the beasts themselves. Amidst them, what must be the princesses' own mounts, pure white thoroughbred camels, which were adorned with pearls and semi-precious stones. Their saddles, unlike the others, were canopied to shield them from the sun.

Five princesses, women or girls, it was difficult to tell, for they were swathed in silk, head to toe and all of their faces, save the slit left for their eyes, leaving absolutely everything to the imagination. King Haydar's most valuable assets, the kingdom's most exclusive and reclusive females.

They would be riding in strict order of seniority, Christopher knew. As they approached, the crowds fell to their knees in obeisance and he followed suit. All eyes were lowered. It was disrespectful to look at the princesses, but on the assumption that the princesses were modestly keeping their eyes to the ground too, Christopher risked a glance.

He remembered now, what he had quite forgotten, that a princess of Nessarah was betrothed to Prince Kadar of Murimon. Now he looked more closely, he saw that the one in front was with child. Prince Ghutrif's wife, he assumed, and so it must be the next one, clad in the colours of the setting sun, who was destined for the kingdom of Murimon. Impossible to determine anything of her, beneath those voluminous layers. He wondered idly whether the prince had been permitted to unwrap his prize before proposing. Most likely the match had been made for dynastic reasons. Bloodlines and power, that was what princes traded in, whether in Arabia or England. The story went that Prinny had agreed to marry Princess Caroline without meeting her. Not exactly the best example of the likely outcome of such random alliances. Though it was most unfair of him to compare the scholarly Prince Kadar with Prinny, it was barbaric, to think that the princess would have no choice in the matter. One reason, at least, to be thankful that the blood flowing through his veins precluded any dynastic matchmaking.

The royal caravan passed by and Christopher got to his feet with the rest of the crowd, his thoughts turning to Tahira. No dynastic power would be traded, no royal treaties nor alliances would be created by her marriage. Her wedding robes would not be dripping with precious jewels, her dowry most likely consisted of linens and pewter, but in one sense her fate would be the same. She would be married to a man of another's choosing. She would be passed from her family to his like a—a parcel. Her worth would be measured by the sons she produced. He knew that it was a common enough fate, he knew that there were far worse, but still, it made him furious. He pictured her, separated from her beloved sisters, deprived of the freedom to escape into the desert night, effectively caged like one of the lionesses in the Tower of London, pacing back and forward in the home forced upon her, withering, her spirit broken.

It appalled him, but there was nothing he could do to change her fate. He couldn't whisk her away on a magic carpet or even a white charger. Appealing as the fantasy might be, the reality was utterly impractical. She had nowhere to run to, no one to take her in, and he certainly had no place for her in his life. So why on earth was he even thinking about it! He recollected that one of Tahira's dreams was to gallop across the desert on horseback. Such a simple wish. He wished he could indulge her whim.

Stupid thought. He had more than enough on his plate without adding any unnecessary distractions. For a start, he had no access to horses. Though there were thoroughbreds aplenty here in Bedouin country, the Bedouins were not exactly renowned for their generosity with their horseflesh. Quite the contrary, in fact, and entirely irrelevant. His entire focus must be on his quest.

Though it was not, for the moment, all consuming. He had to wait on an opportunity to acquire a sample of the turquoise from the mine once the miners had reached the ore seam. In the meantime, he had to find evidence that the mine was worked fifteen hundred years ago, but he could only search for that at night. He had to match his diamonds against samples from other mines in Nessarah. That was a trickier problem, regarding a deal of thought, now he knew the set up in the bazaar. But as to diamond and gold mines in Nessarah contemporary to the amulet—now there he was fortunate, for Tahira seemed pretty sure she'd be able to confirm those. Something which surely merited a favour in return.

He had time on his hands. Why not use it to surprise her, to please her? Cudgelling his brain, trying to recall her other wishes, Christopher smiled softly to himself. A bit of ingenuity, that was all that was required, and some lateral thinking. He prided himself on possessing both. He was already looking forward to the challenge.

Alone at last in her private quarters at the end of a very long day, Tahira lay on her divan on a mound of cushions, staring out of the latticed window to the little courtyard, watching Sayeed, her pet sand cat at play. He was perched on the edge of the fountain, his long ringed tail swishing furiously as he swiped at the fish. It was one of his favourite games, despite the fact that he was almost entirely unsuccessful, for the fish were tiny, and the sand cat's abhorrence of water extreme. Temporarily distracted from her dilemma, Tahira sat up, laughing as the spray of water generated by Sayeed's swiping paw landed on his face, darkening his beautiful pale-gold coat. Hearing the sound of her voice, the cat cast the fountain a contemptuous look and leapt lithely down, padding through the open window, seating himself disdainfully on the cushion beside her.

Tahira tickled his favourite spot on his forehead. Sayeed's purr was more of a low growl. Vicious claws extended, he began to paw at the cushion, shredding the delicate silk. The fur on his front legs was soaking, making the two distinctive chocolate-coloured rings appear jet-black. 'When will you ever learn?' she asked him.

Not deigning to reply, Sayeed began to wash his face with his paws, and Tahira's mind reverted to that fateful moment this morning, when she had spotted Christopher in the milling crowd. She sat up with a sigh. 'What am I going to do? Do you think he could possibly have recognised me?'

The sand cat yawned, and returned to his ablutions. 'You're right, of course he did not,' Tahira continued, hugging her knees, 'I'm just being silly.

Besides, what difference do you think it would make if he did? Are you thinking that Christopher would exploit the situation? But all he's interested in is the turquoise mine, and I've already shared the extent of my paltry knowledge with him.'

Sayeed tucked his paws neatly underneath him and stared at her with unblinking yellow eyes. 'You cannot be imagining blackmail, surely? Christopher is not about to stride into the royal palace to inform my father that I have been breaking free from the confines of the harem, is he?' Tahira shuddered. In fact, she knew Christopher was more than bold and self-assured enough to demand an audience with her father. But blackmail? She shook her head vehemently. 'No, Sayeed, he is not that sort of man. You may take my word for that. It is true, his clothes are threadbare, but he has not the demeanour of a poor man, merely a man who does not care for worldly goods. You are quite mistaken on that score.'

But Sayeed was evidently bored with the topic, and had gone to sleep. Tahira, however, could not rest. She was not the only one with secrets. Christopher was an enigma. This quest of his, to *rid himself* of a family heirloom, to sever all connections with his past, was a paradox. A noble deed which he insisted was ignoble. She knew how painful it was to lose a mother, yet Christopher had devoted six months of his life in an attempt to lose his dead mother's legacy. Such dark emotions possessed him when he looked at the amulet, when he spoke of the past. Hatred? Surely not for his mother. And there was pain too. She longed to know the full story behind the heirloom, though she doubted very much she would be brave enough to ask, and she was pretty certain Christopher would never reveal it. His pain was buried too deeply.

His honour though, he wore like another skin. In the fables which Tahira read to her sisters, the man who protested too much and too often was the man who had the blackest heart. But Christopher's promise to protect her innocence, though made several times more than necessary, sprang from deep within himself. *I do not refer to myself!* She should have known better than to think, let alone suggest, that he did. Christopher was no seducer, but he had known one, and whatever the circumstances, they had affected him deeply. Why?

So many questions likely to remain unanswered, for even if she did dare ask, she did not dare risk being questioned herself in return. Her curiosity must be balanced by caution if she were not to endanger their night-time rendezvous. She so desperately wanted to help Christopher resolve the puzzle of the amulet. And, yes, she rather desperately wanted to spend more time with him too.

Outside, it was dark. She began to change out of her harem clothes, and into her night-time garb. The familiar rustle alerted Sayeed, who yawned and stretched in anticipation of a very different kind of night-time's occupation. By the time his mistress was ready, he was pacing at the door leading to her courtyard, eager to be out hunting.

Tahira locked the door of her private divan and crept out into the courtyard, the cat at her heels. Somewhere in the desert beyond the towering walls, a hawk screeched. Sayeed growled in response, and Tahira laughed softly, her blood fizzing with excitement as she stealthily made for the entrance of the tunnel.

Chapter Four

'Welcome to my humble abode.'

Christopher brought his camel to a halt and dismounted. Following suit, Tahira gazed around her, intrigued. 'You live here?'

'For the moment. It is no palace but it serves my modest needs adequately.' He took her camel's reins and led it over to a small patch of scrub along with his own, where he tethered the beasts.

What he referred to as his humble abode was in fact the abandoned remains of a desert traveller's well. The small cluster of buildings were built of adobe, from a distance blending so well with the surrounding sands so as to be almost invisible which, it occurred to Tahira, would have been precisely why Christopher chose it. In which case she was especially privileged to have been invited into his secret bolthole.

The main house stood more or less intact, with a large wooden door still in place, the windows small slits to keep out the heat of the day. Behind it and to one side stood several crumbling outbuildings, a low perimeter wall marking the remains of a cultivated plot. On the other side stood the well house, with its peaked roof and huge double doors keeping the workings of the precious well safe from the vagaries of the desert and any thirsty wildlife searching for water.

'I have purloined the home of the well-master and his family for my own,' Christopher said. 'These ruins around it would have provided basic accommodation for passing travellers and their camels, I think.'

'Does the well still work?'

'Come and see for yourself.'

He heaved open the double doors and lit the lantern which was standing in readiness by a full tinderbox. The mechanism for drawing up water was relatively simple, consisting of a large leather bucket attached to a thick rope, which was wound around the horizontal strut strung between two forked supports. The winding mechanism was also wooden and looked like a ship's wheel. Christopher loosened the rope. It seemed to plummet a very long way down very quickly. Tahira did not hear a splash, though she could see, from the way his shoulders strained as he turned the wheel and wound in the rope, that the bucket was not coming up empty. He dipped a tin cup into the bucket and handed it to her. The water tasted sweet and was icy cold. 'I've never drunk from a well before,' she said. 'I had no idea it was so delicious.'

Christopher took the cup from her and refilled it. 'What a sheltered life you have led.'

He slanted her a smile, his brows slightly raised, an invitation to confide. Tahira was not so foolish as to do so, but she was tempted, and felt oddly disloyal having to shrug instead. 'Why do you think this place was abandoned, when the well is clearly not dry?'

'It's quite far off the main route to the city. Perhaps they found another well in a more convenient location. Lucky for me. I'm very comfortable here.'

'But how on earth did you find it? You would hardly know it's here.'

Christopher laughed. 'It seems I have a nose for water buried underground, as well as minerals and ores. They say I have the Midas touch.'

'That sounds like a talent that could make a man very rich indeed.'

'If one were so inclined.'

'But you are not?'

'I am not inclined to become a speculator and all that entails. The exhaustive political manoeuvring involved when dealing with avaricious landowners like the Egyptian pashas. The need to be ruthless and cut-throat in business and financial matters. The need to protect your interests when so many covet what you have. None of that appeals to me.' Christopher grimaced. 'It would also be inordinately time-consuming. Time I can spend on my excavations is more precious to me than money. So I am content to sell my services to the highest bidder to fund my digs and in return to levy another, non-financial charge.'

'I don't understand.'

'Like most of the ruling families in Arabia, in Egypt the pashas care very little for preserving their heritage, unless it has an intrinsic value. But they do care a great deal for accumulating new wealth, and that's where I come in. Rather than a share of profits from the gold, diamond, copper, whatever find my survey indicates, I earn myself the right to excavate in their kingdoms, and the promise that they will preserve what I find.'

'That is positively genius,' Tahira said, quite awed by this.

He laughed. 'Ingenious, perhaps.'

'Have you discovered other potential mineral deposits here in Nessarah?'

It seemed to her a natural question, but to her surprise, Christopher's smile died. 'I have, and there are certain individuals who would very much like to get their hands on such valuable information, but I aim to disappoint them,' he said darkly.

But before she could ask him to elucidate, he picked up the lantern and guided her out of the well house, through the ruined garden to the front of the house, where a fire had been set but not lit. 'We've done enough work for tonight. I can continue in the morning, provided I am careful.'

'But what if you are discovered!'

'I won't be. Trust me,' he said firmly. 'I know what I'm doing.'

And he would do it, regardless of the risk. A dangerous man. A reckless man. Suddenly, she didn't care why she was here with him, only that she was. 'Very well, I shall place myself in your hands, whatever it is you have in mind,' Tahira said.

His eyes blazed heat at her unwittingly suggestive words. The look he gave her made her blood heat, and made her wonder if the words had been so unwitting after all.

Then he gave himself a little shake, her a lopsided grin. 'What I have in mind is rather mundane, to begin with. Food. Do you know how to light a fire? No, of course you don't. One look at your hands tells me you are not of peasant stock.'

Tahira froze. 'My family have a certain status,' she said carefully.

'Then let me show you.' Hunkering down, indicating that she join him, Christopher handed her a long spill. 'You can kindle this from the lantern. Light the straw and rushes first, then the—er—the fuel will catch.'

'Fuel?' She peered at it, wrinkling her nose. 'What is it?'

'There's a reason why the Bedouins say that they would rather lose their wife than their camel,' Christopher replied. 'The ships of the desert aren't just a means of getting from one place to the other, you know. They are most generous in their other offerings.'

Tahira eyed the smouldering fire. She took a tentative sniff and got a nose full of smoke for her trouble, but nothing more noxious. 'You are teasing me?'

'I think you must be teasing me. You surely can't be so cloistered?'

She could feel herself colouring, and turned away. 'It appears that I can. You must think me a fool.'

He forced her to turn around, pressing a kiss to her forehead. 'I think you are extraordinary. And I think this fire is ready for cooking. Are you hungry?'

When she nodded, he smiled, reaching behind him for the rush basket which he had brought from the well house. 'Desert hare,' he said, skewering the jointed meat with practised ease, and rubbing it with a handful of delicately scented herbs, before setting it carefully over the fire. 'There's a surprising amount of them in this part of the desert.'

In the desert, men hunted with a hawk and a dog, she knew, but Christopher had neither. Had he a gun? She decided she didn't want to know. The scent of roasting meat was making her mouth water. He placed some flatbreads made from flour, water and salt on a griddle to cook. They puffed up in a matter of seconds. A simple repast, the likes of which she had never eaten, the likes of which would most likely appal her fastidious sister-in-law. Which certainly added to its appeal. Tahira smiled to herself as she watched Christopher tend to their dinner, and settled down to enjoy the ritual of a fire, a meal, and the forbidden company of an extremely attractive man.

'That was delicious,' Tahira said some time later as they drank their refreshing mint tea. 'Thank you so much for taking such trouble.'

'It was no trouble,' Christopher replied, which was not entirely a lie. Hunting for his dinner had become a way of life here in Arabia. Hunting something fit for Tahira to consume—yes, that had been a challenge, but one he'd enjoyed. 'There's no shortage of good hunting out there, if you know where to look,' he said, making a sweeping gesture towards the desert.

'I know. Sayeed, my pet sand cat, has brought me back many examples, though nothing so big as a hare.'

'Sayeed, meaning hunter? He is well named

then. I thought sand cats were feral creatures, hardly suitable as pets.'

'Oh, they are, but I found Sayeed abandoned and half-dead when he was just a new-born kitten. I hand-reared him and nursed him back to health, and so he deigns to tolerate me.' Tahira chuckled. 'And only me. My sisters have learnt from bitter experience to give him a wide berth. He has a penchant for the vulnerable flesh of bare feet. One of his favourite games is to hide behind a divan and pounce on unsuspecting passers-by. Another is to clamber up on to my shoulder and to perch there imperiously. His claws are sharper than scimitar blades, they make short work of my clothing, let me tell you.'

'But you let him out at night? I'm surprised he comes back in the morning.'

Tahira grimaced. 'As I said, usually with a small and bloody sacrificial offering.'

'You should be flattered.'

'Oh, no, I think he merely chooses not to bite the hand that feeds him,' Tahira said. 'And the lure of a nice soft cushion to sleep off his night's exertions.'

Or the lure of a delightful mistress, Christopher thought. Now that they were done with cooking, he had stoked the fire. The flames danced, casting light and shadows on to Tahira's face. She was smiling softly to herself. Having discarded her riding boots, she sat cross-legged. Her feet were high-arched. Her toes were painted with a scarlet lacquer. He had never seen painted toe nails before. He had never before found toes arousing.

'This Midas touch you have,' Tahira said, interrupting his bemused study of her feet, 'is that why you took up surveying?'

'No, it was my interest in ancient sites which came first. I was raised near the city of Bath, which the Romans knew as Aquae Sulis for the hot springs which fed the ancient baths there. Though there is no trace of the original baths now, when I was a boy, we were surveying the River Avon for signs of ancient sewers, and I found a Roman coin there.'

'Your first find! How wonderful. Mine was a mere shard of pottery, most likely from a cooking pot. Were you very young? Did you know what it was? Who did you imagine it belonged to? Do you have it still?'

Tahira's eyes were alight with interest. Christopher smiled, taking the coin from the pouch where he kept it with the amulet, his smile broadening when she handled it reverently. 'I was just a boy, five or six years old,' he said, 'so naturally I imagined it had belonged to a Roman centurion. Some brave, battle-hardened noble fellow in glittering armour, who saved all his emperor's coins to send home to his family. The truth,' he added ruefully, knowing as he did now, that baths and brothels were almost always built together, 'was likely to have been rather different.'

'And so you became a surveyor, because you wished to become an archaeologist?'

Christopher's smile faded. 'I became a surveyor because I had to earn a living, and because it happened to be the profession of the man who passed his love of the past on to me.'

'The same man who was with you when you discovered the coin?' Tahira asked brightly, handing it back to him. 'You said *we* were surveying.'

'Yes. Andrew Fordyce. The same one.'

'A family friend?'

'You could say that.'

A faint frown marred her forehead. His curt tone clearly confused her, but he couldn't do anything about that as he stared down at the Roman coin and the memory of that long-ago, never-forgotten day assaulted him. They were both soaked through from paddling in the shallows of the river, their boots and stockings caked in mud. He recalled the excitement as his chubby fingers closed around the metal disc. 'Mind now, it might be nothing,' he'd been cautioned as he stooped to rinse the mud and grime away, whooping with glee as the ancient markings appeared. And then the proud smile, the pat on the back he'd come to take for granted as the years passed. 'Well done, lad. It seems you've a nose for these things, right enough.'

How innocent he had been. How much he had taken for granted. But none of it was as it appeared. What he had assumed to be love and affection were baser feelings, fed by blood money. Christopher opened his eyes, not realising they had been closed. Tahira was looking at him expectantly. 'I'm sorry?'

'You were a thousand miles away,' she said. 'I was asking what your father did for a living, and why you did not follow his profession.'

'My father...' He caught himself curling his hand into a fist around his coin just in time. 'The last thing my father would wish is for me to follow in his footsteps. And it is the very last thing I would wish either.'

Once again his vehemence puzzled her, and more worryingly intrigued her. He could almost read the questions forming and being discarded in her head. 'We are not close,' Christopher said, before she could ask any of them. 'In fact, it would be fair to say that we could not be far enough apart.' He cast the leaves of his tea into the sand, irked at his lack of self-control.

Tahira frowned. 'But with your mother dead, I would have thought—and you have no brothers, you said. What about sisters?'

I have five daughters, sir. Christopher winced. 'I was raised an only child.'

Her expression softened. 'Oh, how sad. That is, I did not mean—it is only that I would hate to be without my sisters.'

'Though you would happily do without your brother.'

She smiled faintly at this, but was not to be distracted. 'So there was no older sister to step into your mother's slippers, as I did for my sisters? Who then had the care of you as a child?'

Christopher gritted his teeth, tempted to tell her to mind her own business, but reckoning that to do so would only make her more curious, he opted for a form of the truth. 'The wife of the man who taught me to survey.'

'Oh.' Tahira pleated her brow. 'She was your father's housekeeper?'

He chose not to answer this. 'She died thirteen years ago.'

'I'm so sorry. And her husband?'

'He died too. Just last year.'

'Oh, Christopher, how dreadful. Then there is only your father left alive?'

'As far as I am concerned, my father is also dead. Now, I trust you are you done with digging up my past, because I am most certainly done with talking about it.'

She flinched at his tone. 'I did not mean to offend you, and I most certainly didn't mean to upset you, especially when you have done me the honour of inviting me here, and gone to so much trouble to make me feel welcome. I wished only to get to know you a little better. I had no idea the subject of your family was so painful.'

'It is not painful,' he said, as much for his own benefit as for hers. 'It is simply irrelevant.'

Tahira smiled uncertainly. 'You don't think it's rather paradoxical that you should say such a thing? An archaeologist, a man whose raison d'être is digging up the past, but has no interest in his own? You told me that you feel a connection with the past, Christopher, like I do—something tangible...'

'Ancient history, not my past. My personal history has no bearing at all on my work.'

'But your work here has everything to do with the amulet,' Tahira persisted. 'And the amulet connects you to your mother as my Bedouin star connects me to mine.'

'The amulet does not concern us tonight,' Christopher said, thoroughly rattled. Jumping to his feet, he held out his hand to help her up.

'Indeed, I'm sorry. You've had more than enough of my company tonight. Thank you for the lovely meal, and for showing me your home, and...'

'I didn't bring you here just to make you dinner.'

'You didn't? What else do you have planned?'

Imagining her surprise made it easy to cast aside the spectres she had raised. He caught her hand, pressing a fleeting kiss to her fingertips. 'Come with me, and all will be revealed.'

They were making for the nearest dune. Walking across the sands, her excitement mounting with every step, Tahira eyed the large rectangular object which Christopher carried wrapped in a sheet. What on earth could it be? As they began to climb the sharp, steep ridge of the sand dune, her inkling of what he intended became a delightful certainty. Wildly curious as she was, she bit her tongue. Christopher had gone to a deal of effort to please her. The least she could to was permit him to explain in his own time.

He did speak finally, stopping short of the top of the ridge to allow Tahira to catch her breath, though the subject was not what she expected.

'In the winter, in England, it frequently snows,' Christopher said. 'Imagine waking up one morning to find the whole landscape has turned glittering white overnight. Soft, powdery snow is best for sledding.'

'Sledding?' she repeated the word with difficulty, for it was quite foreign to her. 'What is that?'

'I don't know if there is an equivalent in your language. A sled is a sort of chariot which glides across the snow. It can be pulled by horses or dogs. Or, you can just point it down a hill. When I was a boy I used a tin tray—we weren't rich enough to afford a proper sled. Which is where

I got the inspiration for this.' He pulled back the sheet with a flourish to reveal a large metal platter, a very inferior version of the solid silver-and-gold salvers used to serve food in the palace.

Tahira stared at it, completely nonplussed. 'Where did you get such a thing?'

He laughed. 'The means of making your wish come true are my business. Yours is simply to enjoy the experience.'

Which meant he had no intention of explaining himself. Which meant that he had most likely— no, Christopher was right. Best not to know. Best simply to enjoy. 'Are we going to use this thing as a—what did you call it?'

'Sled. We are indeed. My theory is that the sand will act just like snow, and we can slide all the way to the bottom on it.'

'Like a dhow riding an ocean wave,' Tahira said entranced. 'When I said I wanted to slide down a dune, I did not think—thank you, Christopher. This is far beyond what I had imagined.'

'Save your thanks for when we get to the bottom of the dune in one piece. There was a hill, not far from our house, which was just perfect for sledding. Not too high, not too steep, and most importantly not too bumpy. Rather like this dune, in fact. I still fell off regularly.'

Tahira shivered theatrically. 'You must have been soaking wet and freezing afterwards.'

He laughed. 'I was never allowed out until I was wrapped up in so many layers of clothes that I could hardly walk. Fortunately, cold is one of the things we don't have to worry about. Come, let us finish our climb to the top.'

Who took the care to wrap you up in so many layers of clothes? Tahira wanted to ask. His father's housekeeper? It was odd, wasn't it, that he chose to share such personal childhood memories with her unsolicited, yet any time she questioned him about his family, he seemed to retreat. When he talked of finding the Roman coin, and just there, when he talked of this English sledding, it was as if in his memory he was quite alone. Who were these people he had erased? And why?

But to bring it up again would spoil the mood of this precious night that he had gone to such an effort to make perfect for her. She ought to be making the most of it, not pondering ways to make a mess of it. They were nearing the top of the ridge. Christopher was just ahead of her, for he'd moderated his long-legged stride to accommodate her shorter one, continually turning back to check on her progress, to lend her a helping hand. When they finally reached the top, she was panting hard, while he showed no signs of effort. He stood, hands on hips, his pale tunic and trousers, his halo of golden hair outlined starkly against the midnight blue of the night sky behind them, like one of the Egyptian pharaohs he knew so much about, or one of their ancient gods, imperiously surveying his realm. And then he turned towards her and smiled, his eyes crinkling at the corners, and her heart did a little flip. Not a god, but a flesh-and-blood man, who made her blood heat and her flesh crave his touch.

He held out his hand, drawing her into the warmth of his side. 'It is a magnificent sight, isn't it, the desert at night? Quite awesome.'

It was. The dune was so high, she felt as if she could reach up and pull a star down from the canopy of silver suspended above them. The moon glowed pale luminescent gold. The dunes stretched out before them had been sculpted into a complex patchwork of shadowed ridges and plateaux which looked deceptively permanent, though the landscape could shift and change so fundamentally by morning that it would be unrecognisable. Below them, the little complex of buildings which Christopher had claimed for his home, and in the far distance, Nessarah, her home.

'Beautiful,' Tahira said.

'Very beautiful.' Christopher smoothed an errant strand of hair from her cheek, trailing his fingers over the line of her jaw, down her neck, to rest his hand on her shoulder. A feather-light touch, yet it was like a trail of stars on her skin. His fingers fluttered over the sensitive skin at the nape of her neck, then smoothed down the fall of her hair, which was tied back with a silk scarf, to rest on the curve at the base of her spine.

She turned towards him. She lifted her face for his kiss, bracing herself with a hand on his shoulder. His hand cupped her bottom, easing her closer. Her breasts brushed his chest. His breath fanned her cheek. Then his lips met hers in a velvet, night-dark kiss that managed to be both cool and hot, sweet and sinful. A kiss as dark as the sky, which set her alight like the stars. A kiss that drugged and befuddled, like the effect of the desert sun at midday, and which made her shiver, like the breeze at dusk fluttering over her skin. A kiss which blurred the boundaries between her lips and his, her tongue and his, her body and his. A kiss which felt like it could never end, and when it did, left her giddy, so that she would have tumbled down the dune, had Christopher not caught her.

'Wait, not yet,' he said, laughing. 'It was my intention that we slide down together.'

For the first time, Tahira looked straight down the steep slope of the sand dune. Her head spun. 'Is it dangerous?'

His smile was wicked. 'Isn't that half the attraction?'

She laughed, the bliss of their kiss, the thrill of danger without fear, for she knew that despite what he said, he would keep her safe. 'Then let us launch our metal dhow on the sandy wave,' Tahira said. 'I'm ready.'

He set the large salver down carefully, flattening the sand on the ridge to prevent it sliding away, and sat down astride it. 'It's not a magic carpet, but it might just fly. Now you sit down, in front of me.'

She sat between his braced legs. He pulled her tight up against him. Her bottom was tucked into his groin, her back against his chest, his arms clasped around her waist.

'Tuck your feet up tight.'

She managed, just, to do as he bid her.

'Ready?'

Her heart was pounding, excitement fluttering in her belly as she looked down at the sheer drop, and lower down, a different kind of excitement fluttered, as she pressed herself tight against the solid shape of him. 'As ready as I'll ever be.'

He lifted his feet, curling his thighs around her flanks, leaning back, so that his long legs, stretched out in front of him, were clear of the sand. The sled moved only a fraction, suspended for a moment on the top of the ridge, and her heart stopped, and then they plummeted downhill at a speed with made her gasp, close her eyes, and scream with delight as they careered, bounced, slid down the sand dune so fast that she would have been thrown from their precarious chariot, had not Christopher held her so tightly. Somehow, she had no idea how, he kept them both secure, until the very end, when the salver hit a bump and they parted company with their mode of transport. They rolled together, landing in a tangled heap of limbs, covered in sand, breathless, laughing.

'Are you in one piece?'

Tahira had landed on top of Christopher. She had lost her scarf. Her hair was filled with sand. Her lungs were bereft of air. 'Yes.' She tried to push her hair from her eyes, wobbled, and caught herself, bracing a leg on either side of him. She felt the sharp exhale of his breath. Beneath her, between her legs, the part that was the essence of his manhood stirred. She knew this, from Juwan's whispered explanations when first Tahira had been betrothed, but she had not anticipated the responding stirring inside her. When he made to lift her away, she resisted, placing her hands on the sand, either side of his shoulders, and seeking his mouth.

He groaned as their lips met. This time their kiss was fierce. Passion, Tahira thought incoherently, as she surrendered to her instincts, moulding her body to his, relishing her shivering response to the hard length of him pressed insistently against her, to the hardening of her nipples, to the thrust of his tongue, and the sweep of his hands, over her back, her bottom, brushing the contours of her breasts.

He rolled her on to her back. Their kisses became urgent. She was dizzy with them, aflame with them, craving more and yet more, urging him on with strange little cries, pressing herself against him. When his hand enveloped her breast she cried out. Such sweet, shocking pleasure.

When he broke the kiss she moaned in protest, but then his mouth claimed her nipple through the silk of her clothing, and heat flooded her.

Exquisite. The word was made for what he was doing to her with his mouth and his hands, sparking stars behind her closed lids, sending a trail of sensation from her breasts to her belly to the tension building in that most intimate of places. She had the oddest sensation, of soaring and falling at the same time.

And then it stopped. Christopher sat up. 'I can say in all honesty I have never ended a sled ride in that manner before.' He got to his feet, helping her up, brushing the sand from her hair and her clothes. 'But I think we have had more than enough excitement for one night, don't you think?'

She was still lost in their kiss, staring blankly at him. Enough? She wanted more.

But Christopher was looking anxiously up at the sky. 'It's later than I thought, time you were on your way home. May I accompany you, at least as far as the mine?'

Jolted out of her passionate haze, Tahira looked up. 'It is late. Early. No, I can find my way easily enough, thank you. And thank you again for tonight.' She stood on tiptoe to kiss his cheek. 'I don't think a magic carpet ride would have been nearly as wonderful.'

'Probably a lot safer,' he said drily. 'Tahira...'

'There is no need to reassure me every time we kiss. I trust you, and you've just proved once more that I can do so,' she said, blushing. 'Whatever dreadful thing your friend did...'

'What friend?'

'Or acquaintance. The man who you said took unacceptable liberties. I assumed...'

'The man I referred to was neither friend nor acquaintance,' Christopher said curtly.

'Then who...?'

'His name will mean nothing to you. The lesson he taught me means everything to me. I know, Tahira, better than most, how painful the consequences are, how fatal. It is not only my sense of honour which ensures I will never, ever take such vile advantage,' Christopher said fervently, 'it is my sense of myself. I will never be such a man.'

And you will certainly never reveal who this other man is, or what he is to you, she thought, intimidated by his vehemence, her shock at the implications tempered by annoyance, for she had inadvertently spoilt the moment. 'You're right,' Tahira said, 'it's long past time for me to head back.'

Christopher watched until Tahira's camel was out of sight before turning back to his dwelling. He did not like to leave her to ride across the desert at night, despite the fact that she had been doing so unharmed for—how long? She had not said, though she had implied it was some years. She hadn't told him how, exactly, she escaped the confines of her home either. Through a window? A cellar? Did she sleep in a room of her own? He must assume so, for she was adamant that her sisters knew nothing of her escapades. Did her sand cat escape by the same means? And her camel— did she borrow it from the family stable?

Frowning as he went through his nightly security checks, he realised that despite her claim to have told him a great deal about her family, there were some very basic facts of which he was entirely ignorant. The names of her sisters, for example? And the brother and his wife—again, no names. He grimaced wryly. A case of the pot calling the kettle black.

Carefully stamping out the embers of the fire,

he retired to his cottage, braced a length of wood under the latch to serve as a lock, and pulled his meagre bedding out of the cupboard. It would be an easy enough task to discreetly follow her home. Easy enough from there, with his skills as an undercover agent acquired over the last six months, to uncover her history, identify her family. But what purpose would it serve, save to satisfy his curiosity at the cost of his integrity? There were more than enough lies and subterfuges in his life without polluting this one, delightful and honest aspect of it. He should try to reconcile himself to the old adage that ignorance was bliss.

Quickly disrobing, he lay down on the rough mattress, pulled the sheet over him and closed his eyes. Desire had been absent for so long, it was not surprising that it had returned with such unexpected vigour. Tahira's kisses, Tahira's touch, Tahira's soft sighs and sensuous body would go to any man's head—and every other part of his body. He had been starved of female company, of any company since setting out on this self-imposed quest of his, it was no wonder that he found her so very, very alluring. To have met her at the turquoise mine too, the place which he hoped, dreamed, believed would prove to be the turning point in his long journey—it was natural that should add to her appeal. She was an omen of his imminent new beginning. She was his escape from reality.

But she could never be his lover in the true sense. Was he playing with fire? The answer was an unequivocal no. There were some components of his foul heritage which could not be denied. He had only to look in the mirror to prove that—something he avoided doing. Physical traits, yes, but to his dying day, he would deny any link of character. The very thought of proving himself in any way like that man—no, never. Never! The shame would cripple him for the rest of his life, and that was nothing compared to the costs to the innocent.

Damage limitation. Recalling the callous tone in which the words had been uttered made Christopher shudder with distaste. Two lives, dismissed in two words. There was no question of Christopher ever taking such a risk. No risk of him ever crossing that line. Absolutely none.

But that line was a long distance away. He shifted on the mattress, putting his hands behind his head, staring up at the stars through the holes in the cobwebbed roof. He could not make proper love to Tahira, but there were other pleasures they could share without risk. He would like to see her in the daylight. He'd like to see the sunlight rather than the moonlight dappling her skin, to see whether those big beguiling almond-shaped eyes were the darker brown or lighter, whether those luscious lips were truly cherry red, or dark pink. That was no more possible than a complete consummation of their passion, but there was no harm in imagining both.

Chapter Five

Dressing for a formal dinner hosted by the Crown Princess was a long and laborious ritual which usually required at least two handmaidens to be in attendance, but today, once her selection of clothing had been laid out in order, Tahira dismissed her servants from her dressing closet, preferring to be alone with her thoughts. When her mother ruled the harem, she often used to allow Tahira to perform the handmaiden's duties. Mama's closet was always heady with the scent of attar of roses. She would recount the history of each article of formal attire in turn, Tahira recalled. They always paused to take tea when she had finished dressing, before she donned her jewellery. The whole process could take hours.

The *gomlek* was first. Tahira cast off her bathing robe and pulled the loose chemise with its wide sleeves over her head. Mama had favoured bright colours, red and yellow and blue, but she preferred plain white. In times gone by, the garment was left open to the waist, so Mama had said, but nowadays in the harem, women understood the art of concealment. She had laughed at Tahira's confusion over that remark, pinching her cheek and telling her that it was one of the many things she would explain when she was older. One of the many things that she never had the chance to explain.

Tahira's *gomlek* fastened chastely at the neck. Eyeing herself in the mirror, she could clearly see the outline of her breasts, the darker shadow of her nipples through the sheer fabric seeming to invite a caress. Last night, when Christopher touched her, took her nipple in his mouth, her response had been a revelation. Recalling it now, she felt an echo of that warm, sweet melting feeling deep inside her. And his response too, left her in no doubt that he found the curves she took for granted alluring. She was reputed to be beautiful, but so too was every princess in Arabia. Her sisters said she was beautiful, but her sisters viewed her through the eyes of affection. In any case, beauty, real or attributed, was a mixed blessing, as far as Tahira was concerned. Her body was an asset to be traded, one which would buy her a husband who took pleasure in doing his duty—until he tired of her—but not an asset which would provide her with any sort of pleasure.

But when Christopher looked at her, she did not feel as if she was being sized up like a brood mare. When he said she was beautiful, she believed him. When he said he desired her, he meant her, only her, not her royal title or her pedigree or the jewels and gold of her substantial dowry. Tracing her hands over her curves, she saw herself through Christopher's eyes, and liked what she saw. Last night had given her a taste of what desire could be. She smiled to herself. Last night had left her in no doubt that Christopher was capable of giving her so much more.

She pulled on her *dizlik*, the short drawers which tied at the knee. Not always worn, but very necessary when the *salvar* pantaloons were as sheer as the pair she now donned. Struggling with the richly embroidered belt which held the multiple pleats in place at the waist, Tahira wished momentarily for her maidservant's practised assistance. The cerulean-blue organza fell in folds to her ankles, where it was gathered in by two smaller and easier-to-fasten ties. The *salvar*, according to Mama, was in larger harems considered a symbol of status. She had favoured brocade threaded with gold and silver, as Juwan did, but Tahira found such fabrics far too heavy, and was quite content to leave her sister-in-law to reign fashionably supreme.

The next item in the ritual should be the *yelek*, which was laced tight, pulling the waist in and pushing the breasts high, but Tahira drew the line at this. Besides, her *entari* gown fitted neatly enough, the indigo-blue brocade fastened at her waist over her chemise with a row of pearl buttons, the sleeves fitting snugly over her undergarment to the elbow, where they opened up, falling almost to her feet, while the side panels of her robe formed a train behind her, forcing her to walk at what Mama used to call a princess pace.

She was already hot, but her *toilette* was not yet complete. The *koosak* shawl made of the same gossamer as her pantaloons was draped over her hair and fixed with pearl-headed pins. Her *sip-sip* slippers were also blue, studded with pearls, their pointed toes a further impediment to easy motion. She eschewed the *fotaza* turban, which Juwan preferred, and instead placed a little *takke* cap on the back of her head over her shawl. Her Bedouin star carefully concealed, she fastened a pearl necklace in place, added a few thin gold bangles, and she was finally ready.

Her eyes were lined with kohl, her lashes darkened. Her lips were painted vermilion. What would Christopher think of her now? Tahira turned away from the mirror. She did not want reality ever to collide with her fantasy world which last night had been perfect in every way. Careering down the sand dune, her body pressed back against his, it had felt like flying. And afterwards, those kisses. A different kind of flying. Only when she returned to the palace did she plummet back down to earth.

The distant sound of a bell summoning her to dinner made her heart sink. She was worried about her sisters. Ishraq in particular was behaving oddly of late, spending much more time than usual with Juwan. She was horribly aware of the sand slipping through the glass in the inevitable count down to her leaving them. There was nothing she could do to stop her brother arranging another betrothal, but though she told herself she was inured to the event, inside she was screaming denial.

So she wouldn't dwell on it. Instead she would think about the silver pot she and Christopher had found at the mine. What else would they find there? And much, much more importantly, would it connect them with Christopher's amulet? She rather desperately hoped so. It meant so much to him to resolve the mystery, and if the resolution in some way established a connection between them, through her ancestors…

'Now that,' Tahira said to Sayeed, who was finally stirring on his velvet cushion from a long day's rest, 'would be wonderful.'

The sand cat yawned. Tahira tickled him under the chin. 'No adventures in the desert for us tonight, I'm afraid.'

The dinner bell rang again. Tahira adjusted the draping of her shawl, and with a sigh, left the room in preparation for a long and tedious repast.

One night later, Tahira was crouched down on the sand taking a closer look at Christopher's sketches of the site around the mine, made in the full light of day. He had lit a lantern, the moon being on the wane, and the night hazy. 'You are sure that you were not spotted?'

'I chose my time carefully. Mid-afternoon, when the sun is at its hottest, there was no one about.'

'What about the guards? They would not have dared take shelter from the sun,' Tahira said, knowing her brother's reputation for what he called maintaining discipline.

Christopher shrugged. 'There are only two on duty at present, and both were happy to be distracted.'

'How…?'

'Suffice for you to know that they were suitably diverted long enough for me to carry out the inspections I needed.'

He was smiling at her, but there was something in his eyes that warned her not to press him. A dangerous man, who positively thrived on courting danger, she thought, and not for the first time. It was a large part of his allure. He drew her to him in the way that a beautiful, highly polished, lethal blade tempted you to run your finger along its edge, to see for yourself whether it really was as sharp as it looked, unable to resist doing so, despite the fact that your head told you that no proof was needed. Irresistible. Not that she had any inclination to resist.

'So, you have an accomplice,' Tahira said. 'Another person who knows your secret?'

'I have contacts, that is all.'

'Contacts?'

Christopher did not pretend that he hadn't heard her question. He simply gave her a bland smile and turned the subject. 'As you can see, our best chance of finding evidence of settlement is here,' he said, pointing to one of the sketches. 'There are indications of the usual miners' shelters, a few shards of pottery, though we'll need to do some more work to see how old they are. But it's odd.'

'Because our silver vessel is of higher quality than anything which is likely to be found in a miners' village,' Tahira agreed, nodding. 'When I've found the sites of ancient villages, there have been remnants of pottery, beads, some pewter, but nothing like our pot.'

'Precisely. Of course it could have been accidentally left behind by a traveller, or become detached from the luggage of a rich caravan, but…' Christopher tapped his finger on the drawing. 'I don't know, call it gut instinct, but I can't help feeling there's something important we're missing.'

She hoped he was right, but Tahira feared that he might simply be desperate. *It cannot prove fu-*

tile, he'd said to her when she suggested he might never find a home for his amulet. He would not accept defeat, but what would he do if the ore from this mine didn't match? He was so determined not to contemplate failure, she couldn't imagine how he would deal with it, if the worst came to the worst.

But that was a very long way away yet. 'I have some more positive news,' Tahira said. 'I've had time to look back over my own research from the last few years, and I can confirm that both diamonds and gold were being mined here in Nessarah when your amulet was made. I know that's the easiest part of the mystery to resolve, neither are exactly rare here in the south of Arabia, but...'

'It's a big step in the right direction,' Christopher said. 'Thank you.'

His eyes met hers as he kissed her hand, and it was as if her brain was somehow switched off, and her body took over. And then he let her hand go, and she looked away, and she could think again.

'I'm afraid I didn't find any evidence of another turquoise mine though,' Tahira said, fumbling to regain her train of thought. 'Turquoise is not nearly so intrinsically valuable as gold or diamonds, but it is becoming more highly prized for jewellery and decorative purposes nowadays, due to its unique hue, so demand for it is increasing.'

'Hence King Haydar's decision to re-open this mine and corner the market. The man has a penchant for business.'

'It is rather that his son has a penchant for greed,' Tahira snapped, without thinking.

Christopher's eyebrows shot up. 'So it is true, your Prince Ghutrif is the real power behind the throne?'

'He is not my prince.' She could have kicked herself, not only for the unwise words but the scornful tone. 'That is to say, he cares little for his subjects.'

She dared not meet Christopher's gaze. What she needed to do was to change the conversation. 'I know you plan to match a sample of the ore from this mine with your amulet, but what about the diamonds? How do you plan to match those?'

If she did not meet his gaze she would make him more suspicious, so she forced herself to do so, and willed herself not to blush. The startling blue of his eyes was dulled by the night, the odd grey halo of the iris seeming more prominent.

'You speak of Prince Ghutrif with something approaching contempt. An unusual attitude in a region where rulers are loyally revered by their people. Has your family perhaps suffered at his hands in some way?'

Oh, Christopher, if only you knew, she wanted to scream but instead, bit her tongue and said nothing.

He mistook her silence for wariness. 'You can trust me, you know that?'

And she wanted to. A terrible urge to confess, to lay bare the worries about her sisters and her future which had kept her awake long into the night after Juwan's dinner, almost overcame her resistance. She so wanted someone to understand how torn she was. But why should he? She caught herself, aghast. 'There's nothing to tell,' Tahira said. And nothing to be done either, she reminded herself, save to comply.

Christopher's expression hardened just a tiny bit. She had the impression of him retreating, not physically so much as mentally. Then he shrugged, reaching into his tunic for the leather pouch containing the amulet. 'Do you know much about diamonds? The stones in this have a very particular clarity.'

She should be relieved that he had chosen not to pursue her slip, and she should be under no illusions. He had noticed. Tahira stared obediently down at the artefact.

'Most diamonds,' Christopher continued, 'have impurities which gives them a yellowish tinge. Some very rare diamonds have impurities which make them seem blue or red, but these, as you can see, are almost completely clear.'

'And so capable of being definitively matched?'

'I hope so, if I can find a big enough sample—smaller stones, such as can more readily be obtained, are useless.'

And larger ones, such as the crown jewels Juwan kept locked away, quite unattainable, even to Tahira. 'What will you do then?' she asked.

Christopher grinned. 'Gain access to the diamond traders in the bazaar. I tried the other day, but a very large man with a very large scimitar barred the entrance.'

'Not surprising, given the value of the goods contained there.'

'A royal guard, it was.'

'Yes.' He had not dropped the subject after all. 'It is common knowledge that the diamond market is controlled by Prince Ghutrif,' Tahira said warily. 'No one can so much as look at a diamond without his permission.'

'Then I will have to find a way to obtain his permission.'

Alarm bells started to clamour in her head. 'How would you set about doing that?'

'I might pass myself off as a wealthy merchant in order to gain access to the diamond traders. It's a ruse I have used before.'

'But that would require you to show your hand—or at least, your amulet, wouldn't it, in order to compare it with those on sale?'

Her panic was clear enough to her own ears, so Tahira was mightily relieved when Christopher laughed. 'Very true. Perhaps a more direct approach is required. I've had occasion to engineer an audience with the highest possible authority—in Nessarah's case, that would be Prince Ghutrif—when I've found some connections to my amulet's history, though not enough to be conclusive. I've taken the risk, just to be sure I've not missed something vital, to confirm, as far as possible, that I'm in the wrong place.'

'How on earth do you engineer an audience with a prince?' Things could get very complicated for her if Christopher turned up at the palace, and potentially very dangerous for him.

'Drastic measures,' he replied, with one of his

devil-may-care smiles. 'Getting myself arrested is one method, or working my way up the chain of command by refusing to divulge my purpose, it usually works a treat. I had a stroke of good fortune in Murimon, when the chief official there assumed I'd something to do with the Court Astronomer, who happened to be an English woman.'

Murimon! The kingdom which could so nearly have been her home. A coincidence which served to stretch her nerves to breaking point. Should she warn him? Was it wrong of her to keep her identity a secret? But if she told him, what good would it do? 'You are not—Christopher, you're not actually contemplating such extreme action here in Nessarah, are you?'

'Not yet. I've a few tricks up my sleeve to get into that diamond market without having to force my presence on his Royal Highness.'

Which was only a very little bit reassuring, but did at least mean she did not have to reveal her identity just yet. 'I am astonished that you are not languishing in a dungeon somewhere,' Tahira said, torn between awe and horror. 'I knew that it meant a great deal to you to resolve the mystery of your amulet, but I had not quite appreciated you would risk your life to do so.'

'You exaggerate.'

She bit her lip. For six months he had travelled southern Arabia, searching in vain. Six months, alone in foreign lands. There was a reason his scimitar looked well used. Why would a man risk life and limb to give away a priceless treasure? No, *rid himself*, those were his words. What would be so terrible about being forced to keep the amulet? He would not answer, save with a darkling look, and so she asked another question, almost as frightening. 'If you do discover that your amulet belongs here in Nessarah, how do you plan to give it back? You can't just stroll into the royal palace and give it to the King without some explanation and if you do, you'll surely risk being accused of—of—you won't do that, will you Christopher?'

'You know, I hadn't thought that far ahead, but you're right, I need a plan. But that's enough about me and my business tonight, you seem particularly on edge.' He got to his feet, pulling her with him. 'Has something happened? You mustn't worry about our work here you know, we're excavating too far from the mine entrance for anyone to notice.'

'I know. I'm not really worried. Well, only a little bit, that in your haste to finish your quest, you will take unnecessary risks.'

'I would never do anything to jeopardise the outcome.'

'No, I should have realised that.'

'Tahira, what is it? Won't you tell me what's on your mind?'

His voice had gentled. She found herself suddenly close to tears. He smoothed back her hair, letting his hand rest on her shoulder. It felt unbearably comforting. She shook her head. 'It's nothing.'

The wobble in her voice betrayed her. He raised his eyebrow and waited.

'Nothing I care to talk about at any rate,' she whispered, firmly stamping on the urge to tell him everything. 'Things at home are—they are difficult, for the reasons I've already explained. I have known you less than a week, but already I find myself looking forward—you are my one escape from reality, Christopher. I don't want to be reminded of it while I am here with you.'

'Then I will do my best to refrain from questioning you further.'

She took his hand between hers. 'Whatever will be, will be. Let us not waste any more time discussing it, and instead get on with something more productive. Isn't it time we started digging?'

When Tahira left for home, Christopher decided not to return to his camp just yet. There were still a couple of hours left before dawn and the return of the miners, and though the waning moon was providing very little light, it would be worse to-morrow, and almost non-existent the day after that. Best to do something constructive with his time, he told himself, pulling out his sketches of the mine and its surroundings. But he was on edge. Twice, he lost track of his pacing out, and on the third count, realised he was measuring a part of the site which he had already surveyed. Irked, he resorted to simply walking around the perimeter of the outcrop in the hope that some-thing unusual would catch his eye.

Why wouldn't Tahira confide in him? He had no right to demand she did, but there was no reason for her not to, was there? A break in the striations of the rock gave him pause, but on investigation it proved only to be a very shallow cave, which had probably provided shelter in the heat of the day to allow the miners to eat and drink above ground. He sighed. He couldn't prevent her brother from marrying her off, and curling his fists and cursing wasn't exactly constructive. He couldn't do anything, except to help her enjoy the little freedom she had, and tonight he'd messed that up. Had he even thanked her properly for her research into Nessarah's mining history? If so, it hadn't been effusive enough.

'Dammit!' He had come full circle, and he couldn't recall very much of what he'd seen. He should get back to his camp, and if he couldn't sleep—which he was sure he wouldn't—then he would devise a strategy to gain access to the diamond market. He blew out the lantern and left it to cool before putting it in the saddle bag. He pulled on his cloak and tied his headdress over his face. He wondered if Tahira had reached home yet. He wondered if Sayeed, her sand cat, met her in the doorway, or at the window or however it was she regained entrance to her abode. He wondered if she too was regretting their discord. She had had to work hard to hold back her tears tonight.

He wanted to put a smile back on her face. Mentally reviewing her wishes as he mounted his camel, Christopher's mood began to lift. By the time he arrived back at his bolthole, and after carrying out his routine checks for signs of unwanted visitors, he had hatched an outrageous plan. It was risky. If he was caught…

He paused in the act of hauling up fresh water for his camel. It was a completely unnecessary risk to take, all just to please a woman he'd known less than a week, and wasn't likely to know much longer.

Completely unnecessary, yes, but now he'd thought of it, completely impossible not to execute. Imagining Tahira's delight, he made up his mind. If all he could do to alleviate her unhappiness was make some of her wishes come true, then she deserved that he did his utmost to do so.

The Courtyard of the Healers was once, long ago, part of the harem infirmary. Tahira sat in the shade of an orange tree trying to read, but for once the book did not hold her attention. She had been at the mine on three of the last five nights, working steadily at Christopher's side as they exposed what was undoubtedly an ancient miners' settlement. The work was thrilling. She was learning so much from him too, it was a terrible pity she would never be able to put it into practice on her own. But she had resolved not to allow such thoughts into her head. It was the safest way.

Christopher had kept his word and refrained from questioning her, but she knew he studied her when he thought her attention elsewhere.

She frowned, rearranging the cushions, placing a marker in her book. Juwan had warned her this morning to 'expect a joyous announcement regarding her marriage' from Ghutrif, before the birth of his son. In days gone by, Juwan's lying-in would have been the responsibility of the Head Nurse, one of the most powerful positions in the harem, when the kings and princes of Nessarah had taken many wives as well as concubines. No royal male had taken more than one wife for over a century now. The birth of Juwan's child would be overseen by Nessarah's most senior accoucheuse, but the woman was no longer part of the harem.

The royal males of Nessarah still considered several concubines to be indispensable to their well-being. In the unofficial harem, the concubines could call on their own, less senior midwife, Juwan had informed her stiffly this morning, when Tahira had enquired.

'A perfectly adequate woman. As mistress of the entire harem, I am responsible for their welfare,' Juwan had unexpectedly volunteered. 'I tell you, for you will be mistress of your own harem very shortly, and should understand the customs and practices.'

'I am expected to be responsible for my husband's concubines?'

Tahira had been unable to keep the shock from her voice. Juwan, always happy to demonstrate her superior understanding, had smiled smugly. 'Naturally you do not acknowledge them, but you should be aware that their well-being reflects on you.'

'And their children, who will be half-blood sisters or brothers to my own? Am I permitted to acknowledge them?'

'They share no royal blood,' Juwan replied, outraged. 'How can you ask such a thing, Tahira! You are twenty-four years old, you cannot have lived your life behind these precious walls without understanding such a basic fact. Offspring of men's lusts, that is what they are, and as such, they are fortunate to be adequately provided for, once they have been weaned. Did your mother not explain how such matters were dealt with?'

Tahira, feeling quite overwhelmed, shook her head dumbly. 'I knew there were other women, but I did not think—do you think my father—that I have brothers, sisters in Nessarah…?'

'Never say that,' Juwan hissed, giving her a shake. 'I cannot believe your mother left you so unprepared. I cannot believe that I am having to explain to you—but there it is, it seems I must. These are not children of royal blood, Tahira. They are not related to you. The concubines exist to sate a man's lust, for it is greater than that of a woman, and must have an outlet, especially while she engages in the honourable duty of bearing his child, as I am doing. But when these woman bear fruit, it is tainted and must be sent away, you understand? The male children in particular, though they are not of royal blood, there can be no risk taken, lest they get ideas above their station.'

'What do you mean, sent away?'

Juwan laughed shortly. 'Not what you are imagining, though in the past—but we live in modern times. They are given another name, another family. They know no other life. That is why they are taken young, it is much kinder.'

'Kinder? To be taken from their mother…'

'When they are weaned. It is kinder for the woman too, for she may quickly return to her duties.'

'And if she does not wish to?'

'Then she is given a pension, but she cannot keep the fruit she bears, Tahira, under any circumstances. You understand this, I hope, for it is something you may have to enforce.'

'I can't imagine—it seems very cruel. When I lost my mother...'

'A very different matter. You were already ten years old. A baby cannot miss what it has never known,' Juwan said firmly. 'I trust matters are now clear to you. I have no wish to discuss them again.'

'Yes. Thank you.'

Juwan had smiled then. 'I do believe that you will make a very good wife. You are naïve, there is much your mother left undone. But soon, sooner than you may hope, Prince Ghutrif will provide a husband for you.'

Juwan would not be drawn further. The conversation left Tahira deeply troubled and deeply embarrassed by her own blind acceptance of the situation. She had always known, but until now she had chosen to ignore, and not to question. But soon, sickeningly soon, she would find herself in the peculiar situation of being responsible for those women, those children, belonging to her husband, yet whose existence she must not acknowledge. It was taken for granted that a man needed many woman, she had never questioned that, but would she feel different when it was her husband?

Another question it had not occurred to her to ask, largely because she avoided the entire subject of matrimony, but now she forced herself to confront it. The man she would share a divan with, the man who kissed her, touched her, gave her children, would kiss other women, touch other women, give other women children. It was the way of things, it was what she had been raised to, but it felt very wrong.

The only man she had ever kissed was Christopher. The only man she had ever wished to kiss. And a man she fully intended to kiss again, if she was given the opportunity. She lay back against the orange tree, closing her eyes. She thought about Christopher making love to her. His mouth on hers. His hands on her breasts. His lean, hard body pressed against her…

'Tahira, here you are! Surely you are not asleep again! You have been sleeping half the day away of late. You are not ill, are you?'

Alimah and Durrah stood over her, looking concerned. Tahira sat up, smiling at her sisters. 'I was not sleeping, merely musing. Come sit with me. What have you been doing?'

Alimah rolled her eyes. 'Avoiding Juwan. She has promised Durrah and I needlework lessons.'

Tahira repressed a guilty smile. 'You can't deny that you would benefit from them. Your needlework is atrocious, Alimah, and your sister's is not much better, while Juwan's is exquisite.'

'Yes, but her conversation is not,' Durrah said, throwing herself on to the cushions beside Tahira, placing her head on her lap. 'It is all, Ghutrif says, and Ghutrif does, and Ghutrif has decided. Anyone would think she actually likes him.'

'He is her husband,' Ishraq said primly as she crossed the courtyard to join them. 'Better to grow a rose in a marriage bed than a bitter lemon.'

'That's all very well,' Durrah said plaintively, 'but she expects *us* to like him too. She is constantly bleating about how dreadful she feels that she has not yet provided him with a son. It is not her fault.'

'Juwan knows that,' Ishraq said, 'but she can hardly go around blaming our brother, can she? Imagine his reaction if he found out!'

A collective shudder ran around the sisters as

they did so. 'All the same,' Alimah said in a small voice, 'you'd think she would drop the dutiful wife act when it's just us in the harem. Ever since she came here, it's been different.'

'She's a usurper, an interloper, is what she is,' Durrah said staunchly, 'and she knows it.'

'Hush now,' Tahira intervened guiltily, for she knew full well that Durrah was expressing Tahira's own views. 'Juwan is the Crown Princess and as such we must treat her with the respect she is due.'

'You don't.' Durrah pouted. 'She isn't one of us, why pretend? She doesn't understand our jokes, she doesn't read books, she doesn't even paint or dance, and she loathes Sayeed.'

Ishraq and Amirah chuckled. 'Save for Tahira, we all loathe that cat, and Sayeed makes it very obvious the feeling is mutual, so at least we have that much in common.'

'That is true,' Tahira said, relieved to see Ishraq smiling.

Though it was short-lived. Her next sister pursed her lips. 'That cat is growing too vicious to remain here. Look at your hands, Tahira, they are in a disgraceful state.'

They were, thanks to her work at the mine,

and she'd forgotten to tend to them. Guiltily, she tucked them into her sleeves. Not only covered in scratches, but she had two broken nails which it would take a great deal of ingenuity to ascribe to poor Sayeed.

Fortunately, Ishraq was not particularly interested in Sayeed or Tahira's hands. 'Juwan sees our brother through different eyes,' she said. 'As his wife, she knows it is her duty to love him.'

'Well, I for one am glad that's not a duty forced on me,' Durrah exclaimed in disgust.

'Oh, when you marry you will find it easy to love,' Ishraq said assuredly. 'What could be more natural, for you will not only have a husband but a harem of your own, maidservants to command, and when you give your husband a son then you may ask for anything.'

'Really?' Alimah, the youngest of the sisters, stared at Ishraq wide-eyed. 'Anything at all?'

'Jewels. Silks.'

'A horse?'

Ishraq laughed. 'Even a horse.'

'Then I hope that Ghutrif finds me a husband soon, for I would love to have a horse,' Alimah said. 'You would love a horse too, Tahira, I have often heard you say so. Why don't you get married so you can have anything your heart desires?'

'Yes, I would like to know the answer to that question too.' Ishraq's big brown eyes were challenging. 'Do you realise that until you do, the rest of us are forced to bide our time here, doing Juwan's bidding when we could have our own harems...'

'But we'd not have each other,' Durrah exclaimed. 'Ishraq, you can't want Tahira to leave.'

'I want her to get married, so that I can get married,' Ishraq said. 'I'm tired of waiting for her to make up her mind. I want to be queen of my own harem, like Juwan.' She turned to Tahira, her gaze challenging. 'They have three candidates lined up, were you aware of that? Ghutrif's Head of Council is holding preliminary discussions. Juwan wishes the matter decided before she has her son. It is to be hoped, for all our sakes, that this time you manage to hold on to the man in question.'

Though she sensed Juwan's hand behind her sister's words, Tahira knew it would be unfair to blame her wholly. Ishraq was twenty years old, and only demanding what she had been raised to expect. She did not mean to be so hurtful, she was simply—rightly—frustrated. Tahira must not think that Ishraq loved her less because of it. 'That is really what you want, to be married and rule your own harem?'

The response made her heart sink. 'It is all I have ever wanted.'

Chapter Six

The Bedouin Sheikh corralled his horses in a fenced compound adjacent to his encampment. With the legendary Sabr long-distance endurance race due to to be held in a few weeks, the place was a hive of activity, but as dusk approached, all was quiet, save for the soft whinnying of the thoroughbreds as they settled in for the night. There was no guard on the gate. The Sheikh was a very powerful man, with a well-deserved reputation for being ruthless with transgressors. If any man should be so foolish as to steal one of his precious, pure-bred Arabians—branded so as to be easily recognisable—he would not be long for this world. That was all the security the Sheikh required.

Though Christopher knew, from his previous two nights reconnoitring the enclosure that he was the only human soul present, he checked meticulously before climbing over the fence at the furthest point from the gate. Now all he had to do was make his selection, and make damned sure that he had them back before dawn.

Smiling softly to himself, he turned his attention to the horseflesh. Not even at the horse fair had he seen such a magnificent collection. Best to avoid those he'd noted were being trained for the Sabr, one of the Sheikh's grooms would be sure to notice any sluggishness in their performance tomorrow. No point in arousing suspicion, even after the fact. He was keeping a low profile here in Nessarah, but Christopher knew perfectly well that his presence would have been noted. A stranger. A foreigner.

He knew he shouldn't be doing this. It was ridiculously risky. Completely unnecessary. He had made no promise to Tahira, who was blissfully ignorant of his plan to 'appropriate' a couple of horses. But his blood was fizzing with excitement. And really, was it such a great risk, provided he returned them before anyone noticed they had gone?

The damned amulet, all the dark history it represented, had occupied his mind both day and night, since the moment he'd discovered it. It was such a relief to be able to set that burden aside for a short while. A relief to have something else to think about, to plan, to daringly execute. A whim, yes, but what was wrong with that? He had no need to do this, save to give Tahira pleasure, but that was reason enough. If anyone deserved to be pleased it was Tahira.

Now, where was that fine-looking filly he had spotted a minute ago?

An hour later, back at the mine, Christopher waited anxiously for Tahira to arrive. He had completed his daily check on progress underground before stealing the horses, risking a visit before dark, as soon as the last miner departed. There was no sign of any turquoise seams as yet, though Prince Ghutrif's men were making very short work of shoring up the tunnel. Soon, very soon, he would know for certain whether the stones in his amulet were a match. In the meantime, he had unexpectedly uncovered another very interesting piece of evidence some distance from the site of their own excavation which he was looking forward to sharing.

Extinguishing his lantern, he began to make his

way back down the outcrop to look out for Tahira. She was late. Perhaps she'd had second thoughts or had been unable to get away. But a cloud of dust in the distance made him raise his spyglass, and Christopher smiled with relief.

Though her *keffiyeh* covered her face as she neared, he could see her smile reflected in those big almond-shaped eyes. He helped her down, and she pushed her headdress back, and his belly contracted. It felt impossible to release her, so he pulled her close, and then it was impossible not to kiss her. She opened her lips to him with one of those sweet sighs that set his blood roaring. She put her arms around his neck and pressed herself against him. He slid his hand to the delightful slope of her bottom, pulling her tighter, and he let his kiss say the words that he would not even allow himself to think, that he was more than glad to see her. She tasted exactly as he remembered, of spices and heat, exotic and sultry, the distilled essence of Tahira.

When their kiss ended they gazed at each other, quite dazed, and then she reached up to push his hair back from his brow, before pressing a final fluttering kiss to his lips and stepping back.

'Close your eyes and hold out your hand,' Christopher said.

'What is it?' Tahira asked, doing as he bid.

He reached into his pocket and placed his find into her outstretched hand. 'Take a look.'

'Oh!' Her eyes lit up as she gazed at the gold bangle, her fingers tracing the design, which was of a coiled serpent, the scales etched in green enamel. 'Where did you get this?' Her eyes widened. 'Here?'

He took her by the shoulders, turning her around to face the mine. 'You see that fissure between the two main outcrops of rock? It's been bothering me, I'm not sure why—a hunch, I suppose. It's too far from where we've been excavating to be part of the village.'

'It's unlikely that two such highly valuable artefacts could have been accidentally left behind by passing travellers, isn't it?' Tahira clasped the serpent bangle to her breast, her eyes closed, her expression rapt. 'What do you think it signifies?'

'Something very important,' Christopher said, finally giving way to his own excitement. 'Look. The gold is of comparable quality to my amulet, the enamel work similar, and as far as one can be certain about these things, it looks to be about the same era.'

'Christopher! That is wonderful.'

'It's not conclusive…'

'But it's a big step forward! Though it's strange, isn't it?' Tahira turned the bangle over in her hands. 'The eyes of the serpent are missing, but it is obvious they must have been jewels. Why would such a precious object turn up in a min-ers' camp?'

'The most obvious answer is that it was stolen property and nothing to do with the mine. Maybe part of a robber's buried ill-gotten gains that were never reclaimed.'

'Then we must turn our attentions to the place where you found this.'

He slid the bangle over her wrist. The gold took on a new warmth. The eyeless serpent seemed al-most to come alive. 'It suits you,' he said.

Tahira shivered. 'I like it too well, but I should not wear it if we're going to dig.'

'We're not. Keep it on for now. I have other plans for tonight.'

The horses were tethered to a stunted tree just out of sight of the camels. One grey filly, one chestnut colt, both with the distinctive profile and high-carried tail of the Arabian thoroughbred. Tahira stopped in her tracks. 'Where on earth did you lay your hands on such magnificent creatures?'

'I borrowed them.'

'Borrowed?' She eyed him suspiciously. 'From whom? A most generous friend, to lend you two pure-bred Arabians.'

'Not a friend, exactly. And he's not actually aware of how generous he's been.'

There was a teasing light in his eyes, but Tahira began to feel slightly sick. 'You can't mean— please tell me you didn't steal them.'

'Certainly not,' Christopher said indignantly. 'They'll be returned to their rightful owner before first light.'

'Whose horses are these?'

'They are ours to enjoy, for now.'

'If you took them from a Bedouin—you would be committing a less heinous crime if you stole his wife, you do know that?'

'I have no need of a wife, Tahira, either my own or any other man's. Don't you like these horses?'

'That is not the point.'

'Oh, but it is the only point. Come, introduce yourself.'

She could not resist, and as she ran her fingers over the highly-strung horse's muzzle, Tahira's fear gave way to awe, and to excitement. 'I can't believe you took such a risk for me, it is an outrageous thing to have done. Thank you, though I wish you hadn't—but, no, that is a lie.'

She ought to demand that he return the horses right now, but the grey was gently nuzzling her fingers, and the deed was done now, and a few more hours surely wouldn't make any difference. 'She is beautiful, thank you,' Tahira said.

Christopher smiled. 'You certainly have an affinity with horses.'

'I get it from my mother who, as you know from my necklace, was a Bedouin herself. Mama taught me to ride, but I have not done so for many years.'

'Why not?'

She hesitated, but recalling the conversation earlier with her sisters, and Alimah's yearning to learn to ride being thwarted made her speak out. 'My brother does not appreciate my—what did you call it?—affinity with horses, since he has none himself,' Tahira said scornfully. 'Mama was always saying that I had a strong ration of her

Bedouin blood, and that he had none. I'm afraid it was one of the things she was rather—she seemed to enjoy pointing it out,' Tahira said, grimacing. 'She told him that he would be better sticking to camels.'

'Let me guess. When she died, he put a stop to your horse riding.'

'My youngest sister longs to learn to ride, but she has never been permitted to even sit astride a horse. I blame myself. It was not only Mama who boasted of my prowess—when I was younger, I was not above teasing him, and he—my brother has a very, very long memory.'

'So he's vindictive as well as petty and insecure.' Christopher said something vicious under his breath. 'A pathetic excuse for a man. If I could but get my hands on him...'

'No! Please, don't misunderstand me, I would very much like to see him forced to grovel, whether you chose to use those fists you have clenched or that fearsome scimitar, but—' Tahira broke off, exclaiming impatiently. 'You have gone to an immense amount of trouble to arrange this treat and exposed yourself to danger in the process. Let us not pollute the night with my brother's presence.'

Christopher uncurled his fists slowly. He gave himself a little shake, stretched out his fingers, as if to reassure himself that they had not re-formed into fists, then forced a smile. 'Right, now as you can see, even my ingenuity has failed to provide us with saddles, though I've fashioned makeshift reins from some rope.'

'Oh, that is absolutely fine. I can ride bareback,' Tahira said. 'Will you help me up—having boasted about my horsemanship, I'm not going to disgrace myself with a very rusty scrabbling mount.'

But she was pleased—and relieved—to discover that all she needed was his cupped hand to land gracefully on to the horse, even more pleased to discover that it all came back to her, as if it had been a few minutes instead of many years since she'd had the pleasure. The grey filly was frisky but responsive, allowing her an excellent view of Christopher's easy, lithe vault on to the back of the chestnut colt, and instant mastery of his steed.

'Ready?' he asked.

'Where are we going?'

'Wherever you wish. The night is yours.'

As she fastened her headdress over her face, Tahira's eyes met his, and the low flame of desire stirred in her belly. A breeze ruffled the soft cotton of her cloak. Above them, the light haze of cloud cleared leaving a carpet of stars, and crescent of white-gold moon. She adjusted the rope halter, turned the mare towards the flat expanse of desert to the east and, urging her horse into a gallop, prepared to claim the night.

The gentle breeze became a roar in her ears. Her headdress and cloak flew out behind her. She could hear the steady drumbeat of the horses' hooves on the sand, see the puffs of the sand flying up as they raced, the blur of acacia trees, the startled eyes of some desert creature. And on she rode, skirting between two huge dunes, the sand becoming softer, forcing them to slow, allowing her to turn her head to the side, finding Christopher there, just as she had known he would be, keeping up effortlessly but holding back too, content to let her lead.

Was she being reckless, riding so wildly after all this time? Yes, yes, yes, she was. The ground grew firmer. The grey responded happily to the call for another gallop, and Tahira flew off again, giving herself over to the elements, caring not where they travelled, not wanting it to end, until the horse began to labour.

She reined in. Christopher pulled up beside her. 'Another five minutes or so further on, and we will happen upon an oasis,' he said.

She didn't ask him how he knew, though it saddened her that this foreigner should know her own land so much better than she. The oasis was tiny and uninhabited, a small cluster of palm trees, a tiny scrap of lush green screened from the desert on one side by tall thick grasses, bordered on the other by an alluring pool of water, inky-black in the moonlight. Breathless, Tahira dismounted, pulled off her headdress and stooped down to cool her hands in the water, but when she made to drink it, Christopher stopped her. 'This water is suitable for the horses, but it's best not to risk drinking it yourself. I filled my flask from my well. Here, have some.'

'Thank you.' She sipped gratefully.

'You certainly have the Bedouin touch with a horse. I was struggling to keep up with you.'

Tahira laughed. 'Now I know that you are flattering me. You could easily have overtaken me at any point.'

Christopher grinned. 'I was enjoying the view from behind.'

Her face flamed but at the same time desire

took hold, emboldening her. 'Now I am enjoying the view,' Tahira said. She reached up to push the fall of golden hair back from his brow, letting her hand flutter down his cheek, his throat, to rest on his shoulder. 'Thank you,' she whispered, 'for making another of my wishes come true so perfectly.' And then she kissed him, a soft, tentative kiss.

'You don't have to thank me in this way, Tahira. I don't expect it.'

'I know you don't, Christopher. It's one of the reasons why I want to.'

He pulled her closer, his arm tight around her waist. 'You have other reasons?'

'One other.' She kissed him again, this time shaping her mouth to his, running her tongue along his lower lip, relishing his responsive shudder.

'What is it?' Christopher asked, his fingers tangling in her hair, then stroking down the curve of her spine.

'I just want to,' she said.

'Serendipity again,' he said, catching her against him so tightly her feet left the ground. 'Because I can't think of anything I want more.'

One kiss became another, and another, and yet

another as they sank on to the grass apron surrounding the oasis pool, kneeling, then lying, still kissing. She slid her hands under his tunic, flattening her palms over his hot skin, up his back, over his shoulders, feeling the ripple of his muscles beneath, the way his ribs expanded as he breathed, his breath becoming faster, more shallow.

He unbuttoned her tunic, revealing her thin chemise. A sharp intake of breath. 'You are so lovely,' Christopher said, 'so very lovely.'

She believed him. Kisses on her throat. On the mounds of her breasts, the valley between, and his hand, under her chemise, cupping her, his fingers teasing her nipples into tingling peaks that made her moan, that set up other tingles, tension, inside her. And then his mouth covering hers again, and she lost track of what he was doing, surrendering to the sensations he aroused, her skin on fire, pulsing points of sensation sparking all over her body, but when she tried blindly to pull him on top of her, to touch him in return, he shook his head.

'Just you,' he whispered huskily, nipping at her earlobe. 'Trust me?'

'Yes,' she said, though she had no notion what he meant. 'Yes.

Her kisses became urgent. Her body was embarked upon a journey it was desperate to complete, but Christopher seemed determined to slow her down, his kisses gentling, his touch like the fluttering of a feather on her bare skin, his mouth trailing kisses over her shoulders, her arms, the pulses racing at her wrists, then back up, sliding the narrow straps of her undergarment down, sliding her arms free, rolling the flimsy scrap down, to reveal her breasts. He looked at her for so long, she opened her eyes in trepidation, but his were dark, slumberous, his slow, sensuous smile leaving her in no doubt that he liked what he saw. When the journey resumed, he claimed every inch of her tender flesh with his hands and his lips, working her into a frenzy when finally she felt his mouth on her nipples, making her cry out, arch up, sending the sweet tension inside her up a notch and then another and another.

The sash of her trousers was undone. He spoke her name again, another question implied, and her answer was more of a plea than a response. It should have been shocking, embarrassing, what he was doing, whatever he was doing, but she was oblivious to everything now save his touch, the mounting tension like a dragging, drugging ascent, the slick slide of his fingers making her moan, writhe, gasp, plead. And then his mouth was on hers again, his tongue stroking and sliding into her mouth, his fingers stroking and sliding in that most intimate place, slowly, too slowly, faster, then just when she thought she could stand it no more, she fell, shattered, exploded, into a thousand glittering pieces, and it was like flying across the desert on horseback, or careering down the sand dune, though nothing like either really, soaring, exhilarating, wave after wave, leaving her mindless and breathless and feeling utterly, completely alive.

When she finally opened her eyes Christopher was smiling at her, his brows questioning. 'I had no idea,' Tahira said, dazed, 'no idea at all. It is like nothing I have ever—Christopher, I want you to feel—will you tell me what to do, to…?'

He pushed her tangle of hair back from her face and kissed her lightly on the lips. 'There is no need. Tonight was just for you, and it was more than enough for me. I promise.'

They were dressed again, seated side by side, watching the moon's shadow on the water when Christopher took her hand between his. "Have you considered the possibility that you may be happier married, away from your brother and his wife, in your own home? In truth, I don't like to think of you with any other man, but hate to see you so unhappy.'

A lump rose in Tahira's throat. She had been at such pains to hide her misery, yet it did hurt her that none, not even Durrah, her staunchest ally, realised how the situation tore at her loyalties. 'It is my sisters' happiness which I'm more concerned about. We have always been united in all matters, but of late the harmony in the ha—in our home has turned to almost constant discord, and it is all my fault.'

His grip on her fingers tightened. 'You must not blame yourself. It is your brother who is at the root of it.'

'No Christopher, the fault is mine. I have been hiding behind my promise to Mama,' Tahira said. 'She would never have expected me to use it as an excuse to avoid marriage. Like everyone else, she would tell me it was my duty. My sister-in-law says I am unnatural. Perhaps I am. Marriage is the most natural—and I'm struggling to understand why I'm so much against it, now that it is so imminent. Am I being stubborn? Contrary? I don't know. I've tried, I am trying, to accept—

to look forward—but it's the lack of any say in my choice of husband,' she said wretchedly. 'My sister-in-law assures me that love will blossom, but I fear only resentment can flourish in such a marriage. Am I so awful to think so?'

'No,' Christopher said, looking decidedly grim, 'I can perfectly understand that sentiment. To be forced to do another's bidding, and one who has a history of displaying malice towards you too— it is outrageous.'

'Yet it is hardly uncommon, Marriages are arranged in this way across Arabia—no doubt across the world, even in England?'

'Indeed,' Christopher said stiffly, 'for those with property, title, lands, it is the custom to make such alliances, to sacrifice daughters to the betterment of a family.'

'Is that really so wrong?'

'Are you asking me to help you to come to terms with this appalling situation, or asking for my true opinion?'

'Is your true opinion based on experience?'

He made to speak, then stopped himself. Plucking a long strand of wiry grass, he began to twist it into a complicated knot, clearly torn. When he looked up, his expression was bleak. 'What would happen to you if you refused to accede to your brother wishes?'

'I would be utterly disgraced.'

'Yes, but what does that mean?'

'I… I don't know,' Tahira said, for she had not actually contemplated the reality. 'I would be ostracised, I suppose, shunned by all. Not even my sisters would be permitted to speak to me. My home would become my prison.'

'You have no means of your own? There is no alternative to living in your father's house?'

She laughed bitterly. If he only knew what an absurd question that was. 'The very clothes I am wearing are my father's property. Only Sayeed is mine—and no one can own a wild animal. You see now, why I must do as I am bid? There really is no alternative.'

Christopher muttered something under his breath. 'Powerless,' he repeated, when she looked at him enquiringly. 'You have no choice. No will of your own. You are quite powerless.'

'No one owns my thoughts.'

'But as a woman your actions are dictated for you.'

She swallowed. 'That is a very cynical way of seeing things.'

'It is. As I mentioned before, it was recently pointed out to me that I am fortunate to be a man,' Christopher said, his lip curling.

'Who said that?'

'My father.' His eyes blazed with something beyond fury which made Tahira's blood run cold. And then it was over. His fists unfurled. He gave himself a shake. 'He told me the story of a young woman, much younger than you, a mere girl, destined by her family to make an advantageous marriage. Her circumstances changed, but still, they were determined upon the course they had planned for her, whether she wished to follow it or not. Like you, she was quite powerless. We'll never know how it might have turned out.'

'What happened?'

His throat worked. 'She died.'

'I'm so sorry, Christopher.' Tahira touched his hand. 'Who was she?'

From dark, his expression turned carefully blank. 'I never met her,' he said, disengaging himself, getting to his feet. 'But the comparison with you—I cannot help making it, though the circumstances, the stakes are so very different. Being no thoroughbred myself, at least I have been spared such machinations.'

Utterly confused, and now a little intimidated, Tahira knew he had not meant to hurt her with this last remark, knew he could have no idea that in her own way she was a thoroughbred, was being carefully mated, but she was bruised all the same. 'Fortunate indeed,' she said acerbically, 'for if you ever do marry, it will be because you want to, and not because it is your duty.'

He said something vicious in his own language under his breath. 'Forgive me, I have allowed my demons to blind me. Nine months ago, I would not have considered myself fortunate, but you put me to shame. I do have choices, while you—it goes against every grain of feeling with me that you should be bartered and sold for the sake of—what, a few camels, a small patch of land? No, don't answer that.' Christopher forced a smile. 'I am a man of action, it frustrates me beyond words that I cannot help you. You deserve so much better, Tahira, and perhaps you will get what you deserve, against the odds. Any man who can call you his wife will be very lucky indeed. I trust that the man your brother finds for you appreciates you for what you are.'

With a sinking feeling, Tahira thought back to the conversation she had had with Juwan a few days ago. Perhaps it would not be so bad. Or perhaps it would be better if she accepted that it would be even worse, and adjust her expectations accordingly. But for tonight, she'd had enough of it. 'I am not yet betrothed,' she said. 'Here in the desert night, my actions are dictated by no one and nothing more than my inclinations, and right at this moment, what I want is to gallop back on these beautiful horses you have risked so much to acquire.'

The next day was bathing day in the harem. The door to the Corridor of the Bath used by the men of the palace was locked and guarded, the door to the harem opened, and the hamam suite was given over to the female occupants. Emerging from the small outer anteroom where her clothing was exchanged for the single fringed linen sheet tied around the waist and the carved wooden pattens studded with pearls which kept her feet dry, Tahira paused as she always did, to drink in the atmosphere.

The main chamber of the hamam was circular, with no windows but with light flooding in through the high central dome which was supported by five pillars. The room was clad entirely in marble of different shades and striations, from pure glittering white to gold and dark brown, forming beautiful geometric patterns on the walls, on the massage tables and resting sofas, and on the central dais where the main fountain burbled. Around the walls were other fountains, graduating from ice cold to piping hot which filled the marble basins, each dedicated to a different intimate function. Doors set around the circular walls led off to other, much hotter chambers, a steam room, hot baths and icy cold plunge pools.

Though Juwan was not present today, for she found the baths too hot in her advanced state of pregnancy, her retinue maidservants were in attendance, along with many other women and girls, from the kitchen and chamber maids, laundry maids, to the herbalists, seamstresses and the personal maids of the four princesses. Women of all shapes and sizes languished on the marble divans resting after a massage or having their hair braided and oiled. Others gossiped in clusters while their nails were shaped, their feet decorated with henna. In the other rooms, ritual cleansing was undertaken, where the body was first soaked in oils, then given a vigorous rubbing with a cloth to stimulate the skin. Next came the soaping, the rinsing, the soaking in one of the hot baths, the plunge into a cold bath which made the skin tingle all over and finally the liberal sprinkling of the body and hair with attar of rose.

The chamber was abuzz with a myriad of conspiratorial conversations. Here in the baths, all women were equal, the strict laws of precedence abandoned, the hamam handmaidens serving each woman in turn regardless of rank or status. Tahira looked forward to hamam day, listening to the lively gossip, enjoying the relaxed atmosphere and the spirit of equality that allowed her to forget that she was a princess and to feel, for a few hours, that she was simply another woman, like all of those around her, albeit one, unlike some here, who was not permitted to mingle with the world outside these walls.

Today, however, she was restless, unsettled by last night and struggling to understand why, after a dream come true, and the delightfully, blissfully satisfying experience which had followed, she had woken this morning in such a strange, dissatisfied mood.

Forgoing her usual glass of tea and ration of gossip, she lay down on her tummy on the central dais, where it was the custom for women to be left with their own thoughts and to await a masseuse. Part of the problem was that last night had been so perfect. She had learned to suppress her childhood memories of horse riding so as not to endure the pain of missing it. Allowing the hubbub of the hamam to fade into the background, Tahira opened her mind now to those memories and discovered that they were no longer painful but soothing. Mama's face was hard to recall, but she could remember her laughter, the way she threw her head back and gazed up at the sky when she rode, trusting to her horse to guide her, as if she was imagining herself flying, just as Tahira did. Had Mama felt suffocated by the harem? It hadn't occurred to her until now. Mama had always seemed so very content with her lot, but then Tahira had been so young, and she doubted Mama would have confided in her, even had there been anything to confide. Only at the end, when she knew she was dying, had she been forced to speak frankly, and even then…

Tahira blinked away a tear. *Promise me that you will take care of your sisters, because I fear your brother will not.* Aged ten, she had taken her vow so very seriously, a sacred promise. Over the years, she had read so much into these few words. Too much? Was she choosing to interpret her promise selfishly now, twisting her vow into something that Mama had never intended in order to support her deep-seated reluctance to marry? For it was deep-seated, much more than she had realised until last night.

A soft whisper, a gentle hand on her shoulder told her that the masseuse had arrived. Warm oil trickled between her shoulder blades, and the woman started to gently knead Tahira's muscles, which were stiff from the horse ride.

The woman's touch was deft, impersonal, yet she could not relax. Why was she finding it so very difficult to do her duty? She had always, ever since she could remember, instinctively resisted doing Ghutrif's bidding, but she wasn't a child now. She was a grown woman, and she knew her own mind, yet no one save Christopher accepted that she had any right to an opinion, and that was the crux of the matter. As the masseuse began to work on the knots on her spine, Tahira could feel herself becoming ever more tense. She wasn't a thoroughbred horse, to be bought for breeding in exchange for—what was it Christopher had said? *A few camels, a small patch of land!* It made no difference that it was more likely to be an vast herd of camels, and an entire kingdom. She was a person, not a—an object!

Tahira sat up abruptly, grabbing her linen towel. "Thank you, but I am not—excuse me, I think I will repair to the steam room.'

But seated on a marble bench, her skin damp, the only sound the hiss of the steam rising from the floor, the steady drip of condensation running down the walls, her ire rose even higher than the temperature in the room. Christopher was right, she did deserve better. She deserved to have a say in her destiny. She deserved a husband who valued her as a woman, not a—a dynastic brood mare. She deserved a husband who desired her, and only her. Who cared for her. A man she could honour and value in return.

Tahira rarely cursed, but she did now, under her breath. What was the point harbouring such impossible thoughts. All she was doing was upsetting herself—and frightening herself too, for the strength of her antipathy was growing with every passing day. She had to find a way to reconcile herself to her fate, or she would be utterly miserable.

Leaning back against the relative cool of the marble-clad wall, she closed her eyes, taking slow deep breaths in an effort to rid herself of her agitation, but to no avail. If only Christopher had disagreed with her. But Christopher—recalling his bleak expression, despite the heat she shivered.

I never met her. He'd used similar words before. *I never knew her. She died giving birth to me.* Could his mother be the powerless young girl who was to be forced into an arranged marriage? It would explain why he hated his father, wouldn't it? And the demons he'd mentioned last night.

The amulet! If such a very valuable piece of jewellery was a gift from his father to his mother, and he hated his father, then she could understand why he was so determined to *rid himself* of it. But what on earth could his father have done to earn such enmity? Was Christopher's quest some sort of mission of revenge then? Such a very valuable piece of jewellery! She had not the impression that his family were wealthy. Quite the opposite. Could the amulet be the proceeds of a crime?

Her head was spinning with questions and fuzzy with the heat, but at least her anger had dissipated, now she had something far more intriguing to ponder than her own unsolvable problems. If only she could resolve the mystery of Christopher's quest, but that would require her to have the courage to ask her questions, and the tenacity to keep asking them until he answered, which was unlikely! And in the meantime...

A vision of last night floated into her head. Herself lying abandoned to passion, Christopher leaning over her. The solid weight of his body. The tantalising promise of his arousal. The thrill of her own, rising and rising and then exploding. His kisses. The way his eyes blazed fiercely when he looked at her, his own passion writ so clearly on his face. Finally, Tahira began to relax, her shoulders drooping, her limbs becoming heavy. She slid down on to the marble bench, letting the steam envelop her, and the sweet, delightful memory of Christopher's touch wash over her.

Chapter Seven

Returning the stolen thoroughbreds had proved to be a somewhat hair-raising experience. Who could have predicted that one of the mares in the paddock would begin foaling just as he was making good his escape! Christopher had managed to slip away by the skin of his teeth just as what seemed like half the Bedouin encampment arrived on the scene.

Two days later, he was preparing for an even more risky escapade. Thinking back to the aftermath of their horse ride made his body heat. He hadn't intended, hadn't planned, hadn't expected—how could he have, when he'd never before engaged in such a one-sided experience! Except that the pleasure had not been one-sided. Which made it quite unique. Because Tahira was quite unique.

Christopher paused in the act of adjusting his expensive new black cloak, specially purchased with today in mind. He couldn't recall ever enjoying a woman's company so much. When he was with her, the hours flew by. Was it the sense of sand moving too quickly through the hourglass which made their time together so intense? Or was he simply starved of company? Dammit, what the devil was wrong with admitting that he liked her?

'Naught, if you are careful to make sure you don't let your feelings run away with you,' he told himself. 'Nothing at all wrong with caring for her, provided you don't care enough to do something bloody foolish.'

Such as spirit her away on a flying carpet? He rolled his eyes at this. About as likely as anything else. 'In other words, not in the least likely, and you'd better make sure to remember that. You can take her mind off her situation, but you can't alter it. You might think yourself a man of action, but rescuing a damsel in distress is well outwith the scope of your mission here, so you're just going to have to put up with feeling helpless.'

Outside, dawn was breaking. Time to turn his mind to the matter in hand. Christopher pulled on the red *keffiyeh*, adjusting the black *igal* threaded with gold. Unable to furnish himself with the costume of a wealthy English aristocrat, he'd opted instead for the robes of a wealthy sheikh as the next best form of disguise.

Lord Armstrong had provided him with several sets of papers, giving him the option to switch between several identities. 'Though only if there is no other option,' the peer had stressed. 'Strictly a last resort.' Would the wily diplomat consider this such a case? The answer, Christopher thought blithely, was an unequivocal no. A life-and-death situation on the other hand—very possibly, if his subterfuge were discovered. How the real Sir Ferdinand St John Bremner would react should he find his name and his estate and his reputation had been sullied—happily, that was Lord Armstrong's problem. By the time the local agent had informed London of his masquerade, Christopher would be back in Egypt. Hopefully, minus his amulet.

Outside, the morning light was harsh as he saddled his camel and made his way towards the city. He'd have preferred not to have to draw attention to his presence here in Nessarah until he had a sample from the turquoise mine, but he couldn't sit about twiddling his thumbs until then. The only way to gain entry to the diamond market was through Prince Ghutrif. Fortunately his Highness was avaricious, and the local agent Christopher had deployed, with his hints at further lucrative English business, persuasive. The wealthy Sir Ferdinand St John Bremner's request to establish whether Nessarah could provide him with a jewel fit for his new wife's tiara had been granted.

The white walls of Nessarah's huge bazaar shimmered in the sunlight. This time, Christopher strode confidently through the maze of corridors and stairwells to the closed screen which hid the entrance to the diamond market. He had, most reluctantly, left his trusty scimitar and dagger behind, though the knife strapped to his leg gave him some comfort. He did not believe that Lord Armstrong's agent would betray him, but experience had taught him to be wary.

And the stakes were very high. So high that he could not risk being caught in possession of his amulet. He did not need it to make the comparison, however. He knew the stones intimately, and would easily recognise their counterparts.

The guard dressed in the royal livery of crimson and white was not the same man as before, but he was of the same gigantic proportions. This time, however, there was no restraining paw forbidding him entry, but a respectful bow upon receipt of Christopher's written permission bearing the royal seal, before a curtain was pulled back to permit him to gain entrance.

The trade in precious stones was carried out in a large room on the top floor of the bazaar. Light streamed through a huge window in the ceiling, dazzling the eyes at first. There were four booths, each furnished with a low table, a scatter of cushions, and a specialist in the various gems in which they traded. 'Emerald,' the assistant who met him at the door informed Christopher, 'ruby, sapphire and other stones, and over here, diamonds.'

Caution prevailed. He opted first for emeralds, drinking the obligatory glass of mint tea before inspecting the trays of stones which were so reverently placed in front of him. The emeralds were of excellent quality, very large, and of no interest to him whatsoever. He turned them over, held them up to the light, and discussed their various qualities at length, mustering his growing impatience. Finally, with what he hoped was the correct blend of condescension and regret, he informed the emerald vendor that his future wife had blue eyes and fair hair, colouring which would by no means complement these marvellous stones. Thinking that actually, diamonds were more perfectly suited to a woman with night-black hair, olive skin and big brown eyes, Christopher got to his feet and moved on.

Sitting down, he accepted another glass of mint tea. As the merchant pulled out the first velvet-lined tray from the locked cabinet, Christopher's heart began to beat wildly, his stomach muscles clenched tight. There were just three stones on the tray, but they were sufficient for him to know, even without closer examination, deep down in his gut, that they were a perfect match.

'You did what?' The blood drained from Tahira's face. She stared at Christopher in horror. 'It's not possible. To get into the diamond market one requires permission from Prince Ghutrif himself.'

'Which he very generously granted me. Or at least, granted my alter ego.'

She swayed, clutching his sleeve. 'If it is discovered that you impersonated this English man, Prince Ghutrif would...'

'Prince Ghutrif is only interested in the prospect of more wealthy Englishmen buying Nessarah diamonds.'

'You promised him that?' Tahira's voice was almost a wail. 'You must leave Nessarah at once.'

'You're being ridiculous.' Christopher gave her a little shake. 'I haven't met Prince Ghutrif, he has no idea what I look like, where I am camped, and what's more he doesn't care.'

'But then how did you…?'

'I have a local man, a contact, who acted as my intermediary. I passed myself off as a wealthy English aristocrat. Rather successfully, I might add.'

Tahira's alarmed expression turned to one of puzzlement. 'A contact? You have used that word before. What kind of contact?'

'It doesn't matter,' Christopher said impatiently, 'what matters is…'

'That you have put not only yourself but this *contact* in mortal danger by dint of your deception.'

'Tahira, I don't know why you're getting so…'

'Angry? Frightened? No, actually I'm terrified. No matter how important this amulet to you is, it cannot be more important than your life.'

'You're quite wrong. Until I am rid of it, I have no life worth living.'

Her jaw dropped. 'You can't mean that.'

He could. He did. But he was not inclined to explain himself. 'You're missing the point,' Christopher said. 'I succeeded in gaining entry to the diamond market. I managed to compare...'

'Are you a spy?'

'What?'

'Are you here on English government business?'

'No.' But the denial was unconvincing, even to himself. He didn't want to lie to her. 'There is a man in the English government who has supplied me with papers and contacts.'

'By the stars, you *are* a spy. Do you—what are you—have you been spying on me?' She was quite pale, her eyes huge.

'Why on earth would I do that?'

She licked her lips, but did not speak.

'I've thought of it,' Christopher admitted. 'I've thought of following you home. It would be simple enough, to find out who you are, who your family are. It is not lack of curiosity which has prevented me from doing so but respect for you. You have chosen to keep your identity a secret. So be it. I promise you, Tahira, spying is not my business, surveying is. The truth is, I needed the papers to facilitate my quest, to help me move around freely, gain entry to places such as the diamond market, and even to get me out of hot water if necessary, so I persuaded a man at the Foreign Office to procure them for me.'

'Persuaded.' Tahira's colour had returned. 'What did he want in return? Because such men always have a price. We have a saying. "You shake my olive tree and I will shake yours."'

He couldn't help but laugh, though he also couldn't help but wonder how she came by her knowledge. What men did she know? He'd assumed her family were at least moderately wealthy, but clearly they also had some influence. More questions he couldn't ask. 'You're quite right. He wanted information. Nothing sinister, I assure you. Trade opportunities, which kingdoms would be open to it, what they would trade in, that kind of thing. Information that would be of mutual benefit to Britain and whichever Arabian kingdom engaged with them.'

'And beneficial to the man at your Foreign Office who facilitated bringing the two parties together.'

'Indeed. You are most astute.'

Tahira shrugged. 'I know of such men. Who is he, this man at the Foreign Office, how do you come to know him?'

'Let us say that our meeting was an accident, and leave it at that. My report will give him what he wants, what we agreed, but it will fall a long way sort of all the information I have garnered,' Christopher said. 'Arabia is an untapped treasure trove of minerals and ores. That most valuable information I'll be keeping to myself.'

'You know you could make your fortune by selling it?'

'And you know I won't. You still haven't asked me the outcome of my act of derring-do.'

He was relieved to see her smile again, her suspicions and fears giving way to excitement. 'Well?'

'The diamonds are an exact match!'

'Oh, Christopher!' Tahira threw her arms around his neck, her expression, in the light of the nascent moon, finally every bit as elated as he felt. 'That is wonderful news. Though I still can't believe you took such a risk—but you came to no harm. Tell me you will not do anything so foolhardy again.'

He refrained from making a promise he was more than likely to break, if the situation required it, putting his arms around her waist. Immediately his body stirred to life, remembering all too well the shape of her curves, the taste of her kisses. 'We must not get too far ahead of ourselves. The turquoise is still key, the final piece of the puzzle.'

'Soon, though. In a matter of days, they will have mined the first samples.' Tahira must have sensed his sudden stillness. 'Or so I have heard,' she said, looking away, over his shoulder. 'There is much talk of it in Nessarah. The miners are being paid extra to make haste.'

He had heard such rumours, though he had not heard anything about samples. Was her brother involved in the mine in some capacity? That would certainly explain how she came to be here that first night. He hesitated, torn between curiosity and a reluctance to set her on edge again with questions, and she forestalled him with a change of subject.

'I too have news, though mine is dismal. My brother has found a candidate for my hand. If the negotiations go well, my betrothal could be announced within seven or ten days.'

His heart sank. 'So soon?'

There were tears misting her eyes, but she was biting her lip, determined not to let them fall. 'I want—I so very much want to know—to be with you, when you successfully complete your quest, but there is a chance that might not be possible.'

Every instinct urged him to pull her close, to hold her tight, to tell her that he would find a way to prevent that happening, but that would be pointless and meaningless. And wrong. Instead, he kissed her forehead, forced himself to let her go. 'We might be closer to a resolution than you think. Last night I worked on after you left, and I made a potentially exciting discovery. Come and see what I've found.'

Tahira did not need Christopher's assistance to ascend to the gap between the main outcrops of rock, but she liked the feel of her fingers twined with his, the way their legs brushed through their clothing, the way he looked down every few moments, as if he was afraid she had disappeared.

Juwan had made her announcement this afternoon, seeking out the sisters in the Courtyard of the Healers. 'Negotiations are at an advanced stage,' her sister-in-law had declared with a triumphant little smile. 'My husband is very pleased with progress. A man of substance, family and influence. You are most fortunate, Tahira.'

Tahira could not bring herself to speak. It was

Ishraq who asked the questions, Tahira shutting her ears to the answers, as if ignorance would make a mere mirage of her suitor. But later, as Ishraq enviously recited his many reputed virtues, it was impossible not to hear. A paragon, an Adonis, worshipped by his people, a man any woman would be immensely proud to call husband, Ishraq had said. The irrefutable facts relating to the stranger who would own her were lodged in Tahira's mind, ready to surface as soon as she returned to the palace and lay alone in her bed, but for now, she refused to grant them entry. Not while she had so little precious time left here with Christopher.

She held tightly on to his hand as they passed the sites of their previous excavations, up to the gap between the two outcrops, where he picked up a lantern and lit it, holding it high. 'What have you found?' Tahira asked, frowning when they came to a halt. 'It is far too small to be any sort of dwelling.'

'Come further in and see,' he replied, leading the way, lowering the lamp in order to guide her steps.

'What is it? I can tell from your voice that it is— Christopher, don't keep me in suspense, it's cruel.'

He laughed. 'Only a moment longer.' He came to a halt at his small excavation and handed her the lantern. 'Go on, take a closer look and tell me what you think.'

She stooped down to examine the ground he had so painstakingly cleared. 'This is where you found the gold bangle, isn't it?' She took her time, her fingers tracing delicately over the area he had exposed, before she stood up, stepped back, paced around, frowning. 'There is nothing. No evidence of foundations, and I presume you haven't found any other artefacts?'

'As a matter of fact I have, but I'd rather wait to show you it. Look more closely.'

'What for? Is it another entrance to the mine?' Tahira peered down at the dirt and rocks, shaking her head. 'What am I missing?'

And then she saw it, the tiny gap at the base of the rock which his digging had exposed. Dropping to her knees, she examined it more closely, running her hands over the rock's striations, then standing up, running her hands up further. 'I thought it was a fissure, but it's not, is it?'

Christopher shook his head.

'It has been very cleverly done,' Tahira said, her face almost pressed up against the rock. 'An opening has been blocked up with stone and adobe to blend in with the natural rock. Time has done its work most effectively to cover it up, but I am sure of it. This has been sealed very carefully indeed. Someone has been most determined that whatever is behind here should not be discovered. Could it be our thief's treasure trove?'

He waited, clearly enjoying watching her thought process reflected in her face. 'But, no,' she said now, shaking her head, 'that would not make sense. If our thief did exist, he would have wished to recover his loot at some point. This would take a great deal of effort to break through. That, and the effort put into concealing its existence means that it was never intended to be opened up.'

'Exactly,' Christopher said, primly.

She burst out laughing. 'It is not fair, you have the advantage of me. What have you found?' She set the lantern down, gave his arm a shake. 'Please, I am desperate to know.'

He handed her something, wrapped in a piece of cotton. 'This was buried at the concealed entrance.'

Tahira dropped to the ground to open it, crossing her legs and setting the bundle between them.

Slowly, she unwound the protective wrapping—one of Christopher's cloaks had been sacrificed. The effigy was carved from stone, and almost perfectly preserved. She held it reverently as she traced the cat's feet, tail, ears. The paint was flaking in places, but the rings on the tail and legs clear enough. 'It's a sand cat,' she said, smiling, flattening her hand over the head of the statuette, running it down the back as if she were stroking the real animal. 'A perfectly beautiful sand cat. And very, very old.'

Christopher nodded. 'What do you think is its purpose?'

'Purpose?' But almost before the word was out, she understood. 'It's a guardian, isn't it? This pose, sitting sentinel, I have seen drawings of such things. They usually guard—by the stars! A tomb?'

'Of a wealthy and important person too I reckon. Though I fear it has been raided, for that is the only explanation of our finds.'

'But the entrance has been concealed so perfectly.'

'It was most likely raided not long after the burial, before the tomb was properly sealed. A common occurrence in Egypt, I'm afraid.'

'Who could be buried here?' Tahira wrapped the sentinel sand cat back up carefully, and got to her feet. 'I've never come across anything like this in Nessarah. It begs the question, why? Do you think it's possible for us to take down these stones?'

Christopher grinned. 'Do you think it's possible for us to resist? Though it's very well done, I don't think it would be too difficult, and fortunately, we're quite some distance from the mine, it's highly unlikely anyone will notice.'

'My heart is racing. I can't believe it. Could we start tonight?'

'Do you really have so little time left before you are—is your betrothal so imminent?'

In the light of the lantern, she was reminded of their first meeting at the entrance to the mine. His hair had shimmered like gold. His eyes were such a striking blue. A dangerous man, she'd decided and she'd been right, but during the long nights working together, she had come to see that there was so much more to him than that. An honourable man. A troubled man. A man with demons. A thoughtful man. A man who would take ridiculous risks, go to any amount of trouble, to make a wish come perfectly true. A man she had come to care for far too much, despite the fact that he was also a man about whom she knew far too little. A man who, in a very short period of time, she would never see again.

'Tahira?' Christopher gently wiped the tear which tracked down her cheek with his thumb.

She caught his hand, pressing a kiss to his palm. 'My sister says I am very fortunate. He is not old or cruel, the man my brother has found for me. My sister says she would gladly marry him herself. He is a widower, with a small child. A boy. I would not even be expected to provide an heir. He even lives—he lives within travelling distance. I could not have asked for a more suitable and amenable match, Christopher, but still I cannot—I simply cannot bring myself to embrace it.'

He pulled her into his arms, holding her tight. She burrowed her face into his chest, breathing deep of the scent of lemon soap and whatever it was that was particularly Christopher.

She had heard Ghutrif boasting about the mine to Juwan yesterday, promising her a turquoise necklace made of the first ore, when their son was born. If she could find a way to steal a sample for Christopher, it would save him from taking yet another unnecessary risk by stealing a sample himself.

And yet, the more she helped him, the sooner his quest would be over and he would leave for ever. Another thought struck her forcibly. The more she helped him the more likely it was that he would turn up at the palace to hand back the amulet. Reducing the risk to him made the risk of his discovering her true identity terrifyingly likely, and if he then let slip their acquaintance...

Acquaintance! A word that fell a long way short of whatever it was that they had between them. She shuddered. It simply didn't bear thinking about. If the worst came to the worst—or the best came to the best—or the worst came to the best, or whatever combination—she would think of something to prevent him storming the palace. She would have to.

'Tahira?'

She forced herself to look up. Christopher pushed her hair back from her cheek, his expression set. 'There is no chance that this betrothal will come to nothing, like the others?'

At least he had not guessed her true thoughts. Tahira smiled wanly. 'Lightning will not be permitted to strike again. The last time, I was not—I made my indifference clear, and so too did my betrothed.' She hesitated. Christopher was frowning, that frown he wore when he was trying to bite his tongue. 'That previous match was arranged by his family,' she elaborated, which was the truth, though not specific enough to betray her identity. 'In the end, he chose to ignore their wishes.'

The one thing she could not do. The words hung between them, but they'd already said more than enough on the subject. 'Should we make a start?' Tahira asked, far more brightly than she felt.

The hours passed too quickly. After they had stopped excavating, they sat, as had become their habit, chatting and drinking water from Christopher's goatskin flask. Tahira looked up at the sky and sighed. 'I must leave a little sooner tonight. My friend is worried. Farah,' she added. 'My friend's name is Farah.'

The first name she had spoken save her own and Sayeed's. Christopher acknowledged this rare confidence with a quirk of his brow. 'Would Farah happen to have access to a camel?'

'You guessed!'

'I reckoned you would not dare risk taking one from the family stables.' He angled himself towards her. 'So Farah knows that you escape at night? She must be a very good friend if you trust her with such a big secret.'

'None better. Farah was once my maidservant, but she is so near in age to me that she has always been more of a friend. When Mama died, we became closer. Too close,' she said, her smile fading. 'My brother was jealous.'

'It seems all roads in your life story lead to your brother,' Christopher said, grimly. 'What happened?'

'It would have been better if we had kept our distance in front of him, but we were children, and my brother—oh, we thought him just a spiteful little boy. We never considered that there would be consequences to our excluding him from our games. But as the years passed and we became closer, and Farah—I fear that she took her lead from me and was too bold in her dislike of him, and I was naïve enough to show how much I cared for her. It shouldn't have been a surprise when he contrived to have my father unfairly dismiss her, causing her character to be unjustly blackened.' Tahira clenched her fists. 'But it was.'

'And so your friend takes pleasure in thwarting your brother by assisting you?'

'She has always been happy to do so, but to-night—you see, until lately my absences have been well spaced. It is only recently that I've risked escaping so often. Farah is afraid that I will be caught. Which made me worry about what would happen to her if I was. It has been selfish of me not to think that by implicating her I was putting her at risk too.'

'Does she know that you are to be married?'

'She does now. She is pleased for me,' Tahira said, with a bittersweet smile, for Farah had actually been delighted that she would escape from Ghutrif, even though it would mean they would never see each other again.

'So you haven't shared your own feelings on the subject with her, even though you trust her implicitly?'

'No. Nor—Christopher, you must not worry that Farah knows about you.'

'I hadn't even considered it.'

'No one knows of you, or our meetings. You are my secret, and mine alone.' Flushing, startled by the tone of her voice, which gave her words far more meaning than she had intended, Tahira hurriedly pulled her headdress over her face. 'I must go. I don't want to upset Farah any further.'

Urging her sluggish camel into a trot, she wondered with a sinking feeling how many more times she would make this journey. If Farah had her way, it would be none. It would be the same number if common sense prevailed, but Tahira had never felt less sensible. She had never had so much to lose. She couldn't stop now, not with the tomb to be opened, the turquoise to be matched, Christopher's quest to be completed.

The dangers made her head spin, but the rewards made her heart soar. With Christopher she was alive. Why shouldn't she admit that she cared for him, longed to be with him, relished every moment they were together? Their time was so precious, it intensified every feeling, but their time was finite, and so too, she was sure she would discover, were her feelings. It was as if she had leapt from the highest mountain. It was impossible to stop herself, impossible to climb back, so she could enjoy every moment of the wild careening down before coming back down to earth. She would find a way to beat the odds. She would find a way to land safely. But in the meantime, she had no intentions of shortening the fall.

Even by the opulent standards of the royal palace of Nessarah, the library was an imposing room, and one which was very different in style from the rest of the palace. The ceiling was not decorated with traditional tiles but was elaborately moulded, painted in a soft palate of gold and celestial blues, the central fresco depicting a summer sky with light fluffy clouds of the sort never seen over the Nessarah desert. In contrast, the vast floor space was laid with simple polished flagstones, and just as sparsely furnished. Four long, highly polished reading tables doubled as cabinets for storing papers, but there was not a single other item of furniture or any form of seating. A harem sentry guarded the other side of the door through which Tahira entered for her pre-sanctioned private visit. On the opposite wall, light streamed in from a vast arched window.

Every other inch of available wall space was taken up by books and scrolls. Thousands of them, in shelves which climbed to the ceiling. A narrow gallery ran at half-height, reached by a single narrow, spiral staircase which required the intrepid reader to walk around the full length of the library to reach the books on the furthest side. A single freestanding ladder on wheels provided access for the reader to the lower shelves. The library, created and largely populated by Tahira's great-great grandfather, was not a place often visited by her more recent forebears. No catalogue of any sort existed, and she had never been able to divine any system for the placement of tomes on the shelves. In this sense, every visit to the room was a voyage of discovery, but it could also be highly frustrating. As a result she had started her own system. In effect, creating her own library within the library, relocating, book by book, scroll by scroll, the volumes in which she was interested.

Today however, she was not consulting any of those previously read works on Nessarah's history. The book which lay open on the reading table was bound in red leather tooled with gold, and intriguingly entitled *The Art of Love*. It was not the first book she had perused today, but the illustrations in *The Garden of Delights* had appalled her. Such contortions appeared more likely to induce pain rather than delight, and the book, while it contained a great many words in praise of the male member, contained no relevant information on how to minister to it. *The Art of Love*, which she had discovered between a guide to the art of an Italian painter, and a notebook containing household remedies, was a very different matter. There were no illustrations and no poems eulogising male prowess. Instead, the book was a practical guide to giving and receiving pleasure, narrated alternately by a man and a woman.

She had not progressed beyond the early chapters, for the descriptions brought to mind her own experiences. Christopher's kisses. The way her nipple had tightened when he took it into his mouth, the way she had arched under him in response. The tension. And the heat. Which Christopher, according to the book, had been experiencing too. Eyes closed, seated cross-legged on the floor, she tried to imagine what he would feel like. Silk and iron, the book said, but such a combination was too strange. His chest was hard, solid muscle, expanding and contracting as he breathed. He was clean shaven, though his cheek was rough compared to hers. Would his chest be smooth, or would there be a smattering of dark-gold hair? And his nipples? A flush stole over her cheeks, embarrassment mingled with excitement. Her own nipples peaked against the silk of her camisole, proving that the little book was right. Arousal did not require physical contact. But she did touch herself, imagining her hands were Christopher's, imagining his skin against hers, his rough palms on the soft skin of her breasts.

Only when she slid on to the floor, her breathing ragged, did she remember where she was. Thankfully no one would disturb her with the sentry outside. All the same. Tahira closed the book and got to her feet, placing it carefully on her own shelves before wandering over to the window. Though it looked out only to a rather boring courtyard with a rather plain fountain, at least from here she could see the sky. Cloudless again. It would be another clear night for their work at the tomb. It would take them several nights, Christopher had estimated, before they would be ready to break through to whatever was on the inside. He was working longer hours than she. She had asked him to promise not to work when the miners were there, not in daylight, but he had avoided answering her. though he had promised he would not enter the tomb unless she was present.

Ishraq had informed her today that Ghutrif was planning to make the betrothal announcement at an upcoming camel race, organised specially for the occasion, which all of the princesses would be permitted to attend. A camel race was a rare, exciting treat, but Tahira heard this with a sinking feeling in the pit of her stomach. There would be a huge crowd. Ghutrif was making certain, with such a very public pronouncement, that this time the marriage would definitely go ahead.

Fortunately, Ishraq was beside herself with excitement, more than compensating for her elder sister's distinct lack of enthusiasm. It was the one good thing to come of it, for now that she knew Tahira was soon to be wed, Ishraq was her former sunny, loving self. As for Durrah and Alimah— yes, they were upset, but they too were excited by the prospect of attending a camel race and very shortly after, the wedding celebrations. They were thrilled that Tahira was to marry such an eligible man, and were already talking of bridal visits while Tahira—just thinking of anything bridal made her nauseous. She didn't want to marry this man. She didn't want to think about it, so instead she would think about Christopher. Again. Her escape from reality, because reality was simply too unbearable to contemplate. Was that wrong? She didn't care. Tonight, she would once again inhabit her dream world, with her dream man. Tahira closed her eyes, wrapping her arms around her waist and transported herself there.

The large rock formation where they brought their camels to a halt two nights later was not unlike the turquoise mine, the craggy rocks the same russet red colour, the soft sand tinged with the same hue. 'What is this place?' Tahira asked.

Christopher shook his head, dismounting before helping her from the saddle. 'A place where wishes come true, I hope.'

Just like the turquoise mine, there was a fissure between the rocks, though this was much wider, forming a passageway open to the night sky. Tahira followed in Christopher's wake, leading her camel a few short steps before stopping with a gasp of amazement. The low rock cliffs encircled the space to form a natural arena carpeted with soft sand, which shelved down towards a large pool bordered with juniper trees, their foliage lush. On the far side, a narrow cascade of water fell with a mesmeric murmur into the pool like a shimmering sheet of white silk. Through another gap in the rocks, the desert landscape was framed like a painting, a ribbon of similar rock formations growing ever higher into a mountain range until it looked to Tahira that they formed a staircase to the galaxy of silver stars pinned above.

'How on earth did you find this place?' she said, turning to Christopher.

'I have the Midas touch, remember?'

He had hobbled the camels, discarded his headdress and cloak. His hair had grown longer, thick ripples of gold fell over his brow, giving him a distinctly raffish look. The deep tan of his face made his eyes seem as blue as the oasis pool. This man, this fascinating, fiercely attractive, fearless and driven man, had gone to all this trouble for her. A lump rose in her throat. She felt as if her heart were being squeezed, making her breathless, unable to speak her gratitude, so instead she wrapped her arms tightly around his waist, pressing her cheek against the hard wall of his chest, the unique scent of him mingling with the verdant green of the oasis, the salty, heady taste of the desert night.

'Tahira?' Christopher flattened his hand over her hair, running it down her long plait to rest on the slope of her bottom. It was becoming a familiar caress, and it had a familiar effect, both reassuring and arousing at the same time. 'Are you disappointed?'

She lifted her head, smiling up at him, for once caring not that he would see the sparkle of tears on her lashes. 'I am overwhelmed. It is magical. If you'd asked me to describe my perfect oasis it would be just like this.'

'Excellent, then we may now make your dream come true. Shall we?' he said, gesturing towards the pool.

She hesitated, realising somewhat foolishly that he had taken her quite literally at her word. 'When I said I wanted to swim in an oasis I meant—I can't actually swim.'

'It's not too deep. You can walk over to the waterfall, the water won't go above your waist. Or you can float. I can hold you. You'll be perfectly safe.'

Tahira looked at the tempting waters of the oasis. She imagined the cool caress on her skin while Christopher held her. She thought of the delights she had read of in *The Art of Love*. 'I don't want to feel safe,' she said, twining her arms around his neck. 'I want to feel.' She kissed him, licking into the corner of his mouth, running her tongue along his sensual bottom lip. 'And I want you to feel too,' she said.

'Oh, but I do.'

She kissed him again. 'Yes, but tonight, I want you to feel more.'

He stilled. 'Tahira, we cannot… I cannot.'

'There are many ways of making love,' she said, 'and many ways to reach the summit of pleasure together, a merging of passions but not of bodies.'

'What on earth do you know of such things?'

She laughed, enjoying confounding him, excited by the spark her words had kindled in his eyes. 'I've been doing some research. A bit of digging of my own, you might say. From a book.'

'What book?'

'*The Art of Love*. A most—a most educational tome.'

Christopher's smile was sinful. 'Theory has its place but I'm a great believer in the merit of practical experience.'

'I couldn't agree more,' Tahira said, 'but first—don't you think we should experience this beautiful desert pool?'

'Oh, I think we can do better than that,' he replied, unbuckling his belt and discarding his scimitar and dagger. 'I think we should combine the two.'

Chapter Eight

Christopher pulled his tunic over his head, revealing a deeply tanned, lean and very muscled torso, his ribcage expanding as he raised his arms, the muscles of his stomach rippling. There was a smattering of dark-gold hair across his chest, which arrowed fascinatingly down to the belt of his trousers. His nipples were flat, dark discs, completely unlike her own. A scar, a pale, jagged line on his left side marred the otherwise sheer physical perfection of his body. 'How did you come by that?' Tahira asked.

'The result of a slight altercation with a pasha's bodyguard.'

Any other time, she would have asked him to elucidate, but right now, she was frozen, mesmerised by his body, so completely different from the illustrations in the explicit little textbook, so completely different from her own too. She wanted to touch him, but there was a world of difference between theory and practice, a world of difference between her fevered imaginings and the reality of this flesh-and-blood man.

'Tahira, you don't have to do anything you don't want to. You can change your mind at any point.'

'I haven't changed my mind.' Embarrassment made her sound as if she had. If Christopher thought for a moment that she was unwilling, that she needed persuading—she knew enough of his demons to be certain it would put an end to the prospect of having even a swim together. *I would never, ever take such vile advantage*, he had said to her. That discussion had brought their perfect night to an abrupt end. This perfect night had barely begun. She would not make the same mistake twice.

Tahira took a deep breath and unfastened the buttons which held her tunic in place. Blushing, but keeping her gaze fixed on him, she let the garment slither to the sand. There was no mistaking the flare of desire in the way his eyes widened, in the sharp intake of his breath as he looked at her. Her breasts would be clearly outlined under the flimsy chemise, she knew. As his gaze flickered down, she could feel her nipples hardening. He liked what he saw. She liked what it did to him.

Gaining confidence, she kicked off her boots. Her toes curled into the cool, damp sand. She waited, casting him a challenging look and he laughed when he understood her meaning, kicking off his own boots. His feet were surprisingly slender and very pale. Tahira took a step towards him, untying the sash which held her trousers in place.

Colour slashed his cheeks, but his hand caught her wrists. 'Are you absolutely sure?'

She smiled then, knowing that her desire was reflected in her smile, confident now, despite her lack of experience. 'Certain, Christopher,' she said, and this time he believed her. His gaze was riveted on her hands as she untied the sash, letting the wide trousers drop to the sands. A sharp exhale again. He said her name, a low groan as he looked at her, clad only in her chemise and her short *dizlik* drawers, tied with lace at her knees. 'Do you think this is a suitable costume for swimming?'

'There is only one way to find out,' Christopher said, closing the gap between them. Without warning, he scooped her up into his arms and began to wade into the oasis.

Laughing, Tahira put an arm around his neck. Laughter and passion were a heady mix, she discovered as she looked into his eyes, bluer than the water. A blue she would never forget. He held her high against his chest. She dared to brush the soft smattering of hair with her free hand. Rougher than she had expected, his skin hot to the touch. 'Kiss me, Christopher,' she whispered, her mouth a fraction from his.

He let her go, but only to pull her tight up against him. The water lapped around her knees, droplets splashed her back, but she barely noticed as he wrapped his arms around her. 'Your wish is my command,' he whispered. And then he kissed her.

She kissed him back with a new abandon, desire fuelled by confidence, not of experience but of certainty. He wanted her. That was all the encouragement she needed to explore his body, to run her hands over his bare skin, the rippling planes of his muscles, the skin first smooth then rough with hair, hot, then damp with sweat and the cool waters of the oasis. His breathing quickened like hers. His touch became more urgent as hers did, his hands on her back, her bottom, her breasts.

His mouth on hers, deep, scorching kisses that made her moan, that made her frantic. His mouth on her breasts now, that sweet tug on her nipple that made her insides knot.

Their clothing was soaked through. Pressing herself against him, she could feel the hard ridge of his erect member, the potent symbol of his desire. That most intimate of unions was forbidden in every way, it was the line Christopher would never permit himself to cross, but she had already crossed a line. She would begin her wedding night a virgin, but she would be no innocent. There were so few ways in which she could rebel. It gave a sweet, lethal edge to her passion, to do this. One of the few choices she could make. Her secret. The man who would own her could never have this.

She kissed the man she had chosen with renewed fervour. Kissed his mouth and then his throat, and then his chest. His nipple peaked when she sucked on it. He moaned. He said something in his own language as he scooped her back up in his arms, staggering through the deeper waters to the cascade, soaking them both with spray in his hurry. She braced herself for the heavy fall of water, but it was brief. Behind the waterfall was a cave, the floor soft sand. Christopher set her down, and the kissing started again.

More kisses, and more as they sank to their knees, as he tore her chemise from her, to burrow his head between her breasts, cupping her, teasing her nipples, taking her to new heights of delight. If passion was a colour it would not be the scarlet red of heat, it would be the blue of Christopher's eyes, the gold of his hair. Glittering colours, sharp-edged, unforgettable.

They were entwined on the sand now, locked together, face-to-face, but as his hand trailed down her belly to the waistband of her drawers, once again he paused. 'Are you sure you want to carry on?'

Her nerves returned as she reached to undo his belt, but she knew hesitation would be fatal, and she was determined that her satisfaction would not be one-sided this time. She tugged it open, shaking her head at him when he would have stopped her. 'Christopher, I promise you, I want this.'

His chest expanded as he exhaled. His lids flickered closed for a tiny moment. 'You know I will not…'

'I know,' Tahira said, sliding her hand inside his trousers before he could stop her. Silk and iron, the book had said, but as she wrapped her hand around the thick girth of him, there was no mistaking this for anything but hard, hot man.

'Wait.' Gently removing her hand, Christopher eased her out of her drawers, quickly ridding himself of his own trousers, before lowering her on to the sand. 'By the stars, but you are beautiful,' he said, lying down on his side to face her.

They were both completely naked. The sand was cool and gritty on her flank. The cascade was a shimmering, watery curtain which hid them from the world. It was intoxicating. Taking her cue from Christopher, Tahira ran her hands over his body, drinking in every detail of him, too absorbed by the rush of desire for shyness to take hold. Her touch made his breathing fast and shallow, just like hers. When he pulled her to him, her body instinctively moulded itself to his. Their kisses were languorous at first, their hands tentative, learning each other's shape, but every touch seemed to ignite a tiny fire, and soon every flame was connected up, blazing trails from her breasts to her belly to the tension building inexorably between her legs.

When he touched her there, slid his fingers inside her, she shuddered, but when he tried to ease her on to her back she resisted. 'Together,' she said. 'I want—please, Christopher, together. I know we can—that we cannot—but…'

'We can. Do this much. Together,' he said raggedly. 'But I simply cannot…'

'I know.'

She wrapped her hand around the hard length of him again, feeling the blood pulse as she stroked him slowly. Their mouths met in a tongue-tangling kiss, and her eyes closed as she surrendered to the rhythm he set, reassured by the way their breathing syncopated, that everything she was feeling he was too. She lost herself in his touch, in the tension mounting inside her, in the answering throb of him, the indescribable feeling of her climax, slowly building momentum, until it rushed up on her sending her soaring, making her cry out. Christopher's harsh groan as he rolled away from her to spend himself added a new layer of satisfaction, and an odd sense of disappointment. Her body craved something more. Her body craved what he would never, for reasons which were still unfathomable, permit himself to give her.

Tahira forced herself to sit up. She did not trust herself. She would not tempt him to do what he was so certain would destroy him. Who was this man, that she had shared the most intimate of moments with? For a few seconds, watching his chest heaving, his breathing slow, she felt as if she was looking at a complete stranger. Then he opened his eyes. He sat up, pushing her tangle of damp hair back from her cheek and kissed her slowly, and he was Christopher again. Her dream man, who had tonight made another of her own dreams come true.

'Thank you,' Tahira said.

He laughed gruffly. 'No, thank you. That is not what I had in mind when I brought you here.'

'I meant thank you for granting another of my wishes. You have gone to a great deal of trouble to make them very special. And I know this wasn't what you had in mind, I know that all you planned was my swim, but it is sharing all of this, together, that makes it so perfect. I hope you don't regret it?'

His expression became serious. 'Not if you don't.'

'Never.' She smiled shyly up at him. 'I thought the book exaggerated, but quite the contrary.'

Groaning, Christopher wrapped his arms tightly around her. 'It would be better for both of us if this were not quite so—if I did not find you quite so—if our passion were not so—Tahira, you are soon to be married.'

'But not just yet,' she said fiercely, burrowing her face into his chest. 'Please don't tell me this is wrong. I am not yet another man's property. This cannot be wrong, Christopher, it feels too wonderful to be wrong. Please, let us not spoil the perfection of this night.'

He heaved a sigh, but he nodded. 'You haven't even had your promised swim yet.'

Relieved, she leaned in and kissed him. 'And you always keep your promises. Shall we?'

Tahira stepped into the waterfall, letting out a squeal of shock as the icy water cascaded over her. Christopher watched her as she tilted her head back, closing her eyes, her hair streaming down her back, utterly unaware of her beauty. Her body was silky smooth all over, the tradition here in Arabia, he knew, though until today had not seen in the flesh. He wanted to kiss her, to taste every inch of that olive-toned, sweetly scented skin, to lick into the hot, wet core of her. The possessiveness he felt was both misguided and inappropriate, he told himself, a natural consequence of what they had just shared, nothing more. And what they had just shared—was that wrong? He simply couldn't bring himself to think so.

Tahira held out her hand invitingly. He stepped into the cascade, relishing the sharp sting of the water on his skin, cooling his ardour, which had been returning with astonishing quickness as he watched her. It had been too long, that was all. And they had so little time.

He turned away to rinse the sand from his body, and to keep his eyes from the temptation personified showering beside him. Not that he was tempted to test his control any further. Tonight had not been a close call, he had not at any point considered acting on his body's most insistent urges, but it had surprised him how strongly they persisted, how much he had wanted that ultimate possession.

That word again. Tahira could never be his. What he wanted for her was freedom to be herself, and that was something she could never have. He could not ignore the direct comparison to that other woman whose wishes had been similarly ignored, whose fate had been decided by the selfish passion of one particular vile man. Tonight Christopher had proved once again that he was different, that his blood, tainted as it was, did not define him. He should be proud of that fact. He should also be thankful that Tahira's life would at least be comfortable, if not necessarily happy.

But he could not be thankful. The days, which at times these last nine months had passed with excruciating slowness, now seemed to be galloping by with the speed of an Arabian thoroughbred. Something else he should welcome, for it was hurtling him toward the future he yearned for, the moment when he could finally bury his hateful past, but perversely, he wanted events to slow down. Though he was more than ready to wave goodbye to his amulet, he was not yet prepared to say goodbye to Tahira.

'You look so serious. What are you thinking?'

The tiny frown between her perfectly arched brows warned him he was in danger of breaking the spell they had woven around themselves. He could not resist pulling her into his arms again. 'I was thinking that it would be a crime not to make the most of the little time we have.'

Tahira smiled up at him. Her nipples were hard against his chest. His manhood, nestled between her legs, began to stir. She tilted herself against him, twining her arms around his neck. 'I couldn't agree more.'

* * *

Tahira could not escape the harem the next night, for Juwan had organised a dinner to mark the first birthday of her daughter. There were five long narrow tables set out in the formal dining room reserved for the Crown Princess. Juwan sat at the head of the top table, not on cushions as would be the case for everyday dining, but on a low chair with a very high, intricately carved back. Flanking her were Tahira and Ishraq. Alimah and Durrah, as befitted the youngest of the princesses, were seated on the outside. The same pecking order was reflected at the other tables, set at right angles to the top table, which accommodated first Juwan's ladies, then Tahira's, Ishraq's, Alimah's and Durrah's respectively. Tahira shifted impatiently on her seat. They had been at the table for two hours already, and the meal was not even halfway through. Though her little niece had been toasted with pomegranate and lime juice at the start of the meal, the talk had been all of the forthcoming new arrival, whom no one dared suggest would be another mere female.

She was dressed formally as the occasion demanded. A dark-blue silk underdress with long sleeves, plain save for the beaded cuffs, hem and neckline, which weighted it down. The cerulean-blue overdress was sleeveless, fastened by a row of gold buttons studded with pearls, trimmed with gold braid and pearl beading, and lined with the same dark-blue silk as her underdress. A wide sash in many shades of blue, also trimmed with gold braid, was tied tightly around her waist to emphasise the curve of her hips, the swell of her breasts. Thick white stockings and leather, beaded slippers curling up to points added to the heat and discomfort. Her long hair had been oiled and worked into a complex series of plaits which made her head ache, and the turban with its jaunty feather from which hung a filmy mantle of blue chiffon made it feel as if she was balancing a sack of sand on her head.

Her maidservant had assured her that she looked magnificent and even Juwan had smiled approvingly, but Tahira felt as if the entire ensemble was designed to constrain her, to remind her that all too soon her nights of freedom would be over for ever.

As the talk turned from Juwan's son to Tahira's forthcoming betrothal, boredom gave way to misery, and a black mood enveloped her. No one seemed to notice how little she ate, how strained was her smile, how few were the words she contributed to the excited chatter of the outfits to be worn to the camel race and speculation as to the wedding gifts Tahira would be showered with. Everyone assumed she was happy, and indeed who would not be happy, to be betrothed to such a paragon, to be looking forward to a life of such luxury. She was very fortunate, she told herself for what seemed like the thousandth time. Most women would kill to be in her place. And as for her husband—Ghutrif could have done a very, very great deal worse in his choice. Yes, she should consider herself very fortunate indeed.

Then why didn't she? Why was reconciling herself to the inevitable proving almost impossible? Guilt added to the black cloud which hung over her. The reasons for marriage were compelling. She had always prided herself on protecting her sisters' interests. She would be fatally harming their future prospects if she failed to make a match. Looking around as her siblings ate and chattered and laughed, she thought rather sourly that she had succeeded rather too well in concealing her warring emotions.

The air in the dining room was stifling. Not even Farah understood Tahira's plight, though to be fair, she hadn't confided her true feelings to Farah either. Only Christopher knew the extent of her impotent anger. Only Christopher sympathised with her. His outrage and frustration on her behalf could change nothing, but they were a great consolation to her none the less.

'Perhaps a year from now, we will be celebrating the birth of your own son.'

Juwan was smiling at her. Not maliciously, not condescendingly, but a genuine smile. Tahira's guilt increased. She tried to smile back, but the very thought of what she'd have to do with the unknown suitor in order to produce an heir repulsed her.

'And perhaps a year from now, we'll be celebrating my betrothal,' Ishraq said excitedly, to Tahira's relief turning the focus of the conversation away from her.

Yes, it was better for all concerned if her sisters followed Juwan's example, embraced the inevitable, looked forward in happy expectation to their marriages. If Ghutrif did as well by them as he had done by her, she need have no fear for their future. Juwan had been right when she said that the time had come for Tahira to move away, leave her sisters behind. It was the natural order of things. This melancholy thought brought a lump to her throat.

'Don't be sad,' Durrah said, leaning past Ishraq to speak. 'You heard Juwan, we will be permitted to visit you at least twice a year.'

'I'm not sad.' Tahira forced a smile. She was becoming very adept at it. 'I'm simply overwhelmed. It's all happening so fast.'

'A sign of how much your brother cares for you,' Juwan said. 'He is doing everything in his power to hasten your marriage. When your hand is given, the stain of shame which currently clings to you will be forgotten, your character quite redeemed. That day surely cannot come fast enough?'

So much for Juwan having softened her stance. 'No, indeed,' Tahira replied. The stain of shame would be so deep as to be ineradicable if Ghutrif knew about Christopher. Recalling the events at the oasis made Tahira's toes curl with pleasure inside her slippers. Shame was the very last thing she felt. The memory heated her from the inside. Lying beside him behind the cascade, she had forgotten everything, everyone else, save him. His touch. His smile. His voice. Laughter and desire. He knew her in a way that no man ever would, in a way that only her husband should. Tahira's self-satisfied smile wavered. If her husband could understand her as Christopher did, she would be looking forward to her marriage. But understanding was born from trust, knowledge and insight, and this stranger was interested only in her royal blood, in her pedigree and her famed looks, not in the person under the skin. While Christopher—oh, Christopher!

Tomorrow night, she would return to the turquoise mine. They were making excellent progress opening up the tomb. How many more nights did they have left together? Soon she would be able to count what remained in hours and minutes. Would there be time for them to uncover the secrets of the tomb and much more importantly, to solve the mystery of the amulet? If it did belong here in Nessarah, what would Christopher do? The very thought of him bringing it here to the palace was terrifying. But in such an unlikely event, he would ask for Ghutrif, or even her father, wouldn't he? No reason to imagine that he'd encounter her. Or that her name would come up. And so she really had nothing to fear. Though still, the thought of it...

'Tahira, how many times!'

Startled, her eyes flew to Ishraq, but the source

of Juwan's ire was fortunately obvious, scampering down the banqueting table with a large chunk of goat's meat dangling from his mouth. Hugely relieved, Tahira jumped to her feet and with a mumbled apology, snatched up her sand cat and fled for the sanctuary of her divan.

The next night, Tahira's heart was beating so wildly it felt as if it would leap out of her chest, as Christopher finally cleared an opening in the concealed tomb entrance large enough for them to pass through. Until now, it had been impossible to tell what lay beyond, if anything.

A dry, musty smell emerged from the thick blackness. Christopher's hands trembled as he lit the second lantern. His eyes gleamed with excitement. 'Ready?'

'Yes. No. I've never been so nervous in my life.'

'Be prepared to be disappointed. In my experience, these places almost always contain nothing but rubble and cobwebs. Remember, we already have concrete proof in the form of the pot and the bangle that the tomb has been raided.'

'But you think we'll find something of significance, don't you? I can tell by your voice.'

'You're right, I do. Ever since I first came to

this mine I have felt—I have had a feeling…' His voice broke. He took a shuddering breath. 'You are not the only one who is nervous.'

Which admission made her own feelings seem quite trivial. Whatever lay beyond this wall of darkness might determine Christopher's future. *Until I am rid of it, I have no life worth living.* He was utterly convinced of this, and though Tahira still couldn't understand why, nor was any closer to understanding the real story behind his amulet, she could not bear to contemplate what failure would do to him.

Though her heart still pounded, as she picked up her own lantern and checked it carefully, a steely calm stopped her hands from shaking, gave confidence to her voice. 'Well, we won't find out what's in there standing around out here. I'm ready when you are.'

'There is a danger of rock falls. I think it might be best if I go first.'

'We're in this together,' Tahira said, taking his hand, twining her fingers with his. 'And if you expect me to wait out here while you go ahead—you would not be so cruel, and I would not be so obedient.'

To her relief he laughed at that, pressing a swift

kiss to her mouth. 'Onwards and upwards then,' he said, turning towards the opening and holding up his lantern. 'Actually, that should be onwards and downwards. Be careful, I can see a set of steps just inside the entrance.'

He led the way, carefully counting each tread. Six steps, not hewn from the rock but constructed of large stones. 'I think this is some sort of natural cave, though it's been extended considerably,' Christopher said, stopping to examine one of the rock surfaces. 'You can see the chisel marks clearly.'

The air was hot, dry, becoming dustier. 'How long since someone stood where we are?' Tahira asked, her voice a whisper now.

Christopher whispered too. 'If we're right, and this tomb dates from the time my amulet was fashioned, then that is…'

'Fifteen hundred years.' Over-awed, she stared up at him. 'I've been so—so caught up in what this means to us, to you—Christopher are we desecrating a sacred place?'

He shrugged. 'I have very mixed feelings about it, to be honest. This tomb has lain undisturbed for countless centuries. But aside from my personal interest in this site, I'm an antiquarian at heart.

Places like these teach us so much about our history, and how small and insignificant we are in the grand scheme of things. If we treat such finds with due reverence and respect—and trust me, many people don't—then, no, I don't think we're trespassing here, but if you'd rather turn back…'

'Absolutely not,' Tahira said, lifting her lantern high again. 'Let's press on and see what's at the end of this passageway.'

The darkness was all-enveloping, the flickering light from the lanterns penetrating the gloom only a few feet ahead of them. The floor of the passage was thick with sand. More sand had blown into heaps against the walls. The sealed entrance had clearly not managed to keep the desert or the elements wholly at bay. Christopher continued to lead, counting their steps aloud, having to stoop as the ceiling became lower, to the point where Tahira could feel it brushing her hair.

'Twenty-eight. And it ends here,' he said. 'Two more steps, and…' His Arabic gave way to something low and filled with awe.

'What is it, Chris…?'

Her own voice stilled as she held up the lantern to find herself in a perfectly square room. It must have been formed from an inner chamber of the cave, but the walls and ceiling were richly decorated, covered in paintings and symbols. Two sand-cat statues, much larger versions of the one they had uncovered at the entrance, stood sentinel in the doorway. Another was positioned at the far end, at the head of the large stone sarcophagus which was the only other item in the crypt. Sand had collected in heaps in every corner. The decorative plasterwork had crumbled to expose the rock behind it in places. An empty shelf on one wall stood testament to the success of the tomb robbers, but the lid of the stone sarcophagus looked undisturbed. Whoever lay within had been allowed to rest in peace.

A very young woman, judging by the painted effigy on the coffin lid. The air was thin here, it was hard to breathe, the temperature stifling, but Tahira barely noticed any of this as she laid her hand on the image and closed her eyes. A terrible, bone-deep sadness enveloped her. Tears leaked from behind her lids and tracked down her cheeks. Despite the intense heat, she shivered.

'Tahira?'

Strong arms enveloped her. She turned gratefully, clinging to him, listening to the reassuring, steady beat of his heart, her cheek against the damp cotton of his tunic. 'Did you feel it?' she whispered. 'Such sorrow and grief. Did you feel it? And she is so young too. She reminds me of my sister, which would make her fifteen or sixteen.'

'Only sixteen.' Christopher was looking grim.

'I wonder what befell her. Sickness of some sort, most likely. It is tragic, a life cut so short.'

He muttered something quietly in English. 'A tragic complication,' he translated, when she looked at him blankly, then shook his head. 'It's very strange, there is nothing written on the coffin, not even her name.' Raising his lantern, he surveyed each of the walls in turn. 'There's nothing to identify the person who was laid to rest here, which leads me to conclude that whoever buried her wished to erase her memory, possibly because she had been in disgrace. And so she was made an outcast in death.'

'Oh, no, how dreadful. Though I suppose that would explain such pain, as I sensed. I wonder what happened, though I don't see how we will ever find out.'

'One thing is certain, she's of exalted birth. The sarcophagus, the exquisitely painted and lavish decoration. The creation of the tomb itself would have been an expensive and time-consuming undertaking. Then there's the magnificent quality of the items we've found. Could she even be a member of the royal family?'

Tahira's heart leapt. Could this be why she'd felt such a strong connection? 'But the Nessarah royal family have always been buried in the same place, the Mountain of the Kings, since time immemorial.'

'The only way to confirm her lineage would be to gain access to the records in the royal palace...'

'The royal palace!'

Her voice was a squeak. Christopher eyed her quizzically. 'Where else would the history of its inhabitants be held? These murals here,' he said, peering closely at the wall where the colours were brightest, 'don't depict the current palace of course, but they do show a very sumptuous building. And this symbol of a mythical bird—I've seen it on the insignia of the royal guards. There's no doubt in my mind that this is the tomb of a princess of the royal blood. I wonder—by all the stars in the heavens!'

'What is it?' Thoughts whirling, Tahira crossed the small room to join him.

But Christopher seemed quite dumbfounded, his gaze locked on one of the murals, and could only point mutely. The scene depicted the young princess—for Tahira knew in her bones it was a princess—painted in life this time, seated cross-legged in a courtyard surrounded by trees bearing impossibly large lemons and pomegranates. Paint flaked from the image, in places only the outline remaining of the fountain, a cushion, but the image of the young woman was almost perfectly preserved. Ink-black hair. Vermilion lips. Huge brown eyes outlined with kohl. A rich dress of the same blue which Tahira had worn to Juwan's dinner only last night. And around her neck...

'It's your amulet.' Tahira almost dropped her lantern.

Christopher turned to her, his face alight, a smile which on anyone else she would have called serene, and which gave her goose bumps. Reverently, he touched the mural, his eyes drifting closed. 'Finally, my quest is at an end.'

Tahira had reluctantly departed some time ago, much later than her customary hour. She had begged him not to linger too long and risk discovery by the miners, so earnestly that he'd been forced to lie to her for the first time. Now Christopher's lantern was burning dangerously low, the shadows cast on the walls of the tomb distorted, but still he remained, gazing at the image of the young princess wearing his amulet.

It *was* his amulet, no doubt stolen by the same looters who had dropped the silver pot and the serpent bangle. He could not resist taking it from its pouch and comparing it one last time, the fingers of one hand tracing the mural image, the other the real thing. Diamonds and turquoise and gold. And at the centre, not a precious stone after all, but another image. A golden cat, quite clearly and distinctively a sand cat, with turquoise for eyes. Turquoise which Christopher was now certain must have been mined here. Not that it mattered any longer. He had all the proof he needed, though it would have been satisfying to complete the final link in the chain.

It was over. Nine months after that fateful discovery, six long months of searching, and it was finally over. He could put his past behind him, forget all about that dreadful day, claim the future he had been planning for so long. Clutching the symbol of his suffering to his chest, Christopher waited for relief to flood over him, but the emotion he felt was distinctly different.

It was over. His time here in Nessarah was over.

Tonight was a beginning, but it was also an ending. A farewell to the past, but soon, very soon, a farewell to Tahira. His heart gave another lurch. He had known this day would come, of course he had, but because he had been too frightened—yes, he could admit to fear now that he was safe—to consider the possibility that his quest would not be successfully concluded, he hadn't dared contemplate the conclusion of these nights spent with Tahira.

But it was not over quite yet. Before he faced up to that prospect, there were still some loose ends to be tied up. Such as how best to engineer the return of the amulet to its rightful owner, who was presumably King Haydar. And what about the tomb? They'd need to seal it up again as a matter of urgency. Any day now, the mine would be in production, which meant a night guard would be posted. They couldn't risk this sacred place being discovered, for the sake of the tomb's ancient inhabitant, as much as for their own sakes.

He and Tahira both had far too much to lose. Now that he was on the cusp of his new beginning, the very last thing Christopher wanted was to be called to account by some over-zealous Nessarian official, hauled over the coals for trespass, perhaps even temporarily detained on the orders of Prince Ghutrif himself. His various official papers would ensure his eventual release, his trusty scimitar would ensure his eventual escape if need be, but he would be a fool, a complete and utter idiot, to expose himself to such unnecessary peril.

Christopher tucked his amulet safe back into its pouch, and took a last, lingering look at the large stone sarcophagus. Sixteen, not quite a child but definitely not a woman. Buried at exactly the same age as that other woman-child. At least she had been given an official burial in the family vault—or so he must suppose. At least that other young woman had been spared an eternity spent alone, with only guardian cats for company.

He really must go, but still he lingered with his thoughts. Tahira would be married very soon. If she was discovered here, what would happen to her? Nothing worse than the fate she faced, she had told him once, dismissively, but now he pondered the question properly, he feared for her. Her vindictive brother would not tolerate disobedience, but would his desire to punish her be stronger than his desire to have her married?

Though it made his heart sink, Christopher knew he had to put an end to their encounters.

Their work was done. His quest was all but over. They could not justify the level of risk any longer. Picking up his lantern as it flickered dangerously, he made his way back out of the tomb. Dawn was already breaking. There was no time to cover their tracks, he would have to pray that their luck would hold for one more night. Just one, was that all there would be? It felt wrong that their precious time together should end with the sealing of a tomb.

As he crept with stealthy speed towards his camel, he racked his brains for a more fitting ending. Gathering up the reins, hauling his ship of the desert into something resembling a trot, it came to him. Changing direction and heading for the city, he passed a group of miners heading in the other direction. Cursing, Christopher checked that his headdress was pulled over his face. He could have come from anywhere, but there was no denying the mine was the most obvious place. He could not afford to arouse curiosity.

Despite the fact that his dress was unremarkable, this camel a workaday beast, the miners stopped to stare. Was it his lethal scimitar which caught their attention? Whatever it was that made him stand out, Christopher cursed it, turned his head away, and continued on. Tonight, they would have no choice but to close up the tomb. The last grain of sand had just dropped through the hourglass.

Chapter Nine

The euphoria of unlocking the secrets of the tomb had given way to harsh reality by the time Tahira returned to the palace. She had rid herself of the worst of the sandy dust which clung to her by washing in the trough where Farah's camel was stabled—or she thought she had. One brief glance in her own mirror told her otherwise, forcing her to make a more thorough *toilette* when what she really wanted to do was collapse, exhausted, on to her divan. Naturally, as soon as she did so, she was once again wide awake, her mind churning.

It was over, was her primary, most melancholy thought. Christopher had solved the mystery of his amulet's origins. As Sayeed curled up on the divan beside her, she was reminded of the jewelled sand cat depicted in the centre of the amulet, and of the princess who had worn it. Who was she and what had happened to make an out-cast of her? An outcast is what Tahira had told Christopher would be her fate, if she stubbornly refused to marry, but she had envisioned a solitary life, not a lonely death. She shivered again, recalling the strength of the pull she had felt when she touched the sarcophagus. It had been the same when she had first held the amulet. The connection couldn't be denied.

If the amulet belonged to a princess, then Christopher would be desperate to restore it to the princess's descendants. In a panic, Tahira sat up so suddenly that Sayeed swiped at her with his claws in protest. Christopher was a man who acted on impulse. As early as tomorrow—which was already today—he could turn up at the royal palace to hand back the amulet. Which thought kept Tahira wide awake for the remainder of the night.

At breakfast, having almost persuaded herself that she was completely overreacting, when the almost unheard-of summons came, she thought she might faint for the first time in her life. Standing trance-like as her maid dressed her in the elaborate attire required for a formal interview with the

Crown Prince, Tahira felt as if she were watching herself from a distance.

Too late, too late, too late, echoed around and around in her head as she followed the guard from the harem through the corridor leading to a waiting area designed to intimidate the visitor with its porphyry pillars and elaborate ceiling decorated with green and gold.

Too late! No matter that the summons made no sense, for even if he had become aware of her true identity, why would Christopher betray her and thus himself? Panic made a mockery of logic. The waiting room opened on to the Tower of Justice, a euphemism for the famed armoury with its formidable display of shields, spears, scimitars and daggers, all purely ceremonial in these more civilised times, but many with a bloody history.

Arriving at the entrance to the Chamber of the Royal Imperial Council, Tahira could scarcely breathe. As the doors were flung open, her name announced and she stepped forward, at first she thought she had simply overlooked him, but a second, more measured glance around the room revealed no trace of Christopher.

Only her brother seated in splendid isolation at the far end. Tahira dropped to her knees and prostrated herself before him, for once thankful not to have to stand. Ironically, for once, Ghutrif did not wish her deference to be prolonged.

'Rise, Sister. You may proceed and give thanks.'

Familiar emotions began to take over as her panic subsided, not least of which was guilt, as she struggled to reconcile her simmering resentment with the knowledge that her marriage would make everyone happy, including her beloved sisters. Everyone but herself, that is.

The Chamber of the Royal Imperial Council was one of the longest rooms in the palace, and the most sparsely furnished. Save for the rich rugs beneath her feet and the lavish curtains which draped the huge row of stained-glass windows, there was only the throne, gilded and scrolled, on which Ghutrif imperiously sat, observing Tahira from under his hooded lids. As ever, she was struck by the family resemblance. Though his features were undoubtedly masculine, they were also unmistakably brother and sister. If Christopher ever did meet Ghutrif would the similarity strike him too? Perhaps she should confess tonight. But if she did...

'I am waiting, Sister.'

'Your Highness.' She dropped on to bended

knee and took the extended hand, kissing the air a fraction above his skin. 'I must thank you profusely for arranging this most—most worthy match.'

'Worthy?'

Worth a great deal to you, I have no doubt, Tahira thought rebelliously. Fixing her smile, she inclined her head. 'Worthy of our Royal House of Nessarah, I mean.'

'Then it is to be hoped that you make a better fist of representing our Royal House this time around.'

Tahira bit her lip, determined not to rise to the bait. Silence, she had learnt the hard way, was the best way to neutralise her brother's barbs.

Silence stretched. Ghutrif's fingers drummed on the wide arm of his throne. He crossed his legs. He uncrossed them. Tahira stared down at the rug on which she knelt, counting inside her head. She had once got as far as eighty-five. Today, Ghutrif surrendered at forty-one.

'What have you done to yourself? You have the hands of a miner, not a princess!'

Curse the skies! 'Scratches inflicted by my little Sayeed,' Tahira said, with a silent apology to her cat. 'I was teasing him, it was my own fault.'

'That animal is vicious and feral. You know you will not be permitted to take him with you?'

'Then I will release him into the wild,' Tahira said through gritted teeth. At least that way, she thought, to console herself, one of us will retain their freedom.

'The camel race to celebrate your betrothal is arranged for four days hence. The marriage will take place within the month. I am planning a lavish celebration, although naturally both events will pale into insignificance compared to the festivities planned to mark the joyous and long-awaited arrival of my son and heir.'

Ghutrif was smiling that supercilious smile that made her grit her teeth. He was dangling something between his fingers. 'Perhaps that is why I am in such a generous mood, Sister. You may have this small token to celebrate this most *worthy* match I have made for you. Call it a reward for your obedience. I intend to have your wedding jewels crafted from the same material. Not so valuable as diamonds perhaps, but rarer.'

It was a bracelet, formed of polished gems set in gold. The stones were a vibrant blue, streaked most distinctively with copper. Tahira had seen a similar image on the wall of the tomb last night.

She had seen the real things on Christopher's amulet. 'Turquoise,' she said, reaching eagerly for the trinket.

Ghutrif snatched it away. 'Crafted from the first samples taken from my new mine.'

'It is very beautiful. Most distinctive.'

Ghutrif threw the bracelet into the air. Tahira snatched it, fastening it around her wrist with trembling fingers. The gems were a perfect match. 'There is nothing like it in Arabia, nor even in Egypt, I am most reliably informed,' her brother told her with another of his infuriating, self-satisfied smiles. 'The mine will be most profitable.'

Which meant that the mine would be heavily guarded. 'When will it become productive?' Tahira asked, dry-mouthed.

'Such a question from a woman. But I suppose you are concerned that there will be sufficient ore for your wedding jewellery.'

She cast her eyes down in what she hoped was a coy manner. 'You know me so well.'

'Full operations commence immediately after the camel race.'

Which meant they must make haste to close the tomb. Tonight. It could not wait any longer. 'If you will excuse me, Brother, I am overwhelmed by your generosity,' Tahira said. 'And with only four days to prepare for my betrothal—there is much to do.'

'Your new-found enthusiasm is as surprising as it is pleasing.' Ghutrif eyed her warily. 'Go and prepare with my blessing, but this time there must be no last-minute hitches. Have I made myself clear?'

'Completely,' Tahira said, turning her back disrespectfully on her brother and fleeing the chamber.

Never had a day in the harem passed so excruciatingly slowly, Tahira thought, as she headed across the desert towards the mine. It was a beautiful night, the air salty and damp, the sky shimmering, hazy, the stars appearing as if peeking through a gauze curtain. Would this be her last-ever night with Christopher? The crushing sense of impending doom was making her teary, and she was determined not to spoil it with tears, but if this really was to be goodbye— She blinked furiously.

She now had the final confirmation of Christopher's amulet's origin, in the form of the turquoise bracelet, but she couldn't possibly show it to him because he'd ask her how on earth she came by such a thing, and she couldn't possibly tell him the truth since that would mean revealing that she'd been deceiving him all along as to her identity.

Tahira cursed under her breath. All she had left was tonight. She would be much better served by concentrating her energies on not ruining it.

Christopher was waiting for her at the entrance to the tomb. He immediately enveloped her in a fierce embrace which left her breathless.

'I was worried you might not be able to get away,' he said, pushing her hair back from her face. 'You look a little crestfallen, has something happened?'

A lump rose in her throat. Tears burned her eyes. She longed to tell him, all of it, but what good would the truth do, save to ensure that they parted on bad terms? 'I've missed you, that's all,' Tahira said, surprising them both. 'It has been a very long day.'

Christopher looked unconvinced. His eyes, those striking eyes, saw far too much. 'Tahira...'

She pulled his head towards her and kissed him. It was a kiss meant only to silence him, but as their lips clung it became a desperate kiss. She truly had missed him. She would miss him terribly when he left. And Christopher, his hand stroking her hair, the nape of her neck, her cheek, she had no doubt that he felt the imminence of their impending parting every bit as much as she did. They kissed fiercely, desperately, as if they were trying to meld into one entity. When they finally stopped, breathing ragged, cheeks flushed, eyes dark with a mixture of passion and resignation, there was nothing more to be said.

'We must seal the entrance up tonight,' Christopher said flatly, freeing her from his embrace. 'We can't risk it being discovered.'

'I've heard the mine will become fully active imminently,' Tahira ventured.

'Have you?' He waited, but she could tell from his tone that he had no expectation of her explaining how she came to know such sensitive information. Her relief was tinged with another heavy dose of guilt. She hated deceiving him, but she had no choice.

'I've been making drawings documenting the layout of the tomb. It's taken me most of the day. It was worth the risk,' Christopher said with a shrug at her horrified expression. 'I wanted you to have something to add to your collection.'

Tears burned her throat again. 'Thank you.' Would she be able to take these with her? They belonged in the library with the rest of her modest body of work, but Tahira couldn't imagine parting with them. 'Thank you,' she said again, kissing his cheek.

He caught her to him once more, resting his chin on her head. He said something she couldn't understand beneath his breath. Then he let her go. 'It will take us most of the night to seal the entrance. We must make a start, but before we do, I've been mulling something over. It's my amulet. I've always assumed that I'd hand it over to a person, a descendent of whoever owned it, but why do that when the true, original owner is right here?'

It took Tahira a moment to understand his meaning. When she did, to her shame, what she felt first and foremost was relief. 'You intend to leave your amulet in the tomb?'

'It is such an obvious solution, don't you think? I mean, it must have been a personal piece, because if it was part of the crown jewels, it would never have been allowed to be buried with her. It seems to me that this is the perfect place to leave it. Bury the past in the past,' he concluded with a bitter little smile. 'I confess I find it a singularly apt solution.'

Now that she knew he would not be seeking out Ghutrif, Tahira's relief gave way to concern. 'Christopher, what if the painful memories you associate with your amulet refuse to be buried with it? Physical objects can be buried, emotions are more difficult to dispose of.'

'Since when did you become an expert on the subject of burying emotions?'

'Since I was informed earlier today that my betrothal is to be formalised in four days' time.'

'So soon!' He wrapped her in his arms. She surrendered to the comfort of his embrace, the steady beat of his heart, the familiar scent of him, the heat of him. His hand stroked her back as if she were a child, but his voice, like hers, was not steady. 'You are determined to go through with it?'

'You know I have no other option. It is what everyone wants. If I refuse, I would not only make my own life miserable, but that of my sisters too. Married, they will believe me happy and make happy marriages of their own in turn. But if I am outcast—no, it does not bear thinking about. I must set a good example.'

'And allow your brother to blackmail you into a marriage you do not want.'

She took his hand, which was tightly curled into a fist. 'That is between my brother and his conscience, Christopher, if he has one. I choose to make the best of a bad situation. I also choose to stop talking about an outcome I have always known cannot be avoided on this, our last night together.'

'No,' he said vehemently. 'We must close up the tomb tonight, we dare not risk leaving it another day, but let us have one more night to ourselves before you bow to the inevitable.'

Her mouth trembled. One more night, just one more night. It was her heart's desire.

'Tahira, is it too much to ask? If you think the risk is too great so close to your betrothal, I would understand. I would not dream of jeopardising…'

'No, it is what I desire more than anything. I assumed that you would want to leave immediately, that is all. I dared not ask you…'

'Tomorrow then?'

Though it was only one more night, it was one

more than she had expected. Tahira nodded mistily. 'Tomorrow.'

Christopher kissed her hard, swiftly. 'Tomorrow. Now let us make haste. We have a great deal
to do before dawn.'

The silver pot and the serpent bangle sat on the
shelf from which they had been stolen. Christopher carefully laid his amulet on top of the sarcophagus, placing it over the heart of the dead
princess's effigy. Once again, the relief he had anticipated feeling for nine long months still eluded
him. He felt oddly bereft and had to force himself
to let go of the artefact.

How odd that they kept it all these years. As
always, the memory of that day, that loathsome
voice, made him shudder. He released the amulet. Now there was nothing left to remind him,
no object left to mock him, no evidence of his
shame. Now, he was once again free to be himself. Picking up the lantern, he turned to where
Tahira stood watching him from the doorway. She
thought he was making a mistake, he could see
it in her eyes, though she was biting her lip. She
was wrong. He would not regret this. When they

sealed up the entrance, that would be it. Then, surely, he would feel an enormous sense of relief.

He let her lead the way, refusing to look back. Forward, that was the direction he was heading from now on. It took them until dangerously close to dawn, but by the time he saw Tahira off on her camel the tomb was resealed. Christopher was done with the past.

Tahira rode directly to Christopher's temporary abode the next night. After he had tied up her camel, he led her to the fire which he had lit. 'It's very nice but it has no magic qualities,' he said, unrolling a rug with a flourish. 'I'm afraid I'm going to have to admit defeat on the whole flying carpet thing.'

Tahira sank down, running her hand over the tightly woven silk. 'All the same, I shall imagine you travelling on this, being carried by the winds across Arabia to Egypt. Though there's not much room for your worldly goods. A camel and a mule would be more practical.'

'This will suit me perfectly.' Christopher sat down beside her, crossing his legs. 'I always travel light, and now I don't even have my amulet.'

'Our princess is keeping it safe for eternity,'

Tahira said. 'It is such a shame that we'll never know who she was, what tragedy resulted in her being buried nameless and alone.'

'But we can deduce something of her life from the artefacts buried with her—the silver pot, the serpent bangle, and my amulet. And we also have the drawings from the tomb now, to keep her memory alive.'

'So even though she has no name, she lives on, in a fashion.' Tahira's smile was tinged with sadness. 'Were we wrong to cover her tomb up?'

'No!' Christopher took her hand, twining his fingers through hers. 'Definitely not. In Egypt, the tombs which are being uncovered are no longer sacred. They are stripped of all that is of value and then abandoned, or used to house livestock, or more often than not, left open to the elements. Perhaps there will be a time in the future when people value the history of these tombs, but for now—no, I think we did the right thing. In fact, it gave me an idea.'

Christopher was looking decidedly sheepish. 'I wanted to commemorate our time together here by burying something, a record of our brief history,' he said. 'I like the notion that someone like us, with a fascination for the past, might uncover it, in a hundred, a thousand years from now. Only we know what we've shared, and when we are gone—it's a fanciful notion, I know, but I hoped you'd understand.'

'I do, I don't want tonight to be the end,' Tahira said softly, touched to her heart. 'Even though we will never see each other again—you want us to leave some sort of clue—to bury some sort of artefact, so that a part of us will always be together?'

'Yes.' Christopher flushed. 'I did not think I was the sentimental kind, but...'

'It's not sentimental. It's—it's the most perfect—it is perfect.' She kissed his hand. Hot tears dripped on to his knuckles.

'I didn't mean to make you cry.'

She shook her head, wiping her cheeks with the sleeve of her tunic, smiling mistily. 'I'm not. I won't. What did you have in mind?'

Christopher reached behind him to produce a silver casket, the kind used to contain scrolls, and indeed inside there was a scroll. 'Look and see,' he said, taking it out and handing it to her.

There were two sheets rolled together, both drawings. The first was of the rock formation which housed the turquoise mine and the princess's tomb, the distinctive shape, like the battlements of an ancient castle perfectly depicted, the vertical striations of the rock cross-hatched in pencil. The second drawing was of the inside of the tomb, showing the princess's sarcophagus, the shelf containing the silver pot and the serpent bangle, and over the heart of the effigy, Christopher's amulet.

'The place which brought us together, the site of our princess's tomb, the beginning and the ending of your quest.' Her eyes were tearing up again. 'It is perfect,' Tahira said.

'That's not all. Close your eyes and hold out your hands.' The object he gave her was heavy, lumpy. 'Now look.'

Horrified, Tahira stared at the piece of ore which he must have taken from the mine either last night or tonight. In its natural state, the copper streaking the turquoise was more pronounced. Though the mineral was unpolished, it was still a stark contrast with the rough stone which encompassed it.

'As you can see, it is an exact match for the turquoise in the amulet,' Christopher said, grinning.

'If they had discovered you in the mine—if you had told me that you needed further proof, I could have—' She bit off the remainder of her words, colouring brightly. Shock and alarm had made her indiscreet.

'Your brother is an investor in the mine, isn't he?' Christopher said. 'Don't worry, I had deduced as much. It was the only reason I could think of which would explain your inside knowledge.'

'Yes,' Tahira agreed gratefully, for it wasn't exactly a lie. 'But what possessed you to take such a risk?.'

'It simply felt right, somehow.'

She had the strangest feeling, breathless and giddy, looking at him. 'It is right, I do see what you mean, though to have risked so much—but it's done now.'

She placed the lump of ore carefully inside the silver casket. 'The clues to our meeting and to our find, but I think…' Reaching behind her, Tahira undid the clasp of her gold chain. 'Yes, this feels right too. I would like to leave something of myself with the rest.'

'No, you can't bury that. It means so much to you.'

'That's exactly why I want to put it in here.' The little token her mother had given her all those years ago was warm from her skin. 'The Bedouin star,' she said, kissing the trinket one last time. 'My nights of wandering under the stars are over, I don't need you any more.'

'Then I too want to leave something precious to me.' Christopher brought out the pouch which had once contained his amulet, tipping the lonely contents on to his palm. His Roman coin glinted dully in the firelight, the base metal almost black. Like Tahira, he placed it to his lips, before returning it to the pouch. 'May I?'

When she nodded, he put her necklace in beside it and retied the pouch before placing this last item in the casket and closing the lid.

'Where should we bury it?' Tahira asked.

'Over the centuries this well and its buildings will fall completely into ruin as the desert reclaims it. One day, far in the future, someone like us might carefully sift through the foundations, looking for relics.'

'And then they will scratch their heads and wonder how it came to be that a Bedouin necklace and a Roman coin were buried together,' Tahira said, beguiled by the image. 'But you haven't answered my question.'

'Come and see.' He led her into the well-keeper's house, where a deep hole had been dug just inside the main wall. Together they placed the casket inside. 'One last thing,' Christopher said, producing a neatly carved stone cat in a sentinel pose, just like the ones in the princess's tomb, setting it at the head of the precious box. 'To keep the contents safe.'

Tahira watched, quite overcome with emotion as he made light work of filling in the hole. How many years before it was uncovered? Who would find it? What would they make of it? How many times over the years to come would she ask herself those questions? A piece of herself and of Christopher, held safe together. Their secret, waiting to be uncovered long after they themselves had been confined to history.

'I don't want tonight to end,' Tahira said, as they sat back down on the rug laid out in front of the fire underneath the starry sky. 'If this really was a magic carpet, that's what I would wish for, to stay right here always.'

Christopher had not thought beyond this moment. All the effort he had put into the burial of the casket, he'd told himself was for Tahira, but as he pulled her into his arms, he could admit to himself that it was for him too. His own way of preserving these forbidden moments for ever. Stupid thought. Mawkish. But somehow right.

Like their kisses. The most natural thing in the world to kiss her under the desert stars. The taste of her had become so achingly familiar in such a short time. Days. Not even enough weeks for the moon to turn full cycle. He ran his fingers through the heavy silkiness of her hair. She had tied it back loosely tonight, held only with a silk scarf which came easily free, allowing him to spread the rippling waterfall of it over her back. Jasmine. How would he ever smell jasmine again without thinking of her? Her hands fluttered over his shoulders, her fingers tangled in his hair. Her kisses were the heat of the desert, the glitter of the stars, the sultry, heavy air of the desert night.

They sank back together on to the rug and their kisses merged one into the other, drugging and rousing. She whispered his name as no one ever had. Her eyes, heavy-lidded but watching him, reflecting his passion, her skin hot under his touch, the same fire in her blood that heated his. He drank deep of her mouth, then trailed kisses down her throat, to the tempting valley between her breasts. Her fingers plucked at the buttons of her tunic, and when they were open, at the buttons of his. Her hands were on his chest, flattened over his nipples. His mouth on her breasts, and his hands. Soft moans. His own breath, fast and shallow.

Emotion surged with the blood to his groin. Tenderness, wanting, a deep-seated, primal need to be one with her. Her voice urged him onwards, her hands on his back, on his buttocks. And his hands, over her, inside her. The sweet, hot wetness of her desire for him. The hard, driving need of his desire for her. Like nothing before.

Their mouths met again. Such kisses, spinning them to new heights. Her hands on his shaft now as his touch brought her to her climax, as she unravelled beneath him, gloriously naked, unbearably vulnerable, he wanted to gather her to him, to keep her safe, to make her one with him, to complete what they had started, what he so urgently needed.

Completion. He kissed her deeply. She arched under him, her body melding to his, her legs twined around his. Possession. To be hers. He wanted to be hers. He wanted, needed, to be hers. It was the only thing that mattered. The only thing that was right. He could feel her, the tip of his shaft just touching the sleek, hot, wetness of her, the rippling of her climax, the soft, pleading sound of her voice, the heady, deep kisses, her hands on his buttocks, and the primal need to thrust inside her took over. He had never felt anything so perfectly right.

And so irretrievably, unbearably wrong.

His curses rang out into the desert night as Christopher flung himself away, jumping to his feet, his chest heaving, his eyes wide with horror. 'Dear God in heaven, what am I doing.' Grabbing his tunic, he pulled it over his head, tugged on his trousers, panting, cursing, heart hammering, threw her clothing at her. 'Put these on. I cannot—I am—put these on, for the love of God, put them on.'

He couldn't breathe. Tahira was staring at him uncomprehending, but his Arabic had deserted him. *What had he done? What had he done? What had he done?*

He pulled at his hair viciously. Tahira sat up, staring at him wide-eyed. Her mouth was opening and closing but he couldn't hear her for the roaring in his ears. He couldn't stay here and look at her, so gloriously naked, so painfully naked, the evidence of his shame, the evidence that despite everything, the blood which ran in his veins defined him after all.

Shaking his head, he ran for the well house. The first bucket of icy-cold water over his head made him gasp. Another bucket brought him back from the abyss, but only to the edge. One tiny iota of self-control had prevented him from catastrophe. One tiny last iota. He drank from the third bucket, hands shaking, but his breathing slowing.

Tahira.

'Oh, God, Tahira.'

Rushing back out, he found her, fully dressed, huge-eyed and frightened. 'Christopher, what on earth…?'

His grasp of her language returned. 'I'm sorry. By the stars, I am so sorry. I did not mean— I would never—I thought I would never—did I hurt you?'

'Hurt me? No! You frightened me. What happened, Christopher?'

'What I promised I would never do. I am so sorry.'

'But it didn't—you didn't.'

She tried to put her arms around him, but he shrank back. 'You can't trust me. I cannot trust myself.'

'No more can I, it seems.' Her hair was still loose, a wild tangle of curls that she now tried to tie back but failed, her fingers shaking. And her knees, it seemed. 'I have to sit down.'

'I've frightened you. The last thing in the world—'

'Christopher!' The shock of her sharp reprimand startled them both. 'I'm sorry, but I cannot—it was not only you. I was every bit—if you had not stopped, I would have—we would have—but we did.' She laughed, a strange shaky sound. 'We did stop, I'm still fit for my wedding night, thanks to you.'

'You give me too much credit. I wanted—I always thought that there was a line I could not cross, but blood will out.' With a racking, dry sob, he dropped on to the mat and covered his face with his hands. Shame and horror sent his mind lurching into a terrible dark place he had never inhabited before.

'Christopher, please, there is no need...'

'There is every need. You don't understand.'

'What don't I understand?'

'I am my father's son after all. Base-born, base of blood and equally base of mind. I thought myself better than he. Tonight, I've proved myself every bit as vile.'

'Base-born? No, I don't think you mean what you say. You are so upset, I think you are using the wrong words. Base-born means...'

'I am a bastard,' Christopher said, dropping his hands, using the crudest translation of the word he knew. 'My father was not married to my mother. I am a bastard, the product of an act such as I so very nearly—you understand now, Tahira?'

But she shook her head, her mouth trembling, wrapping her arms tightly around her knees. 'You speak in riddles. I don't understand any of it. I feel as if I don't know you at all.' A tear splashed on to her cheek. She shook it away violently. 'This is our last night together. Don't let it end like this, Christopher. Whatever it is that has made you—I don't understand, but I want to. Won't you tell me? Please?'

He opened his mouth to deny her, but the words would not come. 'I have never spoken of it.'

'You think I won't keep your secret?'

'I think my secret will make you despise me.'

'I couldn't. It is simply not possible.'

'You can't be certain of that.'

'Is there anything I could tell you which would make you despise me?'

He answered without thinking, 'Nothing.'

Was that relief on her face? Had it been fear? He had no idea. He couldn't think straight.

'Then tell me, Christopher. Trust me. Please.'

It was all too much. He had neither the energy nor the will to resist her. For so long he had kept it all pent up inside him. No hope of relief. No hope of understanding. The need to unburden himself was overpowering. Christopher shrugged fatalistically, closed his eyes, let himself fall back to that day, nine months ago, and began his tale in a hoarse whisper.

Chapter Ten

London—October 1814

Christopher had deliberately turned up unannounced at the imposing house which occupied a prime site on London's Cavendish Square. Though he dreaded the forthcoming interview and fervently wished that he had not come into possession of the document which had led him here, he desperately needed answers. Whatever the truth turned out to be, no matter how earth-shattering, he simply had to know.

'His lordship is not at home to callers lacking a prior appointment,' the butler informed him, eyeing Christopher's plain black coat and simply tied cravat with some disdain. 'He is an important and extremely busy man.'

'No doubt, but I think you will find that he will be most eager to receive me when you show him this,' Christopher said coolly, handing the man his business card.

The butler hesitated, but he was no fool. Perhaps it was the quiet authority in Christopher's voice, it most certainly wasn't his unostentatious attire, but for whatever reason the servant acquiesced. 'Very well, if you will be so good as to wait here a moment, sir, I will ascertain whether your confidence is well placed.'

Less than a minute later, Christopher was shown into a study on the ground floor. The scent of beeswax polish mingled with the slightly musty smell emanating from the myriad tomes and ledgers which filled the serried ranks of bookcases lining the walls. From the empty grate a faint trace of smoke and coal ash added to the range of prosperously genteel odours.

His heart was pounding in his chest as he approached the middle-aged man seated behind the imposing walnut desk. Lord Henry Armstrong was distinguished rather than handsome, dressed with simple but expensive elegance. His grey hair was sparse on top, there were deep grooves running from his nose to the corners of his mouth and a fretwork of lines across his brow, but beneath heavy lids, his eyes were alert and piercing, his gaze assessing. His reputation as one of the most astute diplomats in government ranks was obviously well deserved. Those eyes met Christopher's for the very first time, making his stomach lurch in a sickening manner. A distinctive deep blue rimmed with grey, they were his lordship's most striking feature and were now widening in disbelief. 'Christopher Fordyce,' he said faintly, getting to his feet. 'Is it truly you?'

Ignoring the proffered hand, Christopher sat down, while his lordship made for the side table, pouring himself a large brandy from the crystal decanter. 'Would you care to join me? No? So be it, but you will excuse me if I avail myself. I find I have need of a stiffener.' He took a large gulp before sinking back on his chair behind the desk. 'Excuse me. If you had given me any prior warning—though I doubt it would have lessened the shock. I confess, I never expected this day to arrive.'

Clearly shaken, Lord Armstrong took another draught of brandy before picking up the business card which the butler had delivered. 'Christopher. So those worthy people retained the name. It was my father's, God rest him.' He stared down at the business card again. '"Land Surveyor, Mineral and Ore Specialist",' he read. 'You followed Fordyce's vocation. I trust he is well?'

'Not particularly. He died two weeks ago.'

'Ah. My sincere condolences.' Lord Armstrong mopped his brow. 'And Mrs Fordyce?'

'Passed away twelve years ago.'

'I am sorry to hear that. They were good people. Your business, sir, does it prosper?'

'I did not come here to exchange pleasantries, but instead to demand some answers from you.'

Lord Armstrong's eyebrows shot up. 'Demand?'

'You heard me correctly,' Christopher said, pleased to note that his steady and calm tone did not betray his emotions. 'For a start, will you confirm that you recognise this document? Is it written in your own hand?'

Christopher pushed the thick parchment across the blotter. The aristocrat's face tightened momentarily before, with an almost imperceptible exhalation of breath, he snatched it up, tugging at the knot on the faded red ribbon which bound it. Lord Armstrong perused the document, his mouth set, his pale complexion turning slowly ashen. When he finally replaced it on the desk, his hands were shaking.

'There seems little point in indulging in obfuscation. I did indeed write it, under instruction from a trusted legal adviser, now long dead. May I ask how long you have been aware of its existence?'

'I found it in my—among Mr Fordyce's private papers while going through his personal effects after the funeral.'

Lord Armstrong imbibed another snifter of brandy. 'You must excuse me. It has been so long, nearly thirty years. A lifetime ago. But those eyes.' His smile was grisly. 'I am afraid there is no denying the provenance of your eyes.'

Revolted, Christopher would have given anything to be able to contradict him but it was inescapably true that his own distinctive blue-grey eyes were an exact match with his lordship's. That was one unspoken question answered. He forced himself to raise the next sensitive topic. 'No mention is made in that document of my…' He cleared his throat. 'My mother.'

'No, for one very pertinent reason.' Lord Armstrong mopped his face again. 'She died giving birth to you,' he said heavily. 'A rather tragic complication.'

'Tragic for her, and an added complication for you, since it left you saddled with me,' Christopher said bitterly. 'Which must have been *most* inconvenient.'

'Inconvenient for your mother's parents, had she lived, since they would have been saddled with you, to use your own terminology.' His lordship frowned. 'There was no question of her keeping you, even if she had wanted to—though I can't imagine why she would have willingly destroyed her marriage prospects. She'd have had no future worthy of the name. However,' he continued brusquely, 'it is a moot point—it simply wasn't an option. You couldn't have imagined that—no, no, stupid question, of course not, it's a preposterous notion.'

The truth was that Christopher had indeed clung to that erroneous assumption. Confirmation that he had been summarily rejected by both his parents was a body blow. This man—yes, he had no difficulty in understanding his instinctive rejection, but his mother—had she lived, would she really have been so compliant? Every feeling rebelled. If he had a child, he'd have moved heaven and earth to keep it.

Lord Armstrong however, took his silence for tacit acceptance. 'So, as you'll have surmised, there were plans in place long before your birth for your—for your...'

'Disposal is the word you're fumbling for,' Christopher interjected icily. Though he knew in his heart the answer to the next question, he steeled himself to ask it. 'You did not offer to do the honourable thing and marry her then?'

Lord Armstrong's look of astonishment was answer enough. To betrayal and rejection he must now add the shame of his bastard blood. 'You need not answer that,' Christopher said.

But Lord Armstrong igrnored him. 'You wish to know the circumstances?' he asked haughtily. 'Why not, it is a common enough tale, I fear. I was very young, and barely had my foot on the bottom rung of the ladder at the Foreign Office. Your mother was no servant girl. If she had been, her condition would have been of much less consequence, but even as a callow youth, my tastes were refined. She was well born, and a great beauty.'

'And no doubt an innocent, until you got your grubby hands on her.'

His lordship permitted himself a slightly lascivious smile, which Christopher found utterly repellent. 'A catch, no doubt about it. Marriage would have been no hardship, but she was destined for greater things. And no wonder. I'll be the first to admit, I simply wasn't in her league back then and so...'

He made a helpless gesture. 'Damage limitation. The merest whiff of scandal would have put paid to her family's ambitions for her, and indeed to my own ambitions too. It was imperative that the matter be hushed up. She was closeted away in the country for the duration of her—her—for the duration. Had things gone to plan, I would not even have been party to the arrangements. Scarlet fever, they told the world it was, which saw her off. As I said, it was a very tragic inconvenience for all concerned. When I learned she had given birth to a son, I personally stepped into the breach, as it were. Quite a responsibility for a young man, but I think you'll agree I did well by you.'

Lord Armstrong looked expectantly at him. The man had the audacity to expect praise for his callous and self-serving behaviour! The room was spinning. Christopher gripped the arms of the wooden chair so tightly that his knuckles showed white. This was not some nightmare from which he would awake. His mother was not his mother. His father was not his father. His life, his whole life, had been built on sand. He had no idea who he was.

'You stepped into the breach?' Christopher said, struggling to assimilate what he was hearing.

'Indeed I did. I believe your mother's family intended to place you in the hands of some wet nurse. Such women cannot be relied upon to give a child the best of care.' Lord Armstrong gave a short, breathy laugh. 'Indeed, that is their very attraction in some extreme cases. Fair enough for a daughter, but a son—well, that is a different matter, even if he is from the wrong side of the— that is—aye, well, what I'm trying to say is that I could not acknowledge you, but you are my progeny after all. And so I secured the services of the Fordyces, a steady, childless couple of good reputation, he with a reliable occupation, I thought—'

'Your thoughts are made very clear in that document,' Christopher said harshly. 'The *transaction*, the terms of payment, the conditions under which ownership of the *goods* were transferred'

'You make it sound as if you were a piece of ornamental furniture, my dear boy.'

The term of affection made Christopher grit his teeth. 'If you consult your bill of sale, you will find that is exactly how you did view me,' he said.

'It is also very clear that you considered the matter firmly closed, your duty fully discharged.'

His lordship's cheeks turned a florid puce. He was clearly not accustomed to having his actions questioned. Christopher snatched up his glass and poured him another brandy. 'Here, drink this. I have not done with you yet, an apoplexy would be extremely inconvenient at this juncture.'

Lord Armstrong drew him a furious look, but did as he was bid.

'You said you were young at the time. How young, precisely?' Christopher demanded.

'I was barely twenty years old, had not even reached my majority.'

'Still old enough to understand the consequences of your actions, I would have thought. And your—my—the woman who gave birth to me?'

His lordship straightened his blotter. 'She was sixteen.'

'Dear God, did she understand what she was doing? Did she know, as you must have, the risks you were taking? A man of twenty years old, seducing an innocent girl of sixteen and not even willing to give the resulting child your name—it is disgusting!'

'You must understand...'

'Oh, I understand perfectly. Both you and my mother's aristocratic family abused their wealth and privilege. In life, and even in death, my mother's fate was determined by others. Status confers the freedom to act in an utterly selfish and completely arrogant manner. I have no desire to hear your mealy-mouthed justifications.'

'Christopher—Mr Fordyce,' Lord Armstrong amended hastily, 'your sudden arrival here has come as a great shock to my system. I have not had time to assimilate—you do understand, don't you, that it is no more possible for me to acknowledge your existence now, than it was then? If it became known that you—dear God, it would ruin me, even more completely than it would have then. My position at the Foreign Office—I have a hard-won reputation for integrity, honesty...'

'And are even more renowned for your naked self-interest and burning ambition, from what I have been able to establish since discovering the evidence of my unwanted lineage.'

'So you admit you have enquired about me?'

'Suffice to know that I want nothing whatsoever to do with you.'

'You are angry,' Lord Armstrong said. 'That is perfectly understandable, in the circumstances.'

Christopher's toes curled tight inside his boots. There was a rushing in his ears. More than anything, what he wanted to do was to slam his fist into that self-centred, self-satisfied, aristocratic countenance. To blacken both of those eyes, so damned distinctive and undeniably identical to his own. To destroy the evidence, obliterate the memory, and start afresh.

But that would have to wait. The document could not be unread. Violence and destruction were not the solution. 'I am not angry,' he said, with a pleasing calm in which only an edge of contempt was audible. 'And as to the notion that I might wish to be part of your life…' Now he did let his contempt show fully, in a bitter little laugh. 'I have my own life, my lord, and I am very content with it. There is absolutely no place in it for you.'

'Then why did you seek me out? What do you want of me, if not my name?'

The man looked puzzled rather than relieved. His arrogance knew no bounds. 'Your name!' Christopher exclaimed contemptuously. 'The very last thing I would wish to own. As is this.' Christopher laid the amulet on to the blotter. 'I take it to be the item of jewellery referred to in the document. The payment for services rendered, though blood money might be a more accurate description.'

Lord Armstrong's thin brows rose so high that they almost reached his receding hairline. 'They didn't sell it? How odd that they kept it all these years. That piece of jewellery was intended to help pay for your education, to provide the Fordyces with the means to raise you as a gentleman.'

'I am eternally grateful they did not, if being a gentleman is defined as someone who is prepared to sell their own child to avoid social embarrassment. This amulet was payment for their co-operation and silence.'

'It belonged to your mother. I was a man of modest means back in those days. Her family gave it to me along with some funds to facilitate the arrangements when she died. Don't you even wish to know her name?'

'To what end? Even had she lived, her identity would have been kept from me. It is ironic that it was her premature death which ultimately allowed me to be privy to yours.'

'I did my best by you, as I continue to do for

all my children. I have five daughters, sir, who consider me a most dutiful father, acting always with their best interests at heart.'

Provided their best interests coincide with your own, Christopher thought cynically, before the import of the words hit him. Five daughters. Which meant he had five half-sisters, blissfully oblivious to his existence. And who would, if he had anything to do with it, remain so.

'I hope,' Lord Armstrong amended fearfully, 'that my mention of the girls—I would not have them dragged into this.'

'My illusions have been shattered, do you think I would wish that fate on five innocent girls?'

'I confess, I am heartily relieved to hear you say that.'

Christopher wanted nothing more than this sordid interview to be over. 'This,' he said, indicating the amulet, 'is Arabic in origin, if I'm not mistaken, and judging from the quality of the stones in it, almost certainly made for the ruling family of an ancient people. Do you know how my—how the woman who gave birth do me came to own it?'

'I know nothing of its prior provenance. But since it was given to the Fordyces in a legally binding agreement, it is now yours to sell.'

'Would it ease your conscience if I did so?' Christopher laughed bitterly. 'No, for you do not possess one. I, however, do and have no desire to benefit from blood money. I came here to return it to its rightful owner.'

'Well, that ain't me,' Lord Armstrong said, looking quite appalled. 'And I doubt very much that your mother's family will wish to be reminded of what they have lost, so there's no point in asking me to give it back to them. If you won't sell it, put it in a museum, if what you say about it being an ancient artefact is true.'

And have the amulet, a potent symbol of the lie his life had been based on, on permanent public display! Christopher shuddered. Unthinkable. 'No. That would not be appropriate. I have no choice but to return it the original owner.'

'Original owner? What on earth do you mean by that?'

He had spoken on the spur of the moment, but as Christopher returned the amulet to its leather pouch, a plan began to take shape in his head, and he knew instinctively that this was the only possible course of action. 'The descendants of the original owner,' he said. 'The quality of the diamonds, the colour of the turquoise, and the purity of the gold are all highly distinctive.'

'How do you—ah, yes, of course.' Lord Armstrong picked up the business card again. 'You specialise in minerals and ores. You have then surveyed in Arabia?'

'I have never been to Arabia. Locating the precise area, matching it with the source of gold and turquoise—as you say, that is my area of expertise. But in order to do so I will require assistance from you, in your own field of expertise.'

His lordship stilled. 'How so?'

'I will require papers to allow me freedom of movement,' Christopher said, thinking rapidly. 'Contacts who will be able to assist me with local information, and the means to extricate myself from—let's say any tricky situations which may arise due to my incognito activities being viewed as suspicious or even hostile.'

His lordship looked aghast. 'I can't help you with any of that. The identities of our agents in Arabia are a carefully guarded secret. Not, mind, that I'm admitting such people exist.' Lord Armstrong drummed his fingers on the blotter. 'Even if I could put you in touch with such contacts, you're asking me to obtain official papers...'

'Secured through unofficial channels. And I'm paying you the compliment of assuming that you know exactly which strings to pull in order to facilitate that.'

More finger drumming set Christopher's teeth on edge. 'You deride my having abused my position for my own ends,' Lord Armstrong said, 'and yet isn't that exactly what you're asking me to do for you?'

Was it? The notion disgusted him. But, no, the man was twisting the situation to his own advantage, as he always did, trying to make him beholden, which was the last thing he ought to be feeling. 'A different matter entirely,' Christopher said. 'You acted to cover up a wrong, to protect yourself. My motivation is restitution.'

'Very noble,' his lordship said, in a tone which contradicted his words. 'Why should I do as you ask? You have made it very clear that you have no interest in exposing me. What is in it for me?'

His lordship spoke belligerently, but Christopher was not fooled. 'You will do as I ask because, bluntly, you will do whatever it takes to be rid for ever of the living breathing evidence of your youthful folly,' he responded coldly. 'You are fortunate that I ask so little, and though I am not a *gentleman* like yourself, you may trust my word when I say it is all I will ever ask of you.'

His words hit the mark. Lord Armstrong resorted to bluster. 'Aye, all very well, but it's no simple matter to obtain such papers. It will take time. There are channels to be gone through, questions to be answered. For a start, how am I to explain the purpose of your visit?'

Christopher struggled to contain his impatience. He didn't want to wait, not another minute, let alone days or weeks or months, before taking action. The sooner the amulet was returned, the sooner he could wipe the slate clean and start afresh. Years of negotiating with Egyptian pashas who, like Lord Armstrong, valued knowledge and power even over wealth, provided him with inspiration. 'You ask what is in it for you. I will tell you. While I am in Arabia, I will carry out a survey for you.'

Lord Armstrong pursed his mouth. 'What kind of survey?'

'A survey of the commercial landscape of whichever parts of Arabia my quest to return the amulet compels me to visit. I will compile a dossier of which kingdoms are open to trade with the west, the valuable natural resources they possess, potential trade routes, who is allied to whom—information which I imagine would be very much welcomed by Lord Liverpool. Our Prime Minister is very eager to promote international trade and bolster Britain's coffers, and would, I am certain, look favourably on anyone who can provide him with such intelligence. Do you really need me to spell out the potential benefits?'

Two thin eyebrows rose in surprise. 'No, you most certainly do not. Now that Napoleon is safely confined on Elba, the opportunities for Britain to expand her influence in the east—'

The lord of the realm who was his father broke off, rubbing his hands together. Smiling for the first time since Christopher made his surprise entrance, he got to his feet and held out his hand. 'I will not offend your sensibilities by saying you are a chip off the old block, but you have yourself a deal, sir.'

'The only thing we have in common is a desire never to set eyes on each other again,' Christopher said, pointedly ignoring the proffered handshake for the second time that day. 'I have written my temporary London address on the back of my card, you may have all the relevant papers and contact information sent there. I do not expect we will have cause to meet again. I bid you farewell.'

Arabia—August 1815

'The encounter I have just described took place nine months ago,' Christopher concluded. 'You understand now why it mattered so much to rid myself of the amulet. It was blood money. It symbolised the lie that my life had been, living with the people whose son I thought I was.'

'Fordyce.' Tahira furrowed her brow, trying to clear her mind. 'The name of the man who was with you when you found the Roman coin we have just buried. The man who shared his own love of the past with you and his profession too, yet he hid the amulet away all those years. He didn't sell it. I wonder why.'

'Guilt, most likely. Or maybe he was afraid. An ordinary hard-working man, a priceless artefact—it would have raised suspicions. I don't know why he didn't sell it, and I don't care. It's buried now, back where it came from, and all those lies with it.'

Christopher had been distraught at the start of his story, shaken to the core by how close they had come to making love. So very close. Tahira shivered, appalled by her own utter abandon, appalled to discover that she was not as relieved as she should be that he had had the willpower to stop before it was too late. The desire to be one with him, to unite with him in the way only a husband and wife should be united, had been so instinctive that she hadn't questioned her actions, driven only by that fierce need—no, it was not a need, it was a certainty. There was nothing more right than making love to him.

And nothing so wrong. Christopher knew that, even if she couldn't bring herself to believe it. But his mood had changed during his confession, he had become angry. He still was. She could see it, a repressed fury, evident in the tense way he held himself, the rigidity of his shoulders, the tightly clasped hands, his set expression. Only his eyes were bleak, with hatred for the English aristocrat who had fathered him, and for the two people who had raised him. He was wrong, surely he was wrong, to think that they did so simply because they were paid? Those childhood memories, not just of the Roman coin but of the snow, the sledding—they had been happy times. It tugged on her heartstrings to see him so tortured, for it was clear that he had not permitted himself to mourn either his lost history or the loss of his putative father, the kind surveyor.

Christopher thought it was all buried and forgotten with his amulet. Did he truly believe that? He desperately wanted to, and they had so little time, a matter of hours, before they parted for ever. Though he resisted when she tried to take his hand, she determinedly twined her fingers with his, pressing a lingering kiss to his knuckles.

'I don't want your pity, Tahira.'

'I am shocked, and I am angry on your behalf, and very sorry indeed for your poor mother, but what I feel for you is not pity. Why would I pity a man who has for the last six months faced untold dangers, taken breathtaking risks, to do what he thought was right? A man who could easily have taken advantage of the connections which the likes of this Lord Armstrong could have given him? A man with such courage, such integrity, such honour, who has taken so much trouble to make our nights together so perfect. I don't pity you, I feel...'

Overwhelmed she blinked furiously, bending her head to press another, more passionate kiss on Christopher's hand. What she felt for him made her heart lurch. What she felt—no, she couldn't let herself feel that. The ultimate taboo. The intensity of this night had whipped her emotions into a shape she mistook for something utterly inappropriate, which would unravel in the cold light of day. 'I don't pity you, Christopher Fordyce,' Tahira said.

'I don't have the right to that name,' he retorted curtly, though his expression had softened, and he no longer tried to escape her touch. 'And as a bastard, I have no right to that other—nor any desire to claim it.'

'What about your mother's name? You chose not to ask it, Christopher, but...'

'I already know more than enough of my mother to torture myself. She was sixteen,' he said. 'The same age as our princess. And he, Lord Henry Armstrong, was four years older, a man of experience, a man who should have known better. If you could see him, Tahira, so full of himself, so utterly callous, so completely untainted by his sin.'

'But didn't you say that it was he who arranged for these kind people to raise you as their own?'

'And buy their silence. If my mother had not died, how different might things have been!'

'What can you mean?'

'You understand now why I compare you with

her, surely? Her father and mine, arranging her life for her, forcing her to comply. Would she have surrendered me, had she lived? Are not the feelings of a mother so powerful, the duty of a mother to a child more vital than her duty to her family?'

'As an unmarried mother,' Tahira said gently, 'she would have been cast out of the society in which she had been raised, and her shame visited on you.'

'The shame was not hers. It was her seducer who should have been shamed,' Christopher said tightly. 'The man who bequeathed me my bastard blood.'

'You must know that whatever blood flows in your veins, it does not change the man you are.'

He jumped to his feet, his face set. 'I thought that knowing how I came into this world would ensure that I would never, ever act as my father did.'

'You did not seduce me!' Tahira exclaimed despairingly. 'Despite every encouragement from me, you did not seduce me!' She too got to her feet. Though she wanted to weep, to throw her arms around him, she dared not touch him. His logic was skewed by his misplaced anger, his interpretation of his history so tangled—but how to help him untangle it now, when the sands of their time together were down to the last few grains? If Christopher wished to imagine a better life, a different life with his mother, who was she to disillusion him? Hadn't she fallen into the very same trap herself? And didn't she know how painful it was, to realise that even a mother would not put her child's wishes over her duty?

'This is the last time we will be together, my last night free in the desert, your last night here in Nessarah,' Tahira said helplessly. 'I am afraid that whatever I say to you now will be the wrong thing, Christopher, but I can't allow you to carry the burden of guilt for what happened between us—what so nearly happened, but did not.'

His arms were crossed across his chest. A light breeze ruffled his hair, blowing the soft, worn cotton of his tunic against the muscled contours of his body. His gaze was averted, fixed on the undulating contours of the desert sands as they formed and re-formed in an endless, shifting pattern of dunes. A dangerous man, she had thought him, from the first moment they met, and a wildly attractive man too. But she knew now that he was also a vulnerable man, a man who felt betrayed, rejected, and lost. A man desperate to wipe the slate of his history clean, yet a man who was set on dedicating his life to uncovering the history of others. Her heart felt as if it were being squeezed, watching him. She felt—she felt far too much. It was not safe to feel so much for a man she was about to say goodbye to, but from the moment she met him, Christopher had made her want to cast caution to the winds. Right now, safe was the last thing she wanted to feel.

'Over there is where you took me sledding,' Tahira said, stumbling over the English word, slipping her arm through his. 'And over there, in the other direction, the oasis where we went swimming—though I never did swim.'

'You floated very beautifully though. I won't forget that image of you, with your hair streaming out behind you, the moonlight on the water, and you...'

Christopher pulled her into his arms, holding her breathlessly tight. 'I have never wanted anyone so much as I wanted you tonight. The other times, the dune, the oasis, though you were temptation personified, I was always—I never once lost control of my desire for you. I was so sure, Tahira, so very much aware of that line my father crossed in begetting me, so certain that I never would allow history to repeat itself. Yet tonight—it was the fact that I didn't think at all which frightened me.'

'But it was the same for me, Christopher.'

'No,' he said gently but firmly, 'it is not the same. The consequences are so completely, unfairly disproportionate. My loss of control would have been your downfall, just as my father's was my mother's.' He shuddered, his hold on her tightening painfully. 'If we had made love, what would have become of us, do you think? All very well for me to tell myself that I would do what they call the honourable thing, in England—marry you—but I will not tell myself that pathetic lie. We are from different worlds. I am a bastard with no name to call my own, certainly none to give to a wife or a child, while you, Tahira, whatever your name, it is obviously a good one. Your brother would never accept me, and you cannot marry a man unacceptable to your family.'

He let her go, only to clench his fists, his mouth curled into a self-deprecating sneer. 'The parallels are painfully obvious. When that man explained the circumstances of my mother's downfall, I thought he too easily dismissed the option of marriage, but though it makes my bile rise to admit it, by understanding how intractable your own family are in the matter of making a good match for you—which brings me back to my point. My act of selfishness would be paid for by you. What would you do, Tahira? What could you possibly do, save proceed with the marriage arranged for you, make a cuckold of your husband before you have even said your vows, and live for ever with the lie, or bring dishonour to your family with the truth?'

His words cut her to the quick, for they were the stark, brutal truth. It terrified her to see how close she had come to the precipice he depicted. 'You are right,' Tahira whispered, shamed. Her future husband was not her choice, but everything she had heard implied he was a good man. He did not deserve a marriage based on lies, a wife who deceived him about the one commodity she brought to the alliance. Yet she still could not bring herself to regret a moment spent with Christopher. 'You are quite right,' she repeated, in an effort to persuade herself it was so.

'Thankfully, it is not a choice you will have to make.' He heaved a sigh. 'Tonight I proved that I can be every bit as selfish, as vile, as the man whose blood runs in my veins—because that's the point, you see. I did not ultimately lose control, but I wanted to. The moral high ground I have claimed is no longer mine.'

'Nor mine.'

'I won't have you say that. You are sacrificing your freedom to do your duty.'

'And am therefore granted the moral leeway you will not grant yourself?' Tahira exclaimed bitterly. 'You deride my brother for imposing his will on me, but aren't you doing the same, by denying me the right to claim some responsibility for my own actions?' Too late, she realised how inflammatory her words were. Too late she remembered that they were amongst her last words to Christopher. But they were said now, and part of her could not regret them.

'I am, as you have pointed out, quite powerless to dictate the course of my life,' Tahira continued, thinking fatalistically that she might as well finish what she started. 'When I'm with you, you allow me to be myself. Can't you see that's the most important thing to me in all of this? You have given me a taste of true freedom, and I used that freedom to choose, tonight, to make love to you. A foolish—far beyond foolish—choice, but my choice all the same. You did not coerce me. And as to the consequences—they are my responsibility as much as yours.'

He did not speak for some moments, but she could see from the way his throat worked that he was struggling with some strong emotion. Anger?

But when he did speak, he sounded shaken. 'Forgive me, I have been thinking only of myself.'

'Christopher, it has been—what you have told me tonight—I cannot imagine what you must have suffered, these last nine months. I am honoured that you have chosen to confide in me, that you trusted me.' Guilt swooped down on her, reminding her that she had not reciprocated that trust. But it was too late for that too.

'I doubt I would, had not we—but enough of my guilty conscience.' Christopher held out his arms, and she stepped gratefully into the comfort of them. 'We have a little time left,' he said, looking anxiously up at the stars. 'Let us sit here together, on our magic carpet, and waste no more time fighting to prove which of us is more culpable.'

Tahira reached up to smooth his hair back from his furrowed brow. 'We are equal,' she said. 'Equally right, equally wrong, equally reckless, and I hope, during the time we have been together, equally happy.'

His fingers warm and gentle on the back of her neck. 'I hope that you will find happiness in the future. You deserve to.'

She put her finger over his mouth. 'No past, no future. Just the present. That's all I'm interested in. Here and now. You and I. Just us.'

With a groan, he kissed her, and with a soft sigh, she melted into his kiss. Lips clinging, hands smoothing and stroking, they sank on to the carpet together. There was an aching sweetness in this kiss that had not been there before, a tenderness in their touch, as if they were made of glass and might shatter.

When it ended they did not break apart but curled into each other, lying on their backs, gazing up at the stars spread across the night sky just for them. More kisses, equally tender, but as the sky turned from indigo to violet and the stars began to fade, their lips and hands became desperate. Passion not spent, but forever suspended, the sense of an ending finally forced them apart.

In silence, Tahira pulled on her cloak and fixed her headdress. Her throat was clogged, her heart heavy, but she was beyond tears. One final kiss before she clicked her tongue for her camel to drop to his knees. Tearing herself from Christopher's embrace was the hardest thing she had ever had to do. 'I will think of you tomorrow, flying back to Egypt on our carpet,' she said.

'Tahira...' His voice cracked. He cleared his throat. 'Thank you. For everything.'

'And you, Christopher. For everything.' She could not bear it any longer. Throwing herself on to the saddle, she kicked the camel into motion. For once the beast heeded her, turning and charging into a fast trot in a jerky movement that almost threw her on to the sands. By the time she had control again, she was so far from Christopher's camp that there was no point in looking back, but she did all the same. He was still there, standing quite motionless.

'Goodbye, my love,' Tahira whispered, unable to deny her heart any longer. 'Goodbye, my own true love.'

She loved him. Now that she would never see him again, she was forced to admit it. She loved him, and it was quite hopeless. Sand flew into her eyes as she made her way back to the palace. She had forgotten to fasten her headdress over her face, but Tahira relished the sting of it on her skin, for it gave credence to her pain. She was in love with Christopher, whatever his name was, and tomorrow her beloved would leave Arabia for Egypt, and two days after that, she would be betrothed to a complete stranger.

As she crossed the desert away from him, every single step her camel took made her heart ache more. Tahira slumped in the saddle, trusting to the animal's instinct for home to guide them back to the stables. Oblivious of the beauty of the fading stars, the changing palette of the sky on this, her last night of freedom, she saw only Christopher. The reckless adventurer she had first encountered. Those eyes, ardent and passionate, tortured and haunted, laughing, serious, furious, sated. Christopher in his shabby desert garb armed to the teeth. Christopher naked. Christopher laughing. Christopher's kisses. Christopher's arms around her, holding her so tightly she could feel his heart beating, delude herself that he would never let her go.

And tonight he had, for the very last time. Misery made her slump further in the saddle. She would have given everything, anything, to be able to turn back, to spend one more night with him.

But there were no more nights, no more hours,

not even another minute. It was over, and instead of wishing for more, she should be thanking the stars that it ended before they surrendered to the ultimate temptation. No wonder making love felt so right. No wonder her conscience had not intervened.

The outskirts of Nessarah were coming into view. What was he doing? Was he asleep? Was he thinking of her? He wanted her to be happy, he had said. His self-control had ensured that her marriage would not be predicated on a lie. She could not imagine being happy with any man other than Christopher, but there had never been any question of her having any sort of life *with* Christopher. Did he care for her? She knew in her bones that he did. Did he love her? No. And even if he did, what difference would it make?

But she loved him and she could not regret it. As she neared Farah's stables and the camel slowed to a walk, Tahira smiled tenderly to herself. 'I love you, Christopher,' she whispered. Her last night of freedom was not yet over. Alone in her divan, she would hold her secret safe, devote herself to thinking only of her love. Time enough tomorrow to try to come to terms with what the future would hold.

Chapter Eleven

Indecisive was one of the last words Christopher would have used to describe himself, but for the last two days, since saying goodbye to Tahira for ever, he'd been unable to make a single decision. No, that wasn't strictly true. He had decided to leave Nessarah any number of times, but he hadn't been able to bring himself to act on it.

He couldn't understand it. His quest was over, his amulet buried, his dark and shameful past put firmly behind him, but the long-anticipated sense of relief continued to elude him. He felt unsettled, unprepared for the future he had been longing for, more haunted than ever by thoughts of the past.

Dredging it all up, reliving it in order to make Tahira understand, that's what had brought it so vividly back. He had been so very clear in his mind that ridding himself of the amulet was the key to wiping the slate clean. He'd expected her to agree, but instead she had questioned him. And her questions, infuriatingly, would not go away.

Why hadn't Andrew Fordyce sold the amulet? Had the man Christopher had always called father simply been too guilty to profit from blood money? Looking back—and Christopher had done a lot of that over the last two sleepless nights— he could conjure only happy memories, not only of his childhood, but of the close working relationship he'd had with his fa—with Fordyce. What's more, despite the fact that they hadn't sold the bloody amulet, Christopher had wanted for nothing. What sacrifices had the Fordyces made? Christopher's schooling, now he thought about it—wasn't hindsight a wonderful thing!—had been far superior to the children of the Fordyce's friends and relations. He'd always believed himself loved, had always loved the people he thought his parents deeply in return. Which is why it had been so painful to discover the damning evidence that he had been duped. Though Tahira didn't believe he had.

Christopher threw open the door of his abode and strode out into the early morning. 'She's wrong,' he muttered under his breath. 'I will not allow her to fill my mind with doubts.'

But was she wrong? Thanks to the Fordyces he had a name—for Tahira was right, no one save himself and Armstrong knew any different. He'd had a happy childhood—there, he could admit that too—and he had been taught a very profitable profession, again thanks to Andrew Fordyce.

None of which changed the fact that Henry Armstrong was a vile seducer, a manipulative conniver, who had walked away from the mess of his own making without a backward glance. Were it not for Armstrong, Christopher's mother would still be alive. Mind you, were it not for Armstrong, Christopher would not exist. Which brought him to another thing Tahira questioned, his idea that his mother might have kept him, against the odds. Unlikely, Tahira thought, though she hadn't actually said so. Not wanting to hurt him? Which forced him to wonder whether she was right about that too. Most likely Tahira understood his mother's situation better than he did. Were she in a similar predicament, she would...

She would never be in a similar predicament, because she was getting married. Christopher cursed long and furiously in a mixture of English and Arabic. He looked out at the beauty of the desert dawn. A distant sandstorm gave a dark golden tinge to the normal palette of pink and orange. It would not hinder his travel plans, for he was heading due north. Today. Though there was the camel race he'd heard about when visiting the bazaar yesterday for supplies. He'd like to see that, it was reckoned to be quite a spectacle. So perhaps he'd leave his journey until tomorrow.

Today, Tahira's betrothal was to be finalised. Would there be a celebration of some sort? For her sake, he hoped she would be able to like the man chosen for her. For his own—he didn't want to think about it. What was she doing at this moment? Was she taking breakfast with her sisters? Or was there some elaborate ritual she would take part in prior to the ceremony—if there was a ceremony? Bathing. Oiling. Those henna designs, the women here painted them on their hands and feet, didn't they, for special occasions.

Tahira. Christopher groaned. Tahira, Tahira, Tahira. He missed her. He'd never see her again. Another thing that didn't bear thinking of. The sun had risen. The sky was a perfect pale blue. Ideal conditions for a camel race? He had no idea, but what the hell, he was kidding himself, thinking he was leaving today. Why not head into the city and find out what all the fuss was about?

The crowds had gathered in the outskirts of the city for the occasion, lining the course in their multitudes. A long row of tents stood off to one side. Various mouth-watering aromas, of roasted goat, delicious concoctions of fruit and yoghurt, toasted coffee beans, and the ubiquitous mint tea wafted from the open fronts of each tent as Christopher wandered through the milling hordes.

Women stood in huddles gossiping and giggling behind their veils, while their menfolk engaged in heated debates over recent form and likely favourites. Children screamed with joy as they ran between the flag poles which marked out the course, some in pairs with silk scarves for reins, mimicking the contest to come. The camels would race around a track which was roughly oblong in shape, which meant that for each lap there would be four tight corners to negotiate.

'And so this stranger who has been in our midst for some weeks is interested in our camels as well as our horses.' The man who accosted Christopher was old, his wiry grey hair tied in the multitude of plaits favoured by some of the Bedouins.

'I saw you at the horse fair some weeks ago,' he said, in response to Christopher's raised brows. 'You are not a man easily forgotten.'

'My colouring is not a common sight in Arabia, right enough.'

The old man shook his head. 'It is your eyes. Not the colour, but you are like me, a man who sees what others do not.' He smiled, revealing a sparkling gold front tooth. 'Do you come to see our royal family today, Mr Foreigner? We will be granted a rare sighting of the princesses, I am told.'

'Indeed, I wondered who that lavish construction would house.' On the opposite side of the track, at the start-and-finish line, a large podium had been erected with benched seating strewn with cushions, a silk tasselled canopy covering the whole. 'Will Prince Ghutrif be in attendance?'

'Today is Prince Ghutrif's gift to the people of Nessarah. Some significant announcement is expected,' the old man said. 'A new gold mine, perhaps. Not yet the birth of the long-awaited heir, for the guns would have been sounded from the palace. Have you attended a camel race before, Mr Foreigner?'

'This is my first,' Christopher said, wondering

if the prince was celebrating the opening of his turquoise mine.

'You will witness a spectacle rather than a race,' the old man was saying. 'Camels, as you will know, take a great deal of encouragement to get going, and once they do, they take a deal more encouragement to stop. Then there is the fact that it is not the most flexible of animals. Have you ever tried to turn a tight corner on camel back?' When Christopher shook his head, the old man cackled. 'I advise you to stay clear of the marker poles if you value your life.'

'But I had heard racing camels were specially bred.'

'You heard correctly. These beasts are fed on a diet of dates and honey, alfalfa and milk. They eat better than I! Such food makes for a smaller hump—reduced still further by depriving the animal of food and drink the day before the race, and so it is easier for the jockey to balance behind it without a saddle.'

'No saddle? I would imagine that would be rather—painful,' Christopher said, wincing.

The old man cackled again. 'A pain eased by the gold given to the winner by our most venerable Prince Ghutrif. Look, he is arriving now.'

Sure enough, the crowd had dropped to their knees, the cries and laughter changing to hushed, reverential greetings. Following suit, Christopher watched furtively as the royal party arranged themselves on the seating under the canopy. Prince Ghutrif was a handsome man, much younger than Christopher had imagined, and slender under his rich robes of gold and scarlet. There was something familiar in his features, the fine arched brows, the brown eyes under heavy lids, explained no doubt by Prince Ghutrif being related to one or several of the other sheikh princes Christopher had encountered on his travels.

There was another man seated in state beside him. A brother? A fellow prince? Now that the prince was seated, the women who must be the princesses, judging from the richness of their robes and jewels, were taking their time to find their seats, their attendants fussing over the arrangement of their silks. Four this time, not the five he'd seen at the market place. The Crown Princess must be too near her time to attend. One, swathed in the colours of the setting sun, was being ordered to change places, to sit not at her brother's side, but beside the stranger, and as she moved Christopher's stomach lurched. Impossible, he chided himself. A trick of the eye, a case of his senses mistaking reality for what he most wanted to see. But his stomach lurched again as she reached up to adjust her veil and her long sleeve fell back to reveal her wrist. And on it, a distinctive turquoise bracelet.

At last, the other three princesses were seated, their maidservants ranged behind them, the guards posted. With a quick, formal farewell to his companion, Christopher made his way swiftly to the other side of the track, and a better view of the royal box. He was being ridiculous, but his pounding heart and dry mouth didn't appear to agree. The set of her shoulders, the tilt of her head, her averted sidelong gaze, were all painfully familiar. If only she were not veiled. If only he could get close enough—but a guard barred his way, and a drum began to beat loudly, and Prince Ghutrif got once again to his feet, the signal for everyone else to drop to their knees.

But Christopher did not, for the woman in the colours of the rising sun had lifted her eyes to look at the crowd. Dark brown eyes, almond-shaped, under perfectly arched brows. Their gaze met and held, and those familiar eyes widened in horror, before the sharp tap of a guard's lance brought

Christopher to his knees. But he refused to drop his gaze. He watched her as her brother continued to pontificate, the things she had told him of her family, her life, her fate, sliding into place like the interconnected pieces of a puzzle. He had fantasised about seeing her in the daylight. Now his wish had been granted. Be careful what you wish for!

'My people, we come together on this most happy of days to celebrate,' the prince announced.

The crowd waited with bated breath to find out what was being celebrated but Christopher, with a sinking heart, already knew. Today was the day Tahira's betrothal was to be formalised. Today was the day that…

'His Royal Highness, Prince Zayn al-Farid, has pledged to marry my sister. I hope you will join with us in celebrating this most joyful and momentous occasion. Please rise, and let the festivities begin.'

Christopher rose, and so did his bile, and his fury, fuelled by the fact that Tahira's brother had not even seen fit to give her name. Fists clenched, he stared at her, willing her to meet his eyes. And she did. As the man she was to marry took her hand and kissed her fingers, Tahira looked up, her free hand stretching towards him, and instinctively Christopher took a step towards her, heedless of anything but the sorrow in her eyes. But a guard barred his way, and he came to his senses, and anger returned full-force as he cursed, turning away from the woman who had lied to him, betrayed his trust, played him for the fool that he was.

He strode across the track, where the camels and their riders were milling, and kept on walking. He couldn't wait to shake the sand from this cursed place out of his cloak for ever.

Tahira thought the day would never end. Seeing Christopher at the camel race, her poor heart had leapt pathetically in her breast, and for a fleeting, foolish moment, she thought he had come to save her from her fate. Why he would do so, why he was still here in Nessarah at all, she had no time to consider, for one glance at his equally shocked expression told her that she was the last person he had expected to see, and she tumbled back down to earth as she saw her betrayal written large on his face.

As the crowd roared, and her brother and husband-to-be dispensed ribbons, trophies and gold, and her sisters relished the spectacle, Tahira's mind raced in quite another direction, out across the desert towards Christopher. She felt quite sick imagining what he must be thinking of her. She had not lied to him, but she knew that the truths she had concealed were tantamount to the same thing.

The races over, back at the palace Juwan held one of her interminable dinners as Tahira's future husband dined in separate state with the menfolk. She gave him barely a thought. Shock had given way to a fierce determination to explain herself to Christopher, but the risks were enormous. She belonged to another now, it would be wrong of her to seek him out, but when she tried to reconcile herself to silence, every feeling rebelled. She had to see him. She had to explain. She had to.

And so she waited, growing more and more tense through dinner, finally claiming to be overwhelmed by the momentousness of the day, to have a headache, to require utter solitude, retiring to her divan long before the meal was finished. Locking her door and making her escape long before the harem lay silent for the night, she was far beyond counting the risk, the possible costs, ignoring Farah's astounded pleas, caring only to reach Christopher, praying to the night stars which lit her way as she careered over the sands at a speed which would have won her first prize this afternoon, that he would still be there.

He was, standing outside the well house, arms crossed, as she approached. He wore his customary tunic and boots, his scimitar hanging at his side, his hand resting on the hilt of his dagger. The breeze ruffled his hair, but as Tahira neared, there was no welcoming smile, and as she drew her camel to a halt, his expression was blank, his eyes hard, the utter lack of emotion more intimidating than any show of anger.

'You shouldn't be here. Not tonight of all nights. Are you mad?'

It took all her courage to command her camel to its knees and to dismount, her knees trembling, her fingers too, as she fumbled over the simple task of tethering the beast, conscious all the time of Christopher watching her, unmoving. 'I had to try to explain,' Tahira said, turning to face him.

'That you have been lying to me from the first moment we met? Poor little rich princess, forced to loll about in the lap of luxury, with her jewels and her silks and her sweetmeats, pretending that all she wants is to get her manicured hands dirty digging up the past.'

'I have never pretended, Christopher, I...'

'And my amulet. Did you know from the start that it belonged here in Nessarah? The diamonds which I went to such lengths to compare, were you laughing up your sleeve at me, knowing full well that they matched the crown jewels? Then there's the turquoise from the mine which your brother owns. You had it on your wrist today and yet you let me risk life and limb to obtain a sample. Are you still wearing it?'

He grabbed her arm, and there was the bracelet she had in her haste forgotten to remove. 'My brother had it made for me, from the first of the ore. I wore it for the first time today and only to remind me of you.'

'To remind you of the man who had bared his soul to you, on the day you became betrothed to another,' Christopher snapped, releasing her with a sneer of distaste. 'As my amulet would forever remind me of you, if I still had it. "A connection," you claimed. How disappointed you must have been when I decided not to return it to your family. An apt double symbol of the trust you betrayed. I am doubly glad I buried it.'

'Don't say that,' Tahira said, covering her face.

'It is the truth.' He yanked her hands away, forcing her to meet his cold, judgemental gaze. 'I bared my very soul to you, trusted you with the sordid truth of my origins, and all the while you were concealing yours.'

'I had to, Christopher...'

'It is ironic, isn't it, that the first person I place my trust in after these nine months living in Hades proved to be yet another person who was not who I thought she was. If I had not stumbled upon that amulet and the document with it, I'd still be quite oblivious of who I am. If I had not stumbled across you today, at the camel race, I'd have been forever oblivious of who you are. A painful parallel I'd rather not have been forced to draw, your Royal Highness.'

'Don't call me that.'

'Why not, it's your name.'

'My name is Tahira.'

'Princess Tahira. You duped me, just as the Fordyces did, and Lord Armstrong too. And I had never thought of myself as gullible either.'

'Stop it!' His voice dripped with sarcasm that

ripped at her flesh. 'I didn't dupe you, I didn't betray your trust, and I didn't lie to you.'

'That very first night...'

Tahira stamped her foot in frustration. 'I didn't tell you the truth the first night because if I had, I'd never have seen you again. And then, having started the subterfuge, the next night I had even more to lose. And the next night, and the next—the more I knew you, the more you knew me—with you, I could be myself, Christopher, not a princess, not—'

'Defined by your blood,' he cut in viciously. '"Whatever blood flows in your veins, it does not change the man you are." That is what you said to me. But the blood that flows in your veins does define you, doesn't it?'

She flinched. 'Yes, it does. And if you'd known who I was, my blood would have put an end to our nights together. While you thought me some ordinary woman, you were happy to consort with me.'

'I have never thought you ordinary.'

'I wish I was,' Tahira said wearily. 'You are angry with me, and I don't blame you. I tried to find the courage to tell you the truth on several occasions, but we had so little time, and I could not bear to risk losing you, the one person who couldn't care less about my bloodline, my pedigree, my connections. All the things you are thinking now, Christopher. Perhaps it was selfish of me to keep the truth from you, but—oh, I have said it all. I didn't want our acquaintance to end, it is as simple as that.'

'Acquaintance! If I had known you were a princess, do you think I would have—?'

'I am certain that you would not have!' Tahira interrupted vehemently. 'That's exactly my point. If you had known I was a princess, you would have run a thousand miles across the desert in another direction, and while you may wish that you had done so, I do not. Whatever you feel now, I cannot regret that we have been—that we have...'

She was trembling. Wrapping her arms around herself, she tried desperately to get her emotions under control. 'I cannot regret a minute of the time I have spent with you. Choose to believe me or not, Christopher, it is the truth.'

His momentary flash of anger was gone. He had himself completely under control again, his expression inscrutable. 'How did you get here?'

'My camel...'

'How do you escape from the harem? I have always imagined you climbing out of a window, but today, I took a good look at that quaint little cottage of yours, otherwise known as the Royal Palace of Nessarah. It's like a fortress, guards everywhere. So how do you do it—wear a cloak of invisibility?'

'There's a tunnel.' He was still angry, she could see the betraying tic in his throat. At least anger was better than indifference. 'A door hidden in the wall of the courtyard which my divan looks on to,' Tahira continued quietly, 'leading down to a tunnel that goes under the palace and emerges in what used to be the old slave market. You can guess its previous use. I came upon the original plans for the palace in the library some years ago, and when I realised what they could mean, I asked to move my quarters.'

'You escape through a tunnel which was once used to bring slaves—concubines into the palace?' Christopher said with a bitter little smile. 'Some would call that sweet vengeance.'

'It was my first archaeological find.' Despite the tension between them, she couldn't help but smile at the memory. 'You can't imagine how excited I was, when I finally located...'

'You told me your first find was a piece of pottery. Another lie.'

Deflated, she found herself at a temporary loss for words. What had she expected, after all? That he would sweep her into his arms and forgive her?

'Your broken betrothals,' Christopher said, and her heart sank further at his tone. 'I saw you once, the day after we met in fact, with your sisters, although I had no idea it was you. You were going shopping at the bazaar. I remembered then, that Prince Kadar was engaged to the eldest princess of Nessarah. He wasn't long crowned when I met him. His brother was—'

'Killed falling off his horse. Prince Butrus,' Tahira interrupted flatly. 'I was originally betrothed to him, and then Prince Kadar inherited me, along with the throne. A most flattering alliance, that would have been.'

'Why did he break the betrothal?'

'I don't know and I don't care, I'm simply glad that he did.'

'Murimon is a far more liberal kingdom than Nessarah. You wouldn't have been locked away in a harem. No need to tunnel out at night, you could have…'

'I don't love him!' Tahira flushed scarlet. 'I did not choose him,' she amended. 'And he did not choose to marry his brother's leavings.'

'Do not talk of yourself in such terms,' Christopher snapped.

'Why not, it's what we princesses are after all, commodities to be bought and sold.'

'You did not seem to me to be particularly unhappy about that when I saw you this morning. You were holding his hand!'

'He was holding mine!' Anger was a relief. 'What was I supposed to do, Christopher? He has just purchased me in a deal that my brother is very pleased with, what's more. When we are married, he will be entitled to do a great deal more than simply hold my hand.'

'I don't want to know about that!'

'Then why bring it up?' she flashed back at him.

'If he really is so repugnant to you, though I cannot imagine why...'

'He is not repugnant. According to my sister—whose name, if your are interested, is Ishraq—no more perfect husband could exist. He is charming and he is kind and he is handsome and all manner of things, but none of them matter, because he is not you!'

The air around them seemed to still. 'What do you mean by that?'

Tahira had nothing left to lose. Christopher

would not forgive her, now that he knew the truth, so why not tell him the whole of it? 'I mean that I'm in love with you,' she said, though by her tone, it sounded more like a declaration of war than love.

Christopher looked first shocked and then horrified. 'You cannot mean that. Princesses are not permitted to fall in love with bastards.'

It hurt. Later, when she thought it over, it would hurt a great deal. For now, Tahira glared at him defiantly. Permitted or not, that is exactly what she had done. More fool her. And more fool her for telling him too. She ought to be relieved that he hadn't believed her.

'Princesses are permitted to do very little,' she said sadly. 'We are, as you have pointed out, defined by our blood. That is the biggest difference between us. You can choose to allow the circumstances of your birth to blight your life, while I cannot escape mine. I searched for any mention of our princess in the palace library, you know. The records are very precise, quite complete, but it is as if she has been eradicated from history. I don't know what heinous crime she may have committed, but I do know if I defy my family's wishes, I too will be effectively eradicated. Ostracised.

As if I have never existed. My one and only purpose in life, as a princess of the royal blood, is to marry. Your blood is bastard—yes, I can use that foul term too— but still, you are more fortunate than I. You are free to choose.'

'Do you now expect my pity, for the life of luxury you have been forced to lead?'

'I don't expect anything from you. You have already given me more—you have done more for me, understood more of me, than anyone, and I want—all I can hope for now is that you will be happy.'

'Why shouldn't I be?'

'Because you are deluded!' The truth burst from her, making her wring her hands in despair. She had not come here to voice any of her doubts, but her doubts were all she could give him. 'You think that all the blame must be placed at the door of the man who is your true father, but it is not so simple, Christopher. If your mother was of such excellent family, what were they thinking, to allow her to spend so much time alone with a man who could not aspire to her hand in marriage? Did she lie, connive to be in his company? And if she did, do you not think that she is in a little way culpable?'

'You cannot know...'

'I know a great deal more of such situations than you! I know the risks a woman will take to escape the shackles placed upon her by her family.'

'The situations are not the same. You are twenty-four years old, she was sixteen.'

'Exactly! Christopher, if she had lived, do you honestly think she would have been allowed to keep you? She was a mere child herself. She may not have found it easy to give you up, but she would have found it impossible not to do so.' She paused, taking a steadying gulp of the salty night air. 'Which brings me to your father.'

'I would rather you did not bring him into the conversation. I have heard enough of your misplaced opinions.'

'Misplaced? Are you sure about that? Why have you not left for Egypt if you are so certain that you are done with the past now that your amulet is buried?'

'That is none of your business.'

He glowered at her. Tahira glowered back, counting. One hundred, and still he did not speak. She girded her loins and broke the silence. 'There is another part of the harem,' she said, 'where my father and my brother keep their concubines.

These women have children. Brothers and sisters who share half my blood, though to say such a thing is not permitted, amounts almost to treason. I will never know them, any more than you will ever know the five sisters you have.'

'Half-sisters, who are entirely unaware of my existence, and if I have anything to do with it, will remain forever so. I know their father for the despicable cur he is, but I will not destroy their love and respect for him.'

'Even if it means depriving yourself of a family you could love and respect?'

'I am not so naïve as to imagine those five females could either love or respect the proof of their father's misspent youth.'

'No, you are an honourable man. And a thoughtful one, and one who deserves better, Christopher. As to your father...'

'If you're going to tell me again that he did me a favour in having me adopted...'

'If you had been his legal son, how much freedom would you have to choose how to live your life? Would you be permitted to leave England, to traipse around Egypt, living in caves and tents, and spending most of your waking hours digging up bones, to quote your own words? I doubt it.'

'The point is a moot one. I'm not legitimate.'

'Nor are the children from the other side of the harem, but like you, they are free of the chains of their birth, free to make their own lives. Like you, they have no shame attached to their name because, like you until nine months ago, they believe themselves to be the legitimate children of another family entirely.'

Christopher looked uncomfortable. 'But they do not have the privileges their birth should entitle them to.'

'No,' Tahira agreed. 'Which is why great pains are taken to ensure that the male children never find out who their true father is, lest they claim a share. Females, however—that is another matter. What female who has lived life outside the harem would fight to be allowed into it? I am accustomed to the life, but it would be cruel to imprison one who was not.'

'Will it be the same—this man you are to marry, will he expect you—will you be confined as you are now?'

The very questions she had tried to ask today, eliciting only such vague answers that she must assume the worst. But she would not burden

Christopher with it. 'The world is changing all the time,' she equivocated. 'As you said, in Murimon…'

'Tahira, you're not going to be living in Murimon.'

'Christopher, what difference does it make to you where I live?'

'You ask that, after all we have—I told you. I want you to be happy.'

How could he imagine she could be when she had just confessed her love for him? Because he didn't believe her, Tahira thought despairingly. And what difference would it make if he did? How many times must she ask herself that question! 'I must go.'

'You should not have come here in the first place,' Christopher said harshly. 'To have arrived here so early in the night, you must have taken a foolish risk.'

'You sound like Farah.'

'Then she is clearly a sensible woman. Does she know of this tunnel you use?'

'Yes, though she would no more wish to return to the harem than…' Flushing, she turned away. 'I must go, Christopher. I am sorry that you believe

I betrayed your trust. I am sorry that you think I lied to you, duped you, all the things you accuse me of—I'm very, very sorry, because all I ever ever wanted—well, I've said it all.'

'Tahira.' He caught her by her shoulders, turning her to him. His arms slid down her arms, but he made no attempt to pull her any closer. 'Promise me you will at least try to be happy?'

A demand? A plea? Was she imagining the hint of desperation in his voice? No more lies. 'I will be happy thinking of you being happy,' she said, pushing the fall of his hair away from his brow.

'You didn't really mean it, did you? When you said—no one could endure to marry another man if they—you didn't mean it, did you?'

She meant it. She would be enduring it. But he sounded so pained, so painfully eager for her denial. Though her heart was breaking, she managed a tiny shake of her head, keeping her fingers crossed behind her back, speaking the words to herself, even as she denied them. *I love you. I love you. I love you.*

Christopher groaned, pulling her tight against him. She tilted her face for his kiss. His lips hovered over hers, and then with a sigh he let her go. 'Goodbye, Tahira.'

This time, it was final. 'Goodbye, Christopher.' *My darling,* she added to herself, for the last time, *my love.*

Chapter Twelve

Four days later

Christopher hauled his camel to a sudden halt. It was no good, he could no longer ignore the undisputable fact that the further he travelled from Nessarah, the stronger the resistance from the invisible thread which had attached itself to him. No matter how many times he told himself it was over, his business in that kingdom was unfinished.

Sliding wearily from the saddle, he found a tiny patch of shade in the lee of a high dune, and dropped on to the sand. For nine months, all he had been able to think about was divesting himself of his amulet, staunch in the belief that by doing so he would bury his past in the process, wipe the slate clean, start again. Replaying that conversation with Lord Armstrong—he would never think of the man as his father—he recalled thinking that his life had been built on sand, that he had no idea who he was.

But he did know now, ironically, thanks to this six-month journey through Arabia, the quest he would never have taken on were it not for his shameful heritage. Traversing so many desert kingdoms, he had been stripped back to his essence, forced to rely on himself, tested to limits he'd had no idea he could endure. His quest had accentuated his natural reckless streak and demonstrated his resilience. He had not once buckled under pressure. He had discovered a talent for complex problem solving and subterfuge, and as the old man at the camel race had pointed out, he had become a man who saw what others did not. In more ways than one. His Midas touch appeared to be significantly more wide-reaching than even he had realised. In fact, contrary to what he'd believed, he'd had no idea who he was before that earth-shattering day, and perhaps he'd never have known, if it hadn't been for Lord Armstrong, who had unwittingly launched him on this very personal journey.

Christopher took a long swig from his goatskin flask. The water was warm from the heat of the day, which was coming to a close. Here was as good a place as any to set up camp for the night. He began to do so, hobbling his camel, which had taken on more than enough water this morning to see them through to the next oasis.

How many of the character traits which defined him did he owe to the man who had sired him? Not a single one. To the people who had raised him, however—so many memories of the couple he had believed to be his parents had assailed him as he made his slow progress from Nessarah. He couldn't recall any sudden blinding moment of clarity, it had come to him slowly, the reason Andrew and Agnes Fordyce had never sold the amulet, the reason they had hidden it away with the accompanying document. Not guilt, but love. Like Christopher himself, they wanted to deny his true heritage, to claim him for their own, raise him without recourse to blood money, as they would have raised a child of their own. But Andrew Fordyce had been unable to destroy the evidence which contradicted this most loving lie, by burning the document and burying the artefact. Andrew, who had imbued Christopher with his love of the past, would have seen such an act as vandalism. The document and the amulet were part of Christopher's history, no matter how much

Andrew Fordyce might have wished to deny it, and so he had compromised, and effectively buried both.

Christopher had deeply mourned his mother, for when she died she was his mother, as far as he knew. Feeling deceived and betrayed, he had not properly mourned his father, the man who had raised him, loved him as his own son, even if they shared not a drop of common blood. Now he saw how wrong he had been, how unjust had been his feelings, and how unforgivable. Finally, nine months after Andrew Fordyce had departed this earth, Christopher bowed his head, covered his face with his hands, and wept freely and unashamedly for his father.

He had slept. When he awoke, night had fallen. Christopher rose, stretching his cramped limbs. The release of his pent-up grief had cleared his mind. He had been seeing things all the wrong way round, thinking that he must redefine himself in the shadow of a man who was not much more than a complete stranger, deny everything he knew of himself simply because the blood which flowed in his veins came from a different source than he'd believed. His blood might be illegitimate in the eyes of the law, but Tahira had been right, after all. He couldn't pretend he had not existed before he had discovered the amulet, he couldn't ignore his history, it was part of him, all of it, and he had to stop fooling himself. Coming face-to-face with Lord Henry Armstrong had changed him, but it had not, as he had feared, defined him. It had been the making of him.

He was his own man. He belonged to no one. It had been a huge mistake to bury the amulet, Tahira had been right about that too. It was the only connection he had to the woman who had died giving birth to him. Not a symbol of betrayal at all, but a precious piece of his heritage. He wanted it back.

Unable to contemplate waiting until morning, Christopher made haste preparing to retrace his steps back to Nessarah by the pale light of the moon. As his camel plodded at a stately pace south, he began to feel oddly lighter. It took him until dawn broke to understand that it was, finally, relief. He was doing the right thing, at last.

The air smelt fresh. Dew glittered on the scrub, darkening his camel's hooves. Gossamer-like cobwebs were spread out between the thorny branches like tiny spun shawls hung out to dry. The heart-shaped blue-and-yellow flowers that bloomed for brief hours only on mornings such as this, brought bright clusters of colour to the sands.

Tahira had wished to spend the night in the desert, to wake up to a morning such as this. The one wish he'd not been able to grant her.

Tahira.

Christopher felt the now familiar lurch in his heart when he thought of her. Which is why he'd tried not to think of her. Tahira, who had discovered an ancient tunnel in the plans of the royal palace. He imagined her, first poring over the plans, then relocating her own quarters in order to search for it. She must have worked at night, right there in the harem in the middle of the palace, risking discovery as she strove to locate the entrance, opened the tunnel up, made her way through it to the outside world. She must have been wildly excited and quite terrified of being found out. She must have struggled to keep such a momentous secret to herself. He admired her fascination with the past which had led to the discovery, the reckless courage which fuelled every forbidden journey to the desert, the fierce, protective love for her sisters that forced her to keep her secret from them. When she'd told him of it, he'd been too angry to see any of this, and she—how disappointed she must have been, to have her achievement dismissed so callously.

His angry reaction bewildered him now, as he stopped at a well to take on fresh supplies. Looking back, he could admit that almost everything Tahira had said to him that night in justification had been true. If she'd told him who she really was, it would have put an immediate end to their time together, time which had become very precious very quickly. Why hadn't he been able to shoulder some of the blame for her deception? Had it ever been a deception? From the first, he'd compromised his curiosity about her, had shut his mind to the questions which he could easily have found answers to, telling himself that it was what she wanted, when actually it was what he wanted too. Because he had known instinctively that the truth would put an abrupt end to everything, and he had deliberately suppressed his suspicions, deliberately refused to piece together the clues she had let fall, into any coherent whole. He'd been shocked when he saw her at the camel race, but it hadn't taken him very long at all to assimilate what it meant.

I love you.

Her voice, her words were so clear that Christopher started, looking foolishly over his shoulder.

I love you.

A princess of the royal blood would never fall in love with a bastard, he had answered. It was not permitted. Groaning, Christopher clambered back on to his camel. His most insistent view, and Tahira had agreed because he'd given her no choice.

I love you.

By the sun and the moon and the stars, she had meant it. She'd told him that she loved him, that most intimate of confessions, that most forbidden of emotions, and he'd forced her to deny it, because...

Because she wasn't free to love him.

Because she was as far beyond his reach as the sun blazing down on his head.

Because it was hard enough, tearing himself away from her when he loved her too.

The camel bleated in protest at the sudden yank on his reins, turning his long neck around to blast a snort of rank, hot breath before coming to a halt, but Christopher didn't notice. He was in love with Tahira. What a bloody idiot he was, for taking so long to see it. He loved her. That was what had made it almost impossible not to make love to her! He wasn't a seducer, he was a blind fool of a man in love.

But what the devil was he to do about it? His feelings changed nothing. His birth made him completely unacceptable to her family. Tahira was set upon doing her duty for the sake of her sisters and for herself too. Though she loved him. Dear heavens, what that did to him, thinking of it? His heart seemed to expand in his chest. She loved him. She loved him and he loved her.

Which brought him full circle. Finally noticing that he was sitting, grinning inanely on a camel standing stock still under the blazing sun of the hottest part of the day, Christopher urged the beast into a walk. He couldn't let Tahira marry another man. He wasn't even going to try to reconcile himself to that, no matter what the facts. She wasn't free, she had no choice but to do as her family bid her, but he was having none of it. She loved him. He loved her. There had to be a way for them to be together. He'd find it. He had three more days to travel to Nessarah to come up with a solution. The final, most important challenge of this Arabian odyssey.

Already, an audacious plan was beginning to form in his mind. Lord Armstrong would receive his precious dossier and not a scintilla more, but Christopher had other valuable bargaining chips up his sleeve. Extremely valuable. All he had to do was find a way to put them to the best possible use.

Nessarah—one week later

When Farah appeared at the window of her divan which led out on to her private courtyard, Tahira, who had been lying sleepless as usual, let out a yelp of horror. 'What are you doing here?' she hissed, pulling her friend quickly into the room and checking the lock on the other door.

'You have to come with me.'

'You told me I must never use that tunnel again.'

'You have to come with me, Tahira.' Farah grabbed a robe from the bottom of the bed and handed it to her. 'Hurry.'

'Why? What has happened? Has my brother...?'

'No, no, nothing like that. I am perfectly safe.'

'And perfectly—I don't know what. You are shaking.'

'That tunnel is horrible.' Farah cast her eyes around the divan. 'And this place. I had forgotten—I could never live here. I had forgotten. I don't know how I could have forgotten. Will you hurry up and get dressed?'

'You haven't told me...'

'Hurry!' Farah gave her a shake. 'He found me, Tahira. I don't know how—I don't know what you told him about me, but he found me, and he's waiting for you now.'

Tahira froze in the act of pulling on a pair of trousers. 'Who found you?'

'That man. Those eyes.' Farah smiled wickedly. 'I knew that there was something—night after night, you risked your neck—I knew it must be for a reason. He is a very persuasive reason.' Her smile faded. 'I hope I have not mistaken...'

'Christopher.' Tahira clutched at her heart, which she was pretty sure was about to leap out of her chest. 'Christopher is here, in Nessarah? But he left, we said our final farewells.'

'Well, he is back, and he is demanding to see you.'

'What does he want?'

'I have no idea, save that it is a matter of life and death and for your ears only.'

Tahira's heart was definitely making a bid for freedom. 'He knows I'm getting married.'

'All of Nessarah knows that.'

'Farah, you know that I love him?'

Her friend enveloped her in a hug. 'I suspected as much. It was why I was so angry with you, because I knew you would end up being hurt. But I know you, Tahira, you will do what you will do, and though I do not know this man, I have seen enough of him to be certain that if I do not bring him to you, he will find another way to reach you himself, which does not bear thinking about. So will you please hurry up before we are discovered.'

Tahira was beyond words when she came face-to-face with Christopher in Farah's home, but so too was he. For a long moment they simply gazed at each other across the small space of the main living area, and then they fell into each other's arms, clinging together like the survivors of a shipwreck, staring as if they were afraid they were looking at a mirage. And then they kissed, and for a long moment, there was no need for words, for their mouths, their tongues, their lips said it all. It felt like a homecoming to Tahira, that kiss, it made everything right with the world. She didn't want it to end, and it seemed nor did he, for when she tried to force herself to break free he pulled her back, almost roughly, and he kissed her again, and again and again, and only when their lungs cried out for air did they finally break apart.

Tahira stared up at his beloved face in wonder, still quite unable to believe he was real. 'I thought I would never see you again. What are you doing here?'

'I realised I had left something behind,' Christopher answered, his smile dazed. 'Something more precious to me than anything.'

'Your amulet? I knew you shouldn't have buried it.'

He laughed. 'You were right, but that's not what I meant.'

Her heart was thrumming in her chest like the wings of a songbird. 'What then?'

'Not what, but rather who,' he said, smiling at her in a way that she was sure would melt her bones. 'You are more precious to me than anything, Tahira. You are the missing piece of me. I love you so much.'

The words she had longed to hear, had dreamed of hearing, brought tears rushing to her eyes. 'Oh, Christopher, I love you too, but we can't—I can't—you know that it's impossible.'

'I thought it was, but now I believe we can make

it possible. Thanks to you, my darling Tahira, you helped me see things clearly for the first time.' He led her over to a stack of inviting cushions, holding her hand between his, his eyes never leaving her face. 'We were meant to be together, and we will be. No force on this earth is going to prevent it.'

His words, so heartfelt, tugged her own heartstrings. 'You have no idea how much I wish that were true, but it cannot be,' Tahira said wretchedly. 'I can't run away with you, Christopher. Ghutrif would not tolerate such humiliation. He would take it as an insult to his authority, and I know him, he is not only vengeful but his influence is immense. He would track us down wherever we fled to, and I can't bear to think what he would do to you. And not only you, my love, my dearest one. He would not believe me capable of acting alone, or of keeping my actions to myself. He would accuse my sisters of collusion. And then there is Farah.' She shuddered. 'It breaks my heart to say it, but I cannot put my happiness over their well-being. Please don't ask it of me.'

'My darling, I know you too well to ever ask such a thing of you.' Christopher's fingers tightened around hers. 'Do you think I don't know what it means to you, to do your duty by your family? Do you think I don't understand that, after all you've told me?'

'Then you understand why it cannot be. I must get married.'

'You must, but it must be to the man you love. With your brother's blessing of course. I will ensure that everything is above board, and no suspicion attached to your sisters or to Farah. But we must be together, Tahira. We deserve no less.'

He spoke with such certainty that she was almost convinced. 'If only...'

'You told me once that you thought the fates had brought us together. You were right, but they didn't bring us together just to solve the mystery of this thing.'

He reached into his pocket and produced the amulet, dropping it into her hands. 'Christopher!' Tahira stared at the beautiful artefact, quite dumbfounded. 'Where did you get this?'

He laughed. 'For such a clever woman, that's a very silly question.'

'You opened up the tomb! But the mine is in full production...'

'I was very quick. And very desperate.'

She curled her hands around the relic, feeling

the familiar sense of connection. 'I am so glad. It belongs to you.'

'It doesn't, it belongs to you. Or rather, it belongs with you, and I hope that one day in the very distant future, you will hand it on to our daughter, and that she will hand it on to hers, and our story, and the story of the first princess who owned this most precious thing, will become a family legend.'

'Please don't. It is too painful to imagine such a perfect future, Christopher.'

'It can be ours. One of the many things I've learned about myself in the last six months is that if I want something badly enough, I'll find a way to get it. I want you to be my wife, Tahira, and I've never wanted anything so much in the world.' His tender expression became serious. 'I thought our blood defined us. I thought it made you an Arabian princess and me an illegitimate Englishman, but I was quite wrong. You have never been a princess to me, you have always been yourself, simply Tahira. I don't care that your blood is blue, and I'm not interested in your pedigree any more than I'm interested in mine. The blood flowing in my veins no more makes me than you. I am not a base-born bastard, I am simply Christopher Fordyce. Do you see?'

She pressed a fervent kiss on his hand, the salt of her tears mingling with the familiar taste of his skin. 'I do see, and I am so glad that you do now, but my brother...'

'Is a man driven by greed and ambition, and will care naught for my heritage when he learns what I have to offer him,' Christopher said grimly. 'Trust me, I understand men like Prince Ghutrif only too well, having one such, unfortunately, rather too closely related to me.'

His father, he meant. The man at the Foreign Office. The man with contacts. The man whom Christopher had vowed never to see again. 'Lord Armstrong,' Tahira said warily, 'the man who is expecting your report.'

'He'll have it, and that will be an end of matters between us for ever. But you may recall, there's a good deal I won't be putting in that report which, as you pointed out yourself, could be worth a fortune, if one was inclined to exploit it.'

'You said you were not so inclined,' Tahira said, frowning in puzzlement.

'I'm not, directly,' Christopher replied, grinning, 'but I know a man who may be.'

Tahira's eyes widened as understanding dawned. 'Ghutrif,' she whispered, awed.

'The very man.'

'What—how…?'

'I have a plan. Do you want to hear it?'

He was smiling again, the smile that connected with her insides, made her want to melt into his arms, but it was his eyes that convinced her, made goose bumps break out on her arms, the skin on the back of her neck lift. 'Do you think it will work, truly? You wouldn't promise something so important if you weren't certain you can make it happen, would you?'

'Never.' He kissed her swiftly. 'Now listen, for we don't have much time before you must get back to the palace and get yourself ready for the summons.'

'Summons?'

'Patience, I'm about to reveal all.'

A few heart-fluttering hours later, Tahira was dressed in her formal best and waiting when the promised summons duly arrived. She had spent what was left of the night fluctuating between wild euphoria and extreme terror. Following the guard from the harem through the corridor leading to the waiting area, she felt as if she was soaring high in a current of air, waiting on a promised pair of wings to arrive before the winds changed, plummeting her back to earth. Past the porphyry pillars, under the elaborate ceiling decorated with green and gold, into the Tower of Justice, her heart thumped painfully in her chest. Christopher would have entered from another door. If he was here. He must be here. She must have faith.

The doors to the Chamber of the Royal Imperial Council were flung open, her name announced as she stepped through. Not so very long ago, the day after they had opened up the tomb, she had come into this room in response to another summons, dreading seeing Christopher because it would mean he had discovered her identity. He had not been there. Now he knew all her secrets, and here he was, garbed in the robes of a rich merchant, standing by her brother's throne with a pronounced arrogance she had never witnessed. Not even by a flicker did he betray himself, playing the part he had assumed to perfection. Not even by a flicker did he betray her either, no warning glance, no reassuring smile, nor any trace of nerves. He trusted her to play her part.

For once, she was glad of her headdress and her veil, for her love had been shining out of her eyes every time she looked at her reflection as she dressed. Her maidservant had noticed and commented. 'I am to be married, remember,' Tahira had said, so rapturously that her maidservant asked if she was ill. Standing before the man she meant, desperately hoping that he would convince her brother to free her from the man he had intended for her, she tucked her shaking hands into the voluminous sleeves of her dress.

'My sister, the Princess Tahira,' Ghutrif said, crooking his finger to summon her. Never had the Chamber of the Royal Imperial Council seemed so long, the throne so distant. His lips were tightly pursed, his long fingers drumming on the arms of his throne. Not a good sign.

Tahira made a formal bow, first to her brother and then to his visitor. She dared not meet Christopher's eyes. Ghutrif would not expect her to speak. She would throw herself on to her knees and beg if it would help, but it wouldn't. Christopher had a plan. She must trust Christopher. He had both their lives and their hearts in his hands.

'As I have informed you, Princess Tahira is already betrothed to Prince Zayn al-Farid. The wedding is set to take place in fifteen days.'

'Fifteen.' Christopher was betrayed into surprise. 'So soon,' he added, recovering himself with a prim smile. 'Then I am both relieved and grateful to have been granted an audience in the nick of time.'

'In time for what?'

Christopher made a little formal bow, hands together, expression supplicating. How Ghutrif would enjoy having his vanity indulged, Tahira thought. 'When I saw the most lovely Princess Tahira at the camel race, she captured my heart instantly.' The gesture which accompanied this statement was theatrical. 'I knew that I must move the sun and the stars to gain your permission to marry her.'

'She is pledged to another, and I'm not interested in the sun and the stars.' Ghutrif narrowed his eyes. 'How did you discern her beauty? How do you even come to know her name. There are four princesses, how can you be sure that this is the one who so very suddenly captured your heart from out of a clear blue sky?'

Ghutrif was no fool. Tahira quite often forgot this. He was shrewd, and he had a nose for mockery. Christopher was making another little bow. 'The princess's beauty is famed throughout Arabia. She was seated in the position of honour at the camel race, and so I deduced she was the eldest daughter, thus learning her name.'

'If you're so clever,' Ghutrif said, his voice dripping with sarcasm, 'then why can you not understand the simple fact that she is already spoken for?'

'When you announced the betrothal, you mentioned only a royal princess. As I understand it, Prince Zayn seeks only an alliance with Nessarah. There are four royal princesses, reputed to be equally beautiful. It is not as if there is any previous acquaintance, nor any particular attachment, is there? Why would not the next in line be just as acceptable as the first? And it would be quite a coup for you, not to mention financially advantageous, your Highness, to have two sisters married instead of one.'

'Prince Zayn has signed a contract.'

'Contracts can be easily amended or redrawn, when other terms offered are more—let us say, amenable.'

Ghutrif's fingers stopped drumming. 'Amenable?'

With a flourish, Christopher produced a scroll and handed it over. 'My terms. I trust you will find them extremely amenable.'

'I will not change my—' Ghutrif broke off as he scanned the scroll, the beautiful Arabic script so painstakingly transcribed by Farah, his eyebrows rising higher and higher on his brow with every line he read. 'This,' he said, trying and failing to hide his excitement, 'is a very interesting document. Untapped ores. New gold and diamond mines. Water sources. How am I to trust this information?'

Christopher spread his hands. 'Dare you risk refusing it? More importantly, I know of your vast power and reach of influence, your Highness. I would be a very foolish man indeed to attempt to dupe Prince Ghutrif.'

'That is true. Very true.' Ghutrif pursed his lips, pretending uncertainty, but Tahira could see the gleam of avarice in his eyes, and her heart began to pound in a different beat. 'You have maps, locations?'

'I have all the information you need to exploit these resources, I assure you.'

'And your personal credentials?'

Christopher handed over a small bundle of papers. 'This one verifies my profession as a surveyor. These are references from Egyptian pashas for whom I have carried out similar work.'

'You did not have my permission to survey Nessarah.'

'Let us just say that I acted on my own initiative.' Christopher executed a small, formal bow. 'You cannot deny that the results are pleasing, but it is up to you, your Highness. You are wise as well as powerful. The information is yours to do with as you see fit, in return for your sister's hand.'

'You hope to buy my sister's hand for the price of some mines which do not yet exist? That is asking for a leap of faith on my part.'

'Firstly the potential rewards far outstrip any risk. Secondly,' Christopher said tightly, for the first time meeting Tahira's eyes with a smile meant only for her, 'your sister's hand cannot be bought, and must be given freely.'

Ghutrif laughed. 'Be careful what you wish for. You may as well know that my sister is something of an oddity. She's already had one future husband die on her, and been jilted by another. Perhaps Prince Zayn might think he is getting the better bargain in Ishraq after all.'

Christopher's fists clenched. Tahira watched in horror as he took a step towards the throne, but before she could cry out, he thought the better of it. 'I am known as a man who likes to take a risk or two,' he said evenly. 'This is a chance I am more than happy to take. So, what do you say, your Highness? Will you take a risk too, on having your name revered by your people as the prince who discovered untold wealth, the prince who secured Nessarah's legacy?'

It was a masterstroke. Tahira bit her lip as Ghutrif positively swelled with pride. 'Very well. We have a deal.'

'There are conditions.'

'Aren't there always! Go on, name them.'

'Princess Tahira and I will be married immediately. A private, intimate ceremony, in the desert, with her sisters as her attendants.'

Christopher made no attempt to hide his smile this time. The warmth of it made Tahira glow. Ghutrif, studying the scroll, did not notice and merely waved his hand vaguely. 'Go on.'

'We will then depart Nessarah for Egypt, where we will make our home. A home in which my wife's sisters will be welcomed on visits at regular intervals while they remain here in the royal palace. Naturally, once they marry, I will seek the appropriate permission from their husbands.'

'Very well.' Ghutrif continued to peruse the

scroll, lifting his eyes only when the silence continued for some moments. 'Is that it?'

'So little to you, but it means a great deal to me.'

'I cannot imagine why, but so be it. You foreigners have some strange customs. Our terms are agreed, I will have the papers drawn up,' Ghutrif said briskly, clearly intent upon concluding matters before Christopher changed his mind. 'There is however one major hurdle to be overcome.' He cast a meaningful look at Tahira. 'Given her history, I would be astonished if my contrary sister chose to marry a foreign stranger whose name she does not even know.'

Tahira could restrain herself no longer. 'I have a choice?'

Her brother drew her a dark look. 'You have no choice but to marry, but it seems you do have a choice between two suitors.'

'Then it is simple.' Tahira got to her feet. 'I choose the man who chose me, rather than the man that you chose for me!'

Ignoring the astounded gasp from Ghutrif, turning his back to the prince, Christopher untied her veil and pushed back her headdress before clasping both her hands between his. 'I ask you most humbly to be my wife, my one and only love, for now and for always.'

She hadn't thought she could love him any more, but she could. He had not only secured her freedom, but he had secured access to her beloved sisters too. 'I want nothing more,' Tahira said, quite forgetting that they were not alone, 'than to have you as my husband, my one and only love, for now and for always.'

Christopher drew her to him. He kissed her hand, not her lips, but she saw the promise in his eyes. For now and for always. And soon.

Epilogue

Three days later, Tahira sat alone contemplating her imminent sunset wedding ceremony. The fates, she thought, had conspired to grant her everything she could wish for on this most auspicious of days. Yesterday, Juwan had given birth to a fine, healthy boy, Ghutrif's much-desired son and heir, whose emergence into the world had been announced to widespread jubilation. The informal celebrations were likely to continue for at least a week, the formal festivities which would follow presaging the wedding of Ishraq and Prince Zayn, granting Tahira and Christopher the privacy for their own nuptials which they so fervently desired. Ghutrif had been easily persuaded to postpone the announcement of Tahira's marriage until after they had departed Nessarah.

Ishraq, to Tahira's profound relief, had been beside herself with delight when informed that she had inherited both her sister's bridegroom and her lavish wedding. When the couple were formally introduced, it seemed, according to Juwan who officiated, that the delight was mutual. Though neither Tahira's sister-in-law nor her eldest sister could understand her preference for the foreigner without kingdom or wealth to bestow on his bride, at the brief betrothal ceremony held yesterday, her younger sisters had been fascinated by Christopher.

'Those eyes,' Alimah said afterwards, making a show of fanning her face with her hand, 'and that smile he has, only for you, Tahira. I do believe his claim to have fallen in love at first sight is true.'

'He sees you as we do,' Durrah had said. 'He knows you as we do, and you know him. I see it in the way you look at him. For you too, it is love, I think, though I am not so sure about the first sight bit.'

A speculative look had accompanied this remark. 'What do you mean by that?' Tahira had whispered, checking that Alimah's attention was focused on sorting through the swathes of silk from which they were to pick their wedding outfits.

Durrah had shaken her head, smiling enigmatically. 'I see your hands have healed from the scratches Sayeed has been regularly inflicting on you. No more broken nails either.'

'Durrah, what are you implying?'

'Tahira.' Her sister had wrapped her arms around her, hugging her tightly. 'You need have no fear, no one else suspects,' she had whispered, 'but you have not fooled me. You have been so very changed, and so very tired too, in the mornings. I don't know how you did it, but please, before you leave, won't you share your secret with me? How do you manage to escape the confines of the harem?'

Horrified, Tahira had steadfastly refused to tell her, extracting a very reluctant promise that Durrah would not pursue the matter. And that, she acknowledged now with a sigh, must be the end of her worrying about it. In a few short hours she would be married and gone from the harem, and in not so many days, so too would Ishraq. With Juwan's son taking up all her attention, Alimah and Durrah would be left a great deal on their own. It was time for her sisters to grow into adulthood without her. Though, thanks to Christopher,

her darling Christopher, their parting would not be final.

The distant tinkling of a bell made her check her watch, and the hour shown on her little jewelled timepiece sent Tahira's heart racing. Her sisters and her maidservants would be here in just fifteen minutes to complete her preparations. She must hurry to complete her last, sad undertaking.

'It is time,' she said with a heavy heart, gently waking Sayeed, who had been sleeping soundly on her lap.

The sand cat yawned, digging his vicious claws into the cushion which Tahira had had the sense to place beneath him in order to protect her finery. She tickled his favourite spot on his forehead, wanting to hear his growling purr one last time, but he was in no mood for caresses. Rested from a long day's sleep, Sayeed was ready to hunt. He jumped down from her lap and padded to the window, his ringed tail held high. 'You are eager to claim your freedom, I see,' she said, blinking back the tears. 'That shall be my wedding gift to you. You are a wild creature at heart. It was wrong of me to try to tame you.'

An impatient mewl greeted this remark. Tahira opened the window and followed him out into the courtyard. For the first time ever, she opened the entrance to the tunnel in daylight. 'Good-bye, Sayeed. Enjoy your freedom.' Her voice was clogged with tears, but her sand cat scampered quickly through the tunnel and out towards the desert without a backward glance. Tahira closed the entrance over for the final time, rearranging the thick trailing plants which covered it. Would Sayeed return and meowl to be re-admitted? Perhaps he would, but not for long. Soon the desert would become his home, as befitted him.

Her own future glowed bright, tantalisingly close. Like Sayeed, she would not look back. Like Sayeed, she couldn't wait to claim it.

The tent had been pitched exactly as Christopher specified at the oasis where he and Tahira had swum, the front open wide to face the waters and the cascade, though far enough back to allow space for their small coterie of wedding guests. No ordinary tent, this one was constructed of silk and brocade, gold-tasselled, the supported poles gilded. Inside, huge garlands of paper flowers were strung out across the roof and down the sides, golden yellow and deep crimson, scented with attar of roses.

The rear of the tent was screened by gauzy layers of chiffon in the same colours. A quick check reassured him that here too, things were exactly as he had requested. Astounding what could be achieved in such a short time by royal command, though perhaps not so astounding, when the royal personage in question had the twin incentives of a new-born heir to welcome into the world, and a sister who had been a persistent thorn in his side to see off. Prince Ghutrif, having assimilated the full magnitude of the dowry which Christopher was furnishing him with, was clearly terrified that his sister's foreign suitor might change his mind. If Christopher had requested a tent spun from gold he reckoned Prince Ghutrif would have found a way to provide it. And if Christopher could have found a way to exclude Tahira's brother from their wedding he would have, but with her father too ill to leave his chamber, they needed the avaricious autocrat to officiate, and to grant their union legitimacy. For Tahira's sake, and for the sake of their children, if they were fortunate enough to have any, the legal status of this marriage must be unimpeachable. Though he had come to terms with his own tainted blood, he would not wish any child of his to struggle as he had done.

A child! Christopher let the drapes flutter back into place, turning his back on the seductive appeal of the bedchamber at the back of the tent. These last few days had been so hectic, he'd had very little time to think of this, his wedding night. Tonight, he and Tahira would make love, and if a child was the outcome—by the stars, if he'd had any idea that this would be the outcome of his odyssey to Arabia—was he ready for this?

Stepping outside, he inhaled the cooling evening air, but though his jangling nerves calmed, they did not wholly subside. His life was about to change for ever. He was about to become a husband, and his wife was a princess of the royal blood. How would she cope with the hardships of life as an antiquarian? Ought he to abandon his future plans? He could, as Tahira had pointed out, make a fortune from surveying. He could keep her in silks, waited on hand and foot by servants. She would never have to get her hands dirty.

I doubt the woman exists, who would tolerate my investing every penny I earn in excavating holes in the ground. Nor would any, I am certain, endure the travails of traipsing around Egypt, living in caves and tents while I spend most of my waking hours digging up bones.

His own words, he remembered, from the first or second night of their meeting.

I would consider that paradise.

Tahira's words. And she'd meant them. She was right too, it would be paradise, with her at his side. Not a princess, but his Tahira, who was marrying him despite the prospect of a life spent far from the lap of luxury. He should remember that. His Tahira, his own perfect love, who would be truly his, as he would be truly hers, in a few short hours.

Christopher made his way to the entrance of the oasis to watch the approaching caravan of camels. White thoroughbreds, he could hear the bells from their reins tinkling faintly. A guard at the front, others flanking the sides. The first camel, with its huge canopied saddle, bore Prince Ghutrif, splendidly decked out in robes of gold and silver. For perhaps the last time, Christopher forced himself to kneel in homage to the man who was about to bestow the greatest gift of all upon him. Two other men behind him in state robes would be the witnesses. Next came the three sisters, in gold and emerald. And finally, in the same gold and crimson which matched his own robes, his bride.

His nerves fled as his eyes met hers. He was

meant to be with this woman. She completed him. Her brother took his place on the make-shift throne in the tent. Her sisters, silks fluttering, sank on to the bank of cushions, the two officials standing behind them. Christopher took his bride's hand in his. Her skin was cool, her fingers slightly trembling, but he detected in her eyes the same certainty, the same profound love. Prince Ghutrif cleared his throat, impatient to begin. For once, Christopher's feelings chimed with the man who was to be his brother-in-law. The sun was sinking. He led Tahira to the low stools in front of the throne, and they sat down together. He couldn't wait to be married.

There were no farewells after the ceremony. Tahira and her sisters had made their adieus in private before leaving the harem, sadness tinged with excitement for each of them, for it was not an end but a beginning. As she watched the royal caravan of camels fade into the distance, Christopher put his arm around Tahira.

'You will miss them profoundly,' he said.

'Yes, but not as much as I missed you, when you left.' She placed her hand over her heart. 'As if you had taken part of me with you. Now I am complete. What have I said?'

Christopher took her hand, placing it over his own heart. 'Almost exactly what I was thinking, while I was waiting for you to arrive. I have never felt so certain about anything in my life, as I did when we made our promises. I love you so much.'

She reached up to push his hair back from his brow. 'I love you too, so much, Christopher. You know that, don't you?'

He smiled, the smile that made her insides melt. 'I do,' he said, his smile turning wicked, 'but just to be absolutely sure, why don't you show me?'

He swept her up in his arms. Laughing, she put her arm around his neck. Above them, the night sky was indigo blue, awash with stars, the moon bright, casting shadows over the reflective waters of the oasis. The tent had been closed over, but lamps had been lit inside. Christopher pushed back the gauzy drapes at the rear and set her on her feet. There was a divan, covered in cushions and silks, scattered with rose petals. Rich rugs underfoot. Her heart was jumping, her pulses racing.

Tahira cast off her headdress, the gold coins which had held it in place tinkling as it fell to the floor. He kissed her then, tenderly at first, his mouth gentle on hers, but Tahira did not want gentleness and when she deepened the kiss, it seemed neither did Christopher. Their tongues touched. He moaned softly, and their kisses heated. Her cloak fell to the floor, pooling at her feet. Then his. His hands cupped her breasts, stroking her nipples, and the sweet, persistent thrum started low in her belly. She tugged at the buttons of his tunic, tearing her mouth from his only to allow him to pull it over his head, moaning, panting as she pressed her lips to his chest to taste him, her hands roaming over his buttocks, the rippling muscles of his back, saying his name over and over, thinking only hazily, *my husband, my husband, my husband.*

More kisses. He laid her down on the divan. The layers of her wedding clothes were cast aside as he kissed every newly revealed piece of her skin, muttering her name, muttering his love, his hands, his lips feverish. Another low growl as he removed the last layer of silk and she sprawled before him, naked. One look at his face, the slashes of colour on his cheeks and his eyes, focused entirely on her, and she could not doubt how much he wanted her. Desire, potent desire, made her reach for him, undo the sash of his trousers. He was fully aroused. Gloriously aroused. Fascinated, she trailed her fingers over the length of him. Iron and silk, the book had said. It was mistaken. Just Christopher, hard and sleek and powerful.

'I want you so much,' she said.

'Tahira.' He kissed her, laying down beside her. 'Tahira, my lovely Tahira, I want you.'

More kisses. His mouth on hers, then on her breasts, her nipples, her belly, and then between her legs. She cried out as he licked into her, fistfuls of the silk sheets between her fingers in an effort to delay, to wait, but she couldn't stop it. He licked, stroked, over, around, inside, and her climax ripped through her, unstoppable, pulsing, throbbing, wave after wave, making her cry out, arch up, reach for him, urgent for the completion which she had been denied for so long.

'Now,' she said, as he lay over her, snatching more kisses, greedy kisses, demanding kisses, 'now.'

'I will be—I will try to be careful, I...'

'Now, Christopher.'

Another kiss, the deepest of kisses, and he was

inside her, and she could not have imagined—it felt so very, very right. Only then did she realise he was holding himself tightly under control, the strain on his face, waiting. She smiled. 'Yes,' she said, kissing him again. 'Yes, please.'

He kissed her. And then he pushed himself higher inside her, and began to thrust slowly, rousing new sensations inside her. Another thrust, and her instincts took over. She moved with him, watching every sensation on his face reflecting what she was feeling. He thrust again, harder, and she wrapped her legs around him. This pulsing, throbbing, climb to her climax was different. She tightened around him, making him groan, making herself shudder, and again he thrust, and again, becoming more urgent, higher, harder, faster, his kisses wild, her hands digging into his back, her breathing harsh, until she could hold on no more and cried out, and he cried out too, pulsing, shuddering, saying her name over and over as he spilled inside her, and there had never, ever been anything so perfectly, beautifully right.

They lay silent and sated for a long time, their skin damp, clinging to each other, shipwrecked on the shore of their lovemaking. The night was long, filled with tenderness and plans and moments where they simply stared in wonder at each other.

'I keep thinking I'm dreaming,' Tahira said several times.

'I can't believe this is happening,' Christopher said.

As dawn broke and the sun made a collage of pinks and crimsons and orange just for them in the sky, they emerged from the tent. The air was salty, fresh. The sand was damp beneath her feet. Tahira turned to her husband and smiled. 'My final wish come true. To wake in the desert. Though I could never have imagined anything quite so perfect. I love you.'

'I love you too.' He kissed her.

'I will never, ever tire of your kisses,' Tahira said.

Christopher smiled. 'The first of a thousand, a million kisses,' he said. 'A lifetime of kisses.'

'A lifetime. A new life. One that deserves a clean start,' Tahira said. Taking him by the hand, she led him into the cool, tempting waters of the oasis. 'I seem to remember you promising to teach me to swim, Husband.'

'I am a man who always keeps his promises, Wife,' Christopher replied with a loving smile.

* * * * *

If you enjoyed this story,
you won't want to miss the
first three books in Marguerite Kaye's
HOT ARABIAN NIGHTS *miniseries*

THE WIDOW AND THE SHEIKH
SHEIKH'S MAIL-ORDER BRIDE
THE HARLOT AND THE SHEIKH

Historical Note

If you happen to follow me on Twitter, you'll know the tag for this book was #spysheikh.

Reading Deborah Manley and Peta Ree's biography of Henry Salt, *Artist, Diplomat, Egyptologist*, provided the inspiration for my hero, Christopher. My own fascination with the discovery of Tutankhamun's tomb, which began with a project in primary school during which I made a papier-mâché death mask (the pinnacle of my artistic endeavours), and my love of the Indiana Jones films, helped flesh out Christopher's character. And reading about the renegade explorer and diplomat Richard Burton in Mary S. Lovell's excellent biography, *A Rage to Live*, inspired Christopher's career—though I've made him a significantly more successful mineral surveyor than Burton.

Having been unable to find a definitive date for the introduction of the term archaeologist, I've used it interchangeably with antiquarian. If this is, as I suspect, anachronistic, then I apologise, and similarly for my use of the term sarcophagus in an Arabian context, which I suspect might be inaccurate but which I felt was best suited to the ambiance I was trying to create inside the tomb.

One of the most moving descriptions of the 'custom' of the aristocracy to hand their inconvenient illegitimate progeny over to a wet nurse and a most uncertain fate was in Amanda Foreman's *Georgiana, Duchess of Devonshire*. Mike Leigh's brilliant film, *Secrets and Lies*, deals with the consequences of modern-day adoption. Watching it again recently, the parallels with history struck me, as they so often do. To what extent are we defined by our genes, rather than our upbringing? What makes us uniquely us? Reading over N. M. Penzer's book *The Harem* when researching this series, I came across the Courtyard of the Princes, where the sultan's illegitimate sons were effectively imprisoned for life, lest they threaten the legitimate line, and the idea for poor Christopher's back story began to take shape. I most sincerely hope that I've done it justice.

Other historical snippets: the library in the royal palace is that of St Florian's, which I have pictures of on my Pinterest board; to my knowledge, there are no such books as *The Garden of Delights* or *The Art of Love*, though I've loosely based them on a reading of *The Perfumed Garden* (translated by Burton as *The Scented Garden*); my description of the baths in the royal palace are inspired by Lady Mary Wortley Montagu's Turkish Embassy letters as well as Penzer's *Harem*; and thanks go to Penzer again, for Tahira's clothing and the translated names for each item.

Any errors or oversights are, of course, my own. There's a comprehensive list of my reading on my website, *www.margueritekaye.com*. I have had such fun writing the *Hot Arabian Nights* quartet. I do hope that you've found Christopher and Tahira's story a fitting conclusion to the series. But if you've still got an appetite for the seductive world of Regency Arabia then watch this space for my new quartet which opens up in a glittering new fantasy kingdom and a highly unusual marriage of convenience.

MILLS & BOON®
Hardback – August 2017

ROMANCE

An Heir Made in the Marriage Bed	Anne Mather
The Prince's Stolen Virgin	Maisey Yates
Protecting His Defiant Innocent	Michelle Smart
Pregnant at Acosta's Demand	Maya Blake
The Secret He Must Claim	Chantelle Shaw
Carrying the Spaniard's Child	Jennie Lucas
A Ring for the Greek's Baby	Melanie Milburne
Bought for the Billionaire's Revenge	Clare Connelly
The Runaway Bride and the Billionaire	Kate Hardy
The Boss's Fake Fiancée	Susan Meier
The Millionaire's Redemption	Therese Beharrie
Captivated by the Enigmatic Tycoon	Bella Bucannon
Tempted by the Bridesmaid	Annie O'Neil
Claiming His Pregnant Princess	Annie O'Neil
A Miracle for the Baby Doctor	Meredith Webber
Stolen Kisses with Her Boss	Susan Carlisle
Encounter with a Commanding Officer	Charlotte Hawkes
Rebel Doc on Her Doorstep	Lucy Ryder
The CEO's Nanny Affair	Joss Wood
Tempted by the Wrong Twin	Rachel Bailey

MILLS & BOON®
Large Print – August 2017

ROMANCE

The Italian's One-Night Baby	Lynne Graham
The Desert King's Captive Bride	Annie West
Once a Moretti Wife	Michelle Smart
The Boss's Nine-Month Negotiation	Maya Blake
The Secret Heir of Alazar	Kate Hewitt
Crowned for the Drakon Legacy	Tara Pammi
His Mistress with Two Secrets	Dani Collins
Stranded with the Secret Billionaire	Marion Lennox
Reunited by a Baby Bombshell	Barbara Hannay
The Spanish Tycoon's Takeover	Michelle Douglas
Miss Prim and the Maverick Millionaire	Nina Singh

HISTORICAL

Claiming His Desert Princess	Marguerite Kaye
Bound by Their Secret Passion	Diane Gaston
The Wallflower Duchess	Liz Tyner
Captive of the Viking	Juliet Landon
The Spaniard's Innocent Maiden	Greta Gilbert

MEDICAL

Their Meant-to-Be Baby	Caroline Anderson
A Mummy for His Baby	Molly Evans
Rafael's One Night Bombshell	Tina Beckett
Dante's Shock Proposal	Amalie Berlin
A Forever Family for the Army Doc	Meredith Webber
The Nurse and the Single Dad	Dianne Drake

0717 GEN STD LP

MILLS & BOON®
Hardback – September 2017

ROMANCE

The Tycoon's Outrageous Proposal	Miranda Lee
Cipriani's Innocent Captive	Cathy Williams
Claiming His One-Night Baby	Michelle Smart
At the Ruthless Billionaire's Command	Carole Mortimer
Engaged for Her Enemy's Heir	Kate Hewitt
His Drakon Runaway Bride	Tara Pammi
The Throne He Must Take	Chantelle Shaw
The Italian's Virgin Acquisition	Michelle Conder
A Proposal from the Crown Prince	Jessica Gilmore
Sarah and the Secret Sheikh	Michelle Douglas
Conveniently Engaged to the Boss	Ellie Darkins
Her New York Billionaire	Andrea Bolter
The Doctor's Forbidden Temptation	Tina Beckett
From Passion to Pregnancy	Tina Beckett
The Midwife's Longed-For Baby	Caroline Anderson
One Night That Changed Her Life	Emily Forbes
The Prince's Cinderella Bride	Amalie Berlin
Bride for the Single Dad	Jennifer Taylor
A Family for the Billionaire	Dani Wade
Taking Home the Tycoon	Catherine Mann

0817 GEN STD HB

MILLS & BOON®
Large Print – September 2017

ROMANCE

The Sheikh's Bought Wife	Sharon Kendrick
The Innocent's Shameful Secret	Sara Craven
The Magnate's Tempestuous Marriage	Miranda Lee
The Forced Bride of Alazar	Kate Hewitt
Bound by the Sultan's Baby	Carol Marinelli
Blackmailed Down the Aisle	Louise Fuller
Di Marcello's Secret Son	Rachael Thomas
Conveniently Wed to the Greek	Kandy Shepherd
His Shy Cinderella	Kate Hardy
Falling for the Rebel Princess	Ellie Darkins
Claimed by the Wealthy Magnate	Nina Milne

HISTORICAL

The Secret Marriage Pact	Georgie Lee
A Warriner to Protect Her	Virginia Heath
Claiming His Defiant Miss	Bronwyn Scott
Rumours at Court (Rumors at Court)	Blythe Gifford
The Duke's Unexpected Bride	Lara Temple

MEDICAL

Their Secret Royal Baby	Carol Marinelli
Her Hot Highland Doc	Annie O'Neil
His Pregnant Royal Bride	Amy Ruttan
Baby Surprise for the Doctor Prince	Robin Gianna
Resisting Her Army Doc Rival	Sue MacKay
A Month to Marry the Midwife	Fiona McArthur

0817 GEN STD LP

MA, L H